"Unique, captivating, and sexy . . . Everything you've come to expect from Sunny and more. . . . A[nother] [rema]rkable addition to Mon[a Lisa . . .] [foll]owing this amazing se[ries . . .] [the] degree of intensity this [book . . .] eroticism of the story[. . .] [characte]rs are constantly evolvi[ng . . .] —Heart

"The latest chap[ter . . . Mona Lisa] series is a pulse-pounding erotic adventure . . . narrated in first person by the heroine in a strong yet emotional voice. Sunny creates a fascinating world that's violent and sexual."
—*Romantic Times*

"Fans of this erotic fantasy saga will appreciate this powerful entry . . . Once again it is the secondary characters that provide strong support to the plot, which makes this an endearing tale . . . Another winner." —*Midwest Book Review*

MONA LISA AWAKENING

"Darkly erotic, wickedly clever, and very original!"
—*New York Times* bestselling author Bertrice Small

"A terrific debut sure to appeal to fans of Anne Bishop or Laurell K. Hamilton . . . Sunny's characters stayed with me long after I finished the book."
—*New York Times* bestselling author Patricia Briggs

"A spellbinding tale full of erotic sensuality and deliciously fascinating characters."
—*New York Times* bestselling author Lori Foster

"A refreshing contemporary urban erotic horror thriller that grips the audience." —*The Best Reviews*

"A lively writer . . . Erotica fantasy that is fresh, engaging, and a damn fun read . . . Sizzling sex scenes."
—*Sensual Romance Reviews*

continued . . .

MONA LISA CRAVING

A NOVEL OF THE MONÈRE

SUNNY

BERKLEY SENSATION, NEW YORK

THE BERKLEY PUBLISHING GROUP
Published by the Penguin Group
Penguin Group (USA) Inc.
375 Hudson Street, New York, New York 10014, USA

Penguin Group (Canada), 90 Eglinton Avenue East, Suite 700, Toronto, Ontario M4P 2Y3, Canada
(a division of Pearson Penguin Canada Inc.)
Penguin Books Ltd., 80 Strand, London WC2R 0RL, England
Penguin Group Ireland, 25 St. Stephen's Green, Dublin 2, Ireland (a division of Penguin Books Ltd.)
Penguin Group (Australia), 250 Camberwell Road, Camberwell, Victoria 3124, Australia
(a division of Pearson Australia Group Pty. Ltd.)
Penguin Books India Pvt. Ltd., 11 Community Centre, Panchsheel Park, New Delhi—110 017, India
Penguin Group (NZ), 67 Apollo Drive, Rosedale, North Shore 0632, New Zealand
(a division of Pearson New Zealand Ltd.)
Penguin Books (South Africa) (Pty.) Ltd., 24 Sturdee Avenue, Rosebank, Johannesburg 2196,
South Africa

Penguin Books Ltd., Registered Offices: 80 Strand, London WC2R 0RL, England

This is a work of fiction. Names, characters, places, and incidents either are the product of the author's imagination or are used fictitiously, and any resemblance to actual persons, living or dead, business establishments, events, or locales is entirely coincidental. The publisher does not have any control over and does not assume any responsibility for author or third-party websites or their content.

MONA LISA CRAVING

A Berkley Sensation Book / published by arrangement with the author

PRINTING HISTORY
Berkley trade edition / January 2008
Berkley Sensation mass-market edition / December 2008

ISBN: 978-0-425-22554-7

BERKLEY® SENSATION
Berkley Sensation Books are published by The Berkley Publishing Group,
a division of Penguin Group (USA) Inc.,
375 Hudson Street, New York, New York 10014.
BERKLEY SENSATION and the "B" design are trademarks of Penguin Group (USA) Inc.

PRINTED IN THE UNITED STATES OF AMERICA

10 9 8 7 6 5 4 3 2 1

To Cindy Hwang,
who nurtures and grows her garden of authors well.

ONE

THE CRESCENT MOON gleamed bright in the star-studded sky, a beacon of light in the darkness. Not chasing it away. No, darkness was fine. Darkness was our domain, the time when we roamed and played and hunted. We slept the days and roamed the evening twilight. And when the sun fell over the edge of the Earth, that was when we rose. The lunar rays didn't chase darkness away, so much as crown it. Make it glisten and glow with shadows and light.

We weren't vampires. We were something older, much older than those legends. We were what begat those first whispers that eventually wound their way into folklore: The Monère, children of the moon, a people who had fled their dying planet over four million years ago. Supernatural creatures faster, stronger, more beautiful than mere humans.

I was the exception to that. The beauty part, that is. I was the pigeon among all the peacocks. Plain, with straight dark hair and shadow-danced eyes. The exotic almond tilt of my eyes was my only attractive feature. At five feet eight, I stood as tall as the shortest of my men, and was built more like a long-distance runner—lean, pared down like an athlete, with a light, modest bosom. I hadn't inherited my mother's lushness, which was fine by me. It was a body I was comfortable with. And my simple looks . . . well, the plainness was not so surprising. Not in a Mixed Blood, which is what I am. A quarter of me is human, the other three-quarters of me is Monère, a people I'd only just come to know existed. And the reason for that? My mother, Mona Sera, a Full Blood Monère Queen, had tossed my mongrel self away at birth, like garbage. I'd been raised among the humans. Grew up thinking of myself as such until puberty hit and the moon's gifts of greater strength and sharper senses, far more acute than any human's could ever be, made it clear that I was more.

I was more than even what I had first suspected. I was a Monère Queen, the newest one crowned. The first Mixed Blood Queen to ever exist in their long and bloody history. Unfortunately, I was doing more than my share of adding to the bloodiness of that history. I'd just returned from High Queen's Court, called before the Council to explain my role in Mona Louisa's death, the Queen who'd ruled here before me in Louisiana.

Mona Louisa of Louisiana. Had a ring to it now that I rolled the words together, didn't it? No longer. She was dead. Not by my hand, though I'd done my best to kill her after she'd torn my lover's heart out from his chest and killed him. When Gryphon died, I had wanted to die, too. But not before ensuring that Mona Louisa departed this Earth first. After I'd seen that goal accomplished, I'd been grief-maddened and had submersed myself in my Bengal tiger form—something I'd suppressed, ran from all my life, that dark, dangerous beast chained inside me. In my grief-storm of pain and loss, I'd finally embraced that animal part of me. Lost myself wholly, mindlessly, in my other self, roaming the forests for a fortnight until my human and animal minds had merged, come one into the other, and I found myself once more aware of who and what I am—a part-human Monère Queen who had abandoned her people for half a month.

One of my people ran beside me now. An enormous wolf with a beautiful, lush pelt of silver-gray, and autumn brown eyes that gleamed as if a light shone within him. And it did. Lunar light. He was not a true wolf but a Full Blood Monère warrior shifted into his animal form. He romped with me now in joy of the night, and I ran with him in celebration of our time, of our strength, of our being, lithe and light in my human form, springing ahead of him, veering sharply aside so that he leaped in front. I followed then, chasing after him. We danced like that for a time, like children playing, or in our case, like living creatures who still had life, who should celebrate that life while it yet remained in them.

Life and death were fickle, sometimes bleeding one into the other. Gryphon, my first love, had died but he'd made the transition to demon dead. He resided now in another realm. In Hell. I would see him again one day. Mona Louisa, the bitch Queen I'd tried so hard to kill and had failed to, was also dead but not entirely gone. She'd drank demon blood and had become more than Monère . . . and I had sucked her light and essence into me. That part of her, that demon-tainted part, resided in me now.

I ran in human form because, now that it was triggered, that demon essence within me partially blocked my tiger self, preventing it from coming out fully. I wondered if the opposite were true, if my animal self prevented the full manifestation of that demon sliver that lurked within me like a dark, insidious shadow.

Others thought I ran the night in my animal form with

my master at arms by my side to keep me safe. But I'd really come here, away from the others' keen ears, to speak to him privately.

Deep in the midst of the forest, we came upon a small clearing. Nestled there was a small hut. The west cottage, it was called. I'd never been here before and looked upon the charming little structure with pleasure. It was a tiny thing with yellow siding, a green sloping roof, and matching green trim. The door was unlocked. I pushed it open and stepped within. It was a simply furnished but comfortable abode, used as a hunter's cabin. A place where Monère warriors shifted back into their upright forms. A place to clean up and wash off the blood after hunting in their animal selves. There were several other cabins like this spread out among our vast acreage.

Nails scraped the wooden floor as the wolf entered the cabin and crossed over to me. A natural wolf, *canis lupus*, stood thirty inches tall at the shoulders and weighed 150 pounds. *Canis Monère*, on the other hand, was much bigger. Or at least the one before me was. His weight was closer to 250 pounds. And his shoulders topped a natural wolf's height by more than half a foot. No wonder the timber wolf that I'd encountered at High Court, a wolf that had looked upon me as food, had backed away beneath Dontaine's growling threat.

A shimmer of light, a pulse of power, and Dontaine stood before me naked and unadorned, breathtakingly handsome with hair as blindingly bright as sunshine, and eyes a lush and deep verdant green in his human form. He was tall, and what I would have called of average build. But average was not a word you used with Dontaine. With broad shoulders, arms roped with sinewy strength, a chest sculpted with rippling muscles that flowed like flesh-silk beneath his pale, flawless skin, he was more heavily muscled than Gryphon, my beautiful, dark, departed angel, and much less massive than my towering Amber, my Warrior Lord, my other love.

Dontaine's hand reached out and I felt that electric, jolting dance upon my skin, a sensation that came from him alone. He touched me. And his touch was not like that of a guard but of a new lover—my new lover.

"Mona Lisa." He whispered my name and title both. The emotions that crossed my face when I looked at him, truly looked at him and saw him—not just the surface beauty but the generous, valiant heart that lay beneath it—made his eyes swirl a deeper green.

He was achingly handsome with bold and noble features, like a blond sun god. And like most men blessed with fair face and exquisite form, he had the confidence, the touch of arrogance that usually came with the looks. And he wasn't just beautiful but powerful, even for a Full Blood Monère warrior. He had been Mona Louisa's favorite, before she had tried to kill me, her territory forfeited to me as punishment. She'd tried to regain it, and one of the means she had used was the tall, sumptuously handsome man who stood before me now, looking at me with soft wonder in his eyes. He'd been left behind to spy and betray me, but he hadn't. He'd saved me instead. Not just once, but again at High Court when I had been questioned there for Mona Louisa's death.

I'd taken him not just into my body but into my heart. In the midst of sadness and loss, I'd found love again, unexpectedly. It was because I loved Dontaine that I needed to talk to him now. So that he did not continue to look at me that way—with love and happiness.

It had only been one day since we'd returned from my testimony at High Queen's Council. And we'd spent most of it reassuring my people here that I would not be blamed or punished for Mona Louisa's death, that everything was okay. But that was a lie. While things may be okay

Council-wise—or as much as it could be after a stir like that—*I* wasn't okay. And only Dontaine knew the truth of this.

I stepped back from my lover's touch. Dropped my eyes from his compelling male beauty, from the tempting loveliness of his form, from the raw and tender heart he offered up to me with those expressive green eyes. I took a hard step back from it all and said, "We need to talk, Dontaine."

A beat of silence. When he spoke, it was with quiet tension thrumming in his voice. "That never bodes well."

I guess that was a rule that held true not only for humans but for the Monère also.

"I will dress," he said quietly, and I retreated to a corner chair as he opened the armoire and began to pull on clothes. I would have stared out the window had there been one, but there was none in this simple cabin. I passed the time instead with an intricate study of the wood-planked floor.

I felt his presence as he neared and sat by my feet. There were no other chairs. I would have felt better had he stood instead of seating himself on the floor below me, a gesture that placed him lower than I, made him even more vulnerable to me.

My eyes lifted from my perusal of the floor, met his, and flicked away. I couldn't say what I had to say to him while looking into those unshielded eyes.

"Dontaine." Just his name for a moment, so lovely upon my lips. Then came the blow. "We cannot be lovers."

He didn't say anything, so I rushed to fill in the pregnant silence. "I care for you. You know that." It was a truth that he'd seen in my eyes. "But you also know that there is something very, very wrong with me. You've asked no questions."

"There has been no time. No opportunity."

"There is now. Do you have any questions for me?"

A strained silence. Then he asked not what I would have asked after all that confused madness that had occurred two nights ago, but what was most important to him. "Why can we not be lovers?"

His hands, long-fingered and elegant, an aristocrat's hands, were folded neatly around his bended knees as he sat there on the wooden floor. I focused on those hands, remembered how they had felt on me, in me, caressing me, and looked blindly away.

"You and I know that it was not my beast's hunger that almost overwhelmed me at High Court." Though that was what we'd told everyone else. Even Tomas, my other guard who'd been there that night, believed it to be true. "It was bloodlust, Dontaine. Demon bloodlust."

"It is because of Halcyon, the Demon Prince. When you accompanied him." Dontaine's words, more of a statement than a real question, referred to the time when I had returned with Halcyon to Hell. When my Demon Prince had been so severely injured because of me . . . always because of me, it seemed . . . that he could not make the trip safely home by himself. Hell was a dangerous place, even for its ruler.

I closed my eyes, picking my answer carefully, tiptoeing among all the lies to pick a truth that I could tell him. "Not in the way you think. I wasn't infected then. But you're right, it does involve Halcyon." It certainly involved his blood, which Mona Louisa had taken from him against his will, breaking one of their greatest taboos—drinking a demon's blood. She'd blood-raped Halcyon. And I, in turn, had light-raped her. Now both of their essences dwelled within me. And all of this had to remain a secret. Unknown.

Blaec, the High Lord of Hell, Halcyon's father, had killed a score of Monère warriors and their Queen—Mona Louisa, the demon blood violator—to keep this secret: that drinking their blood can multiply a Monère's power, endowing them with demon dead strength. I did not want the next blood bath to be that of my men.

"It involves Mona Louisa, too," I said, and told Dontaine nothing he did not already know. He'd seen my brown eyes turn blue, turn into Mona Louisa's eyes. "How, I cannot say. Only that it was the reason why the High Lord of Hell killed her."

"But he spared you. Does he know that you have some of their essence in you?"

A good question. The High Lord had seen me drain Mona Louisa of her light, her energy. He had spared me, believing that keeping my Monère secret—my extremely rare, extremely dangerous gift of Mortal Draining, that light-drinking thing I had done—would ensure the keeping of his demon secret. But the real reason he had spared me was because his son, Halcyon, had named me as his mate. Because after six hundred years alone, he had found love.

Still . . . that was before Blaec knew that his demon secret dwelled as a living presence within me. That it had infected me. That it evidenced within me everything they tried to keep hidden from the Monères. Would he still have spared me had he known this? I would know soon enough. Lucinda, Halcyon's sister, had been at High Court, and her presence there had brought out the demon taint in me. There'd been no hiding it from her. She knew what existed within me—what was changing me—and would have reported that to the High Lord and to Halcyon. Death resided within me, most likely lay before me.

"Lucinda will have told them by now," I said. "If the High Lord, or if Halcyon . . . if they come to kill me, you are not to try to stop them or seek revenge."

Dontaine froze into a stillness that unnerved me.

"They will be within their rights, Dontaine. Do you understand?"

He shook his head, his voice sounding harsh and strained. "No. I do not understand."

"It was something that *I* did. Something I brought upon

myself. I'm sorry to lay this burden on you, but if anything happens to me, you are the only one who knows. The only one who can testify before the Council that I hold Halcyon and the High Lord blameless."

"For executing you," he said. "If two of our Queens are killed by demon hand, even if it is by the High Lord himself again, it will not sit well with the High Queens Council."

"What will they do? Go to war with them?" My laugh was short and bitter. "They would be slaughtered. As would you, all of you here. Everyone I love and hold dear." I closed the distance between us, gripped his hand tight. Felt his electric touch dance with shocking little jolts upon my skin. The sensation was sharper, more painful than normal, betraying his leaking distress. "Dontaine, promise me that you will not lift your hand against them if they come for me."

A hard, painful jolt shot from his hand to mine, making me gasp. He drew his hand away so that we no longer touched. "Are you asking me, or ordering me?"

I searched his eyes, those green tumultuous depths. "You are my master at arms. With command comes great responsibility. You hold our people's safety in your hands. Would you see your mother, your sister, killed for no purpose? Would you throw away their lives—your life—so easily? I ask it of you, but if I must, I will order it. Must I, Dontaine? Must I demand it of you?"

His eyes dropped away from mine. "Mona Lisa . . . What you ask of me . . ."

I went into his arms then because I loved him. Because I was hurting him, and I did not want to. I went into his arms because the torment I glimpsed in his beautiful eyes just plain broke my heart.

Contact with him lanced me for a sharp, electric second before he brought his forceful presence back under control.

"Please, Dontaine. I love you. I want to keep you safe.

All of you—Jamie, Tersa, Rosemary, Thaddeus, Chami, Tomas, Aquila, and Amber. You are my family. The most important beings to me in this world. Please help me keep you all safe. I could not bear it if I lost someone else I loved."

His hands cupped my face, lifted it up to his so that I saw his brilliant, gleaming eyes, the chiseled lines of his face fierce and raw with emotion. Perhaps he would have kissed me then. Perhaps I would have let him. A foolish thing to do when it was infinitely safer to push him away. Safer for him.

I don't know if I would have given in to that momentary folly. I don't know what would have happened afterward. All I suddenly knew was that my gums were burning as if fire had set them aflame. That my teeth were aching. That I had a sudden thirsting urge for blood, to feel it sliding hot and sweet down my throat.

This was what had happened to me at High Court—the promise of fangs. That promise suddenly became reality. My teeth elongated and pushed upward and outward through my gums like small mountains erupting. I gasped because it hurt like hell. Then gasped again when I felt a sharp sting and looked down to see blood welling from the hand I'd drawn up to my mouth and pricked. I'd accidentally cut myself on the sharpness of my own teeth . . . on my *fangs*.

"Dear Goddess," Dontaine whispered. Cold fear skimmed the surface of those two words.

I pushed away from him and stumbled out the door. Away. I had to get away from him. I fled outside into the cool night, and in the breeze that glided over my skin, I felt him—the demon presence outside that had brought forth the demon presence within me. And not just any demon, but one I knew intimately. "Halcyon."

He came to me out of the darkness, my elegant Demon Prince. I sensed him as I'd never sensed him before, like a heartbeat. Only his heart did not beat, he did not breathe. He—like the other demons—was dead, demon dead, and we were not supposed to be able to sense them this strongly. That was what made them so dangerous—that they could approach us almost undetected. That and their far greater strength, both mental and physical.

The last time I'd seen Halcyon, he'd been weak and bloodied, his chest ripped to shreds by a whip. He was not weak now. Others would have looked upon him and seen an average man in looks, height, and build. He was only a bare head-tilt taller than I, slender and trim, with dark hair, dark eyes, just like me. He had a quiet presence rather than a shouting one. A reserved air. An air of loneliness. An apartness from others that had pulled me to him since the very first time I became aware of him in a sun-dappled meadow.

A Monère warrior who did not know the Demon Prince would have seen him and dismissed him in strength and power. Never would have guessed that before him stood the ruler of Hell, someone far stronger than our greatest Warrior Lord.

I'd never feared Halcyon as others did—his great strength, those lethal nails. He'd been kind to me from the very first, and not just kind but a friend . . . and then a lover in a dream or a vision—you might call it a dream reality. Whatever it had been, the feelings between us had certainly been real.

Even when I'd seen Halcyon shift into his alternate demon form—huge, monstrous, ugly—and kill another demon in battle over me, even then I had not really feared him. But now I did. Because I didn't just feel Halcyon's presence, I felt his emotions. He *ached* with sadness. Almost overwhelming grief.

The cabin door opened. Dontaine stepped out, a silver dagger gleaming with naked threat in his hand, and I felt Halcyon's grieving sadness flash into anger.

"Dontaine, leave us," I said, my voice carefully calm.

My master of arms, my lover, did not obey me. Instead he came to stand beside me. "I'm sorry, I can't."

"I'm sorry, too." With a blow that took Dontaine unaware, I struck him, careful with my strength because I was more than just Monère strong now. I caught his unconscious body as it went lax, and carried him inside to the cabin, laid him gently down on the bed.

One last secret touch of that sun-bright hair. Then I straightened and stepped out to meet my fate.

Two

"I SMELL HIS scent on you," were Halcyon's words upon
my return. I didn't know how to answer him. Amber
and Gryphon had shared me without jealousy. I'd have said
that Monère men did not know the meaning of the word,
but that was not true. The one person they had been jealous
of had been Halcyon. The Demon Prince's interest in me
had driven them crazy with resentment and fear. I had no
inkling of what Halcyon's reaction might be to my sleeping
with another man, even if it had been to save us both. Since
I wanted to keep Dontaine alive, I said nothing.

Halcyon gave a little smile, and again that wave of sadness flowed over me, through me. "I will not harm him," he
said, and held out his hand to me.

I walked to him, took his hand without hesitation, felt
the faintest brush of those sharp nails across my skin—
lethal nails that could cut off a demon's head with one
deadly swipe—and didn't flinch. Why should I? If I was to
die, I knew he would make it as quick and as painless as

possible. But before I died, I wanted to know one thing. "How is Gryphon?"

I know. Contradicting myself here, asking him about another lover. But Gryphon and Amber had come before Halcyon. He did not seem to resent them. Dontaine, on the other hand, had come after Halcyon. Therein might lie a very big difference.

"He is well, adjusting to his new existence." There seemed to be more he wanted to say but didn't. He led me instead farther into the forest, away from the cabin, and I went with him willingly. We walked for a time, no words, but a wealth of emotion, *his* emotion, flooded the silence until I could no longer bear it. "Don't be sad, Halcyon."

He led me to a toppled tree fallen long ago, and urged me to sit there on the trunk. "Hell-cat," he whispered, his endearment for me, and again I felt that welling, immense sorrow. "I'm not going to kill you."

His words were a surprise and a relief to me. "Then why are you grieving?"

"Grieving—how appropriately stated. Oh, Mona Lisa." He closed his eyes for a moment as if it pained him to look at me. When his lashes lifted, he looked into me with more than just his eyes as he feathered the back of his fingers across the tip of my fangs in a whisper-light caress. "All that my sister said is true. You have become *Damanôen*."

"It sounds pretty," I said, for a condition that was not. But after the initial bloodlust that had come welling up with the bursting of my fangs, the hunger had faded. I felt it still, but only like a faint, nibbling urge. "If you're not going to kill me then why are you so sad?" I asked.

"What you feel is what you called it—grief. I'm grieving for what we have lost."

"What have we lost?"

"Time," Halcyon said. "An afterlife of togetherness. You have such great mental strength, you would have existed for a long time in my realm." After Monères died, those with enough psychic power transitioned to Hell and became demon dead, living there for as long as their mental energy sustained them. Some of them existed for hundreds of years, like Halcyon.

Something stirred in me, prickled my calm. "Have I lost my afterlife?"

Halcyon gazed at me sadly with eyes the color of dark chocolate. "You are *Damanôen*, demon living now. You cannot become demon dead afterward."

I'd been shortchanged already. As a Mixed Blood, I would have probably only lived a hundred years, a human's lifespan instead of the three hundred years of life most Monère enjoyed if they were not killed before then. Now on top of that I'd lost the promise of afterlife. It was a devastating blow.

I drew in a deep breath and thought, *At least I'm still breathing*. A lifetime had been gained and lost; I was just back where I first started. *So you didn't really lose anything*, I told myself.

Sure.

The ache in my heart said differently.

"Well, at least I've got eighty more years of life," I said.

Another swelling ache of pain from Halcyon.

It made my heart beat faster. "Don't I? Halcyon, you said you weren't going to kill me." Now that hundreds of demon years had been chopped off of my existence, the remaining few human decades were even more precious.

He closed his eyes and somehow drew down a light veil so that I was no longer bathed in his emotions. So that my own started to rise up instead.

"Not now," he said. Two very innocuous words apart. Strung together like that, they became very foreboding. Very portentous.

"What the hell do you mean? *Not now*. So you're going

to kill me later?" I felt that calmness, that resigned feeling of peace slipping rapidly away from me.

Fuck that, a voice inside of me shouted, *I don't want to die.*

"Calm," Halcyon murmured and I felt that rising heat within me smooth back down like turbulent waters soothed. "It will be easier if you remain calm."

"What will be easier?"

"Controlling the new demon nature you have acquired." *His* demon nature. It had been Halcyon's blood Mona Louisa had ingested. "How well you can control it will determine how long you shall live."

"What do you mean, Halcyon? I'm getting pretty tired of asking all these questions. Why don't you just tell me what's going to happen?"

Like a symphonic swelling, that sadness came wafting out from him again. "It is something that is better shown," he said, and like that the grief shut off. Completely this time, like a limb suddenly chopped off. And in that absence, my demon bloodlust came rushing back into me like a thirty-foot wave held back for a time but no longer contained. It smashed down on me. Drowned me in want and throbbing need.

"Christ!" I gasped. My nails sank down several inches into the tree trunk I'd unconsciously gripped, my fingertips aching and throbbing just as my teeth had before my fangs had erupted. I didn't know if it was because I had shoved them through hard wood, or if it was because my nails where changing into sharp dagger tips like Halcyon's. I didn't *want* to know. Didn't want to see. So I kept them buried, like an ostrich sticking its head in sand, and desperately fought that wild hunger, that bloodlust, that was urging me to pounce on Halcyon and sink my fangs into him.

I would *not* be that stupid. Because if I was, forget eighty years, my life wouldn't even last eighty seconds. *No, no, NO! Do not jump him.* But it was like trying to hang onto an oil-slicked ledge. My grip, my control, was starting to slip. I was hanging on only by my mental fingertips, slipping, slipping, starting to fall . . .

A majestic stag, its antlers spanning almost four feet across, emerged from a thicket of trees. A wild animal that did not behave like a wild animal, it came right up to me like a tame pet, his large, liquid eyes calm and tranquil, his body a contained fountain of blood that called wildly to me.

"Drink," Halcyon said, and his voice, his command, broke the last strands of my tenuous control. I fell on the stag like a ravenous beast, which is what I had become. I plunged my fangs into the deer's neck with no care, no finesse, with only greed and crazed need. And drank and drank and drank. Hot glorious blood gushed down my throat, that pulse of life beating into me, flowing hot and sweet and coppery good, taking the burning edge off, partly quenching the overwhelming need so that it no longer overwhelmed thought. So that I could think once again, become acutely aware of what I was doing. Become horrified by it.

I pulled my fangs out from the meaty flesh with a wet, sucking *slurp*, and fell with a cry away from the animal onto the ground, my hand covering my mouth. Now normal nails, I noted in one corner of my mind while I sucked in air, feeling my stomach, full of blood, churning with horror and distress.

Blood spurted out in tiny gushes from the stag's neck, a gentle outflow. Halcyon put his mouth over the ragged bite wound—what I had done—and lapped up the blood until it no longer flowed.

"Our saliva can both thin blood and thicken it," Halcyon said, drawing away. "When you are done feeding, simply picture the blood clotting, and it will stop."

As if responding to a silent command, the big animal lumbered calmly away, disappearing into the forest.

"If you feed your hunger instead of fighting it, you will be able to control it better. It does not take much blood." With a natural grace that was a part of him, Halcyon caught my hand and pulled me up from the ground to perch once more on the tree trunk. I sat there numbly with my body trembling, my fangs stained red with blood.

"Your control," he said calmly, bluntly. "*That* will determine if you live or die."

Oh. I even understood the reasoning. The Monère. We were a people that lived in secret among the humans. Anything that threatened that hidden coexistence, say a wild Mixed Blood boy raiding and killing a human farmer's domestic livestock . . . he would be eliminated in a blink. Anything that stood out, that called attention to us like that would not be tolerated or allowed to live. The equivalent of that, in the demon dead's case, would be my fangs. That would draw a lot of attention. Because, quite simply, the Monère did not have fangs in our human form. Only the demon dead did. Which boded ill for me because I still had them. Fangs. As in long, sharp, pointy canine teeth protruding from my mouth. They would cause quite a stir among the Monère if they were seen. It would make them wonder how I'd acquired that demon trait . . . and whether I had other traits of theirs, like their greater strength, which I did. Both explanations—Mortal Draining (me—my fault) and drinking a demon's blood (Mona Louisa's fault)—would get me killed. The first one by the Monère Queens, because if they knew what I could do, I'd be too dangerous for them to tolerate . . . or risk having my ability spread to others. The second would get me just as dead by the demons, who had already wiped out an entire Queen's force to keep their secret quiet.

The problem was, now that my fangs were out I didn't know how to make them go away. And Dontaine—Christ!—he'd already seen them, striking a bolt of fear through me like lightning. *Don't think of him. Don't think of him.* Because if I could sense Halcyon's emotions, he could probably sense mine. I hoped and prayed that he couldn't read my thoughts, though. That he did not know that Dontaine had already seen my fangs. Shit! I had thought of it again.

"I can't read your thoughts," Halcyon said, which of course made me believe quite the opposite. "Your face, the way you stiffened. It's easy enough for me to read from your expression that you just thought of something you did not wish me to know . . . and that you feared that I might."

Okay, I could buy that explanation. Horace the steward and Bernard Fruge, Dontaine's father, had read me like that.

Halcyon paused. A human might have sighed, but he was demon dead, he did not need to breathe. And they rarely did so unless it was to speak or to scent our fear or arousal. "When you felt my sadness," he said, "I was calming your demon. I can help you that way if I choose, because it is my blood residing in you."

"You linked us together."

Halcyon nodded.

"Are we linked now?"

"No. I have withdrawn my aid. You stand by just your control alone, and it is not bad."

But is it good enough to let me live? was the million-dollar question. Apparently so. He hadn't sliced off my head yet. It seemed for the moment that I was good. But I wanted to know beyond the moment. "How do you . . ." I gestured to my fangs. "How do you make them go away?"

"In time, you will be able to make them appear at will or suppress their emergence if you wish. For now, they will subside when I leave you. It is my demon presence that pulls forth your own."

"And my nails. Will they become like yours? Or my eyes . . . will they glow red?" Like Halcyon's did with rage—flickering fiery red as if the very flames of Hell were ignited in him.

"I do not know. What you are now, what you will become, no one can predict. What you did . . . no one has done that before."

His words left a leaden feeling in my stomach. As if I had swallowed down a bar of steel, and it weighed me down like a dropped anchor.

I'd been an oddity before—the first Mixed Blood Monère Queen. Now I was even odder yet with not just human blood mixed in with the Monère, but with demon spirit added in, too. Totally bizarre. And from what he was saying, I might become even more so . . . if I managed to live that long. Great. Just freaking great.

"Your father called what I did Mortal Draining. I got the impression that others had that ability in the past, that I'm not the first one to do this thing."

"No. But that you were able to become *Damanôen* that way . . ." Halcyon shrugged. "No one else has ever done so."

"What . . . they usually just drank down demon blood, right?"

"That is correct."

"And you killed them all. That's what your sister, Lucinda, said. I believe her exact phrasing was: *My kind hunted and killed things like you long ago*. Real inspiring words, you know."

"You are being sarcastic, very like yourself. That is a good sign." He spoke totally without humor.

"Answer the question, Halcyon." And because he was the ruler of Hell—even if I was not going there, dammit!— I tacked on at the end, "Please."

"You are asking why we killed off all others like you in the past, but are letting you live?"

"Yeah, that's what I'm asking."

"Most Monère who became that way did so through blood rape as Mona Louisa did with me." Blood rape. It seemed to be an actual phrase used by demons, not something I'd thought up in my head. "Those demons would of course tend to kill those who had violated them so, if they were able. Other *Damanôen* were killed either because they could not control themselves—they went rampaging mad—"

I must have gone sheet-white, because Halcyon hastened to add, "But you have not shown that tendency."

"It's early yet," I whispered.

"It manifests fairly quickly," Halcyon said, his voice once again that soothing, gentle tone. Its brief effect on me was totally ruined by his next words. "Others like you were eliminated simply because they were able to sense us."

I swallowed. "A living demon detector, able to sense your presence. I can see how other demons would not like that. So, they were hunted down and killed off because of that."

"Yes," Halcyon said softly. "There were never many *Damanôen*, and the few that existed were often quickly killed. Knowledge of them, that they once existed, has been lost."

"More like carefully contained, I'd say."

Halcyon nodded, acknowledging this. "Lost, contained—however you put it, the fact remains that it has become a secret knowledge among the demons, erased from Monère awareness."

"And you and your father would like to keep it that way."

"Yes. Both my father and I would like to keep it that way."

Circling us back to that crucial question: Of whether or not I had good enough control to keep that secret hidden.

Not just the drinking demon blood thing, but that Monère could become like demons while yet living. Fangs popping out tended to give that away.

I didn't know how to ask this. Couldn't bring myself to ask him straight out: *Will you kill me if I draw too much attention to myself?*

I said instead, "Halcyon, what will we do?"

His answer surprised me. "There are two ways we can handle this. We can try and hide it. Or we can try the opposite—not trying to hide it. Diverting them instead from the real reason for your demon-like change."

"If I have a choice in this, I'm all for *not* trying to hide it. I think I would fail in the endeavor to hide it," I said honestly. Fail and die. And now that I knew I would not be enjoying a long afterlife, I sure as heck did not want to depart this life anytime sooner than I had to. "What do you propose?"

"That I claim you publicly as my mate ten days from now at the next Council meeting. Others will presume that any changes, any strangeness you manifest, even those of becoming more demonic . . . they will assume that it comes from our union."

Diversion. Creating smoke elsewhere to hide the true cause. "I think that's a *brilliant* idea, Halcyon."

Turmoil flashed in his eyes.

"What is it? What's wrong, Halcyon?"

His voice, when he spoke, was low. "I do not want it just to be false diversion. I want it to be true. I want you to be my mate in truth."

"Oh." One little word to express everything that I suddenly understood. He loved me. Wanted our union to be not just official but real, and feared that it would not be so. That I would agree to it simply to save my life.

Where I once would have hesitated, here I did not. Because I'd come to learn that life could be fleeting. That love was precious where you found it, something to be cherished. Something to grab ahold of with both hands and one's entire heart. "Yes, Halcyon. I will be your mate. In truth, in love, with everything that I am . . . even the demon part of me that is you."

He looked into my eyes, deep into me, and laughed joyously. I was suddenly in his arms, and that remaining thirst for blood that throbbed in me still, became channeled into hunger of another kind. One that involved flesh, yes. But not to eat it. Well, at least not literally.

I felt the tide of need shift within me and welcomed it with delight. With eager hands that roamed and sought and found smooth skin, muscled flesh. With trembling heart that wanted, wanted, wanted him. His love, his laughter. That look in his eyes as he caressed me gently with the back of his knuckles.

"Mona Lisa."

"Yes, love me."

"I do."

"Show me," I said, my fingers flying, unbuttoning his clothes, unzipping mine. He stood there docilely, letting me undress him, watching as I shed my own clothes. But his eyes . . . his eyes were anything but docile or tame. They burned with need, with sexual heat, with heart's desire.

Naked, we came together. And that first touch of flesh to flesh shuddered a cry from me, a sigh from him. He laid me upon the ground, came down on top of me, and I opened my heart and body to him.

"You are mine," he said, his chocolate brown eyes burning down into mine, watching me, connecting us that way. Watching me as he pushed slowly into me and connected us that way, too. He entered me, slid luxuriously in, and we both groaned. My eyes fluttered shut.

"No. Look at me, Hell-cat. Let me see you. Let me know you. Let me inside of you. Yes," he whispered as he stroked within me, his face, his body, his eyes a breath above mine, giving us an intimacy that was as deep and poignant as how he felt moving within me. "You hold me so tight, so warmly. My home," he said, and with another wet slide, pushed back into me. "You are my home."

Gentle, so gentle he was. And then his eyes slid down, fell upon the side of my neck. Then, and only then, did I become aware that his strokes in and out of me . . . they were timed to the flux and flow of my heart. As my blood pumped within me, so did he time his movements within me. My pulse quickened at that realization. At the knowledge of where he looked, what he desired. As it did so, his own rhythm accelerated.

Pleasure had weakened me, making me yielding, lax. Making me a soft, receptive sheath for his piercing flesh— a deep penetrating blade that plunged in and pulled out. Now with that one look, that caressing touch upon my neck, everything tightened in a dark and dangerous, convulsive thrill. Halcyon groaned at my tighter clutch, his rhythm thrown off for one faltering second at that gripping pleasure. That inner tightness and awareness. "Ah . . . sweet Hades."

He pulled out, plunged back into me, his movements sharper, a touch more forceful. Less harmonious. More invading.

Blood. I became so aware of it beating within me. Coursing in me as he moved within me. No longer a soft pulsing flow, but one gaining speed and momentum, beginning to pound. Another dark thrill chased through me, tightened me. Blood. I suddenly desired it between us. And so did he.

"Drink," I said. And tilted back my head, offering him my neck.

"Hell-cat." Just those two words spoken in a rough, velvet rasp. His head lowered as he accepted what I offered, as he took what we both needed. His soft lips pressed over my beating pulse. The tips of his sharp fangs pressed against my skin, caressed it. I shivered. Groaned. My hands buried themselves in the thickness of his hair, held him to me there. One stroke, two—sharp fangs gliding over soft skin. And then he pierced me. And with that first taste of my blood, the dynamics of our lovemaking changed. As my red life flowed into him, what was soft and sweet became darker, more dangerous.

He growled, his body hardening as every muscle tensed. Then he unleashed himself, a sudden, hard pounding force, ramming himself into me, and I cried out in ecstasy.

"More," I demanded, "more!" And he gave me more. He drove into me as he drank me down, as if the speed with which he pumped himself increased the speed with which my blood pumped into him. Maybe it did. All I know is that I wound tighter and tighter as he pistoned himself in and out of me with almost frenzied fury while he gulped me down, propelling me upward until I shattered into a million pieces of light. A million pieces of rapture.

I saw him above me, his skin dark gold like a gilded angel, as he called forth my inner light—the moon's rays that dwelt in all her children. The night filled with the light that glowed from my skin, that burst from me as I burst apart, convulsing, shattering in climactic bliss. And above me, I felt not light but power swell from him. A burst of energy as he seized above me and pulsed within me, splashing his liquid heat into me, a small return for the fluid he had taken from me. He threw back his head and roared his release, his fangs crimson bright with my blood. And I felt the exchange equal. Was more than happy with it as he collapsed on top of me and let me bear his full weight, a pleasure all to itself, to feel a man sprawled on top of you like that with every muscle lax, all desire sated, every need fulfilled.

When my light faded back into me and darkness covered

us once more, Halcyon turned his head and licked my wound closed so that it no longer bled. Easing out of me, he rolled to the side, pulling me with him to snuggle against him, his eyes warm upon my face. "Hell-cat," he said softly.

"You didn't use any of your mental powers."

"I wanted our first real time together to be just you and me. No mental enhancement, no question of compulsion. Just me, my body, pleasing you."

I ran my hands over that body, enjoying the feel of it—that smooth skin, those light muscles. The strong shoulders, powerful arms.

I realized that my fangs were gone. Just normal teeth once more.

"It certainly pleased me," I purred, whispering a kiss against his lips now that it was safe. Now that there was no bloodlust. "*You* please me. Your mind, your body. Separate or together." He kissed me back, pressed warm lips to mine.

A sound suddenly intruded, pulling him back from me, rolling him away. He moved so quickly, they both did, that I didn't realize at first what was happening, just saw dark hair against light hair, and caught the quick flash of a blade. I heard Halcyon growl, heard the other man curse, and realized that it was my master of arms, Dontaine, my other lover, awake and enraged, his green eyes flashing with murderous intent.

I screamed, "Dontaine, no! Halcyon, stop! Both of you!"

They grappled together, grunting, growling, fighting. An entangled mass rolling on the ground, heeding me not.

"Stop it!" I screamed.

Dontaine was suddenly flung away. He sailed through the air for a dozen feet before hitting a tree with a hard *thunk*, branches snapping and breaking beneath his weight as he dropped to the ground. He jumped to his feet and rushed Halcyon again like a crazed bull, his shirt slashed, blood staining it.

I'd worried about Halcyon's jealousy and his anger. I hadn't thought of Dontaine's. He went after the Demon Prince armed with just a silver dagger and mindless rage.

Halcyon stood poised like a matador as the bigger warrior charged him. His slender body was tense, almost eager, his eyes hard and gleaming, with a cruel little smile on his face. His lethal nails were curved and ready at his side, Dontaine's blood adorning the tips like red fingernail polish.

He held no malice toward me. That was what I had told Gryphon about Halcyon the first time I had met him. I hadn't feared the Demon Prince, then. That was not true now. Malice emanated from Halcyon in thick, palpable waves as he watched and waited for Dontaine with that eager gleam in his eyes.

"That's it, warrior," he crooned. "Come to me."

I didn't let him. I tackled Dontaine, gasping as we hit the ground hard. Dontaine twisted, protecting me as we rolled. A nice sentiment, a natural instinct, but not what I wanted. What I wanted right now was obedience from him. I ended on top of Dontaine.

"Mona Lisa, are you all right?" He sounded concerned. He sounded sane, intelligent, reasonable. Not at all like a suicidal idiot.

I snarled and grabbed him by the shirtfront. "I command you as your Queen to stop! Right now. *No fighting!*"

He yielded, in his eyes, in his body beneath mine. But not in words. I slowly peeled myself off of him and rose to my feet. "Say it, Dontaine." My voice was hard, flat, and brittle. As brittle as how I felt.

"No fighting," he said and rose to his feet. His body trembled as he looked over my head, behind me. Not in fear, but in anger. In rage.

Carefully, I stepped back to the side, positioning myself so I could see them both. And understood immediately what had set Dontaine's anger ablaze once more. Halcyon's nakedness. That golden skin was uncut and dry . . . all but his shaft that glistened with wetness, coated by my juice where he had sheathed himself inside of me.

"Halcyon, could you dress, please?" I asked. Walking back to where my own clothes law strewn on the ground, I pulled them on quickly. Dontaine stood where I'd left him, like a dog straining against an invisible leash, held back only because of that restraint. No less savage because of it.

I went back to him. Touched him soothingly. "You knew Halcyon was my lover. I told you that, and you took the news calmly. Why did you attack him now?"

"Because he infected you! You must stay away from him lest he infect you even more."

Fear spiked through me as Dontaine's words betrayed to Halcyon the very thing I had tried to keep hidden from him. God, how tired I was of being afraid.

One of my new abilities was a falcon's clarity of vision, Gryphon's gift to me. To see clear down to one's soul. I turned Dontaine's face down to me, looked into his eyes, and saw the real truth in him. "Dontaine. It is not just fear for me that made you try to kill the High Prince."

Fine tremors shook Dontaine. Heated his eyes with a tangle of emotions. "True. I want to kill the Demon Prince because you turned from me as a lover, yet you continue to accept him."

"He is safe," I whispered, a part of me crying at the pain I saw in those eyes. "He cannot be affected by what is in me. I do not fear for him as I do for you."

"And he cannot get you pregnant as I can," Dontaine said bitterly. Another harsh truth that I could not deny. Halcyon was demon dead. He could not bring forth life. Dontaine, on the other hand, was descended from a potent

fertile line, rare among the Monère, and usually prized because of it. But not so with me. His potency, in my eyes,
was a huge detriment. I could not risk becoming pregnant,
infected as I was with demon darkness.

All of Dontaine's strengths were detriments with me.
First, the unusual Half Change state that he was capable of
achieving, arresting his change halfway into his wolf form so
he became that terrible, horrendous embodiment of human
legend—werewolf. A gift usually prized for its rareness. I
had shied from its ugliness—the part-man, part-animal hy-
brid. Monstrous, I'd called it. Not an ability I wanted to gain
for myself. I could gain others' gifts by having sex with them,
and I could pass my gifts along to them in turn. That was how
I had acquired Gryphon's keenness of vision, and some of
Amber's great strength. In exchange, they had obtained from
me the ability to withstand sunlight, to not burn beneath its
hot rays.

Sex and Basking—a Queen's ability to call down the renewing rays of the moon and share it with her people. That
was what the Monère society was based upon. Or perhaps
it was even simpler than that. Maybe it was just based on
power: Warriors gaining it by Basking and having sex with
Queens; Queens gaining it by sleeping with her men—a
great many, varied number of them. One big fuckfest of
power and pleasure.

I'd rejected Dontaine once. And again a second time after he'd offered what he saw as the most valuable part of
himself—his potency, his ability to give me a baby—when
he'd found me grieving at the knowledge that there would
be no living remembrance of Gryphon, that I wasn't pregnant with his child as I had hoped. I'd hurt not only Dontaine's heart, but even more unforgivably, I'd pricked his
male pride. I saw it all there in his eyes, and didn't know
what to do about it. He was too angry to heed his words.
Had in fact spilled out in a heated rush the very knowledge

I'd knocked him unconscious to keep hidden—that he was aware of my demon infection, as he called it.

I shouldn't have pulled my punch, worrying about my strength when I'd knocked him out. I should have hit him harder, kept him out of it longer. Maybe knock some more sense into him. He could scarce have any less of it.

I turned away from him to plead with Halcyon instead. "Don't kill him."

Menace still emanated from the Demon Prince. His words, though, were calm. "If he restrains himself, I will not. Mostly because you will need him."

His words drew Dontaine's attention as nothing else could have. "What do you mean?" Dontaine demanded roughly.

"Your Queen will need a source of blood near her at all times. Even when she learns to call wild creatures to her, fresh animal blood will not be so easy to keep at hand. She will need someone to drink from should her bloodlust stir. A little drink of blood to sate the hunger, and she gains much control over it. Would you be willing to let her feed from you?"

"Halcyon—"

My Demon Prince turned to look at me. "Hell-cat, what you have cannot be passed to him in that way. You cannot 'infect' him, as you fear."

And what the Demon Prince offered to Dontaine was clearly a balm to the warrior's wounded pride—to be needed by his Queen.

"She can have anything of me that she desires," Dontaine said. And like that, his aggression began to fade. He sheathed his dagger . . . while I wanted to plunge it into him, so pissed off was I by how badly I'd bungled things with my new lover . . . and how easily Halcyon had fixed them. But he was the ruler of Hell, after all. Soothing one Monère warrior's wounded pride had to be a piece of cake compared to handling a realm full of dangerous, blood-thirsty demons.

It was my first lesson in rulership. And I accepted it, bitter though it tasted in my mouth. "Thank you, Dontaine."

My eyes flashed gratitude to Halcyon, or at least tried to, for restraining himself. For not slaughtering Dontaine. For handling the situation without bloodshed.

"I will leave you now," Halcyon said. The barest brush of those sharp nails—a sweet and dangerous caress across my cheek—and he started to walk away.

"So soon?" Disappointment coated my voice as I followed after him. "You just got here," I said almost plaintively.

He stopped, turned around. "Hell-cat," he murmured, and I felt the mental brush of his power, invisible lips pressing against mine in a brief, phantom kiss. "I am being prudent. I expended a lot of energy. It would be wiser for me to go now and recover. I will tarry longer next time, I promise."

I could not argue with him for being careful. The last time he had come here had ended disastrously for the both of us. "How will you get back to the portal?" I asked. The nearest one that I knew of was in New Orleans, almost an hour's drive away.

"The same way I got here. By car."

"You took a taxi?" I asked.

"Yes, and he waits for me patiently by the roadside where I had him stop when I first sensed you."

"You bespelled him," I said. "In which case, the cab will still likely be there. But this is my land, Halcyon." Or would it now be our land, I wondered, when we were mated? I pushed the thought away for later examination, and concentrated on the important matter here and now. "The last time you came here, you left gravely injured. We will see you safely to the car."

"I would enjoy your company," Halcyon said with a smile, and held out his hand to me. I took it, my hand slipping naturally into his, and walked companionably beside him. The barest hesitation, and then Dontaine joined us, too. And if it was a little awkward for a moment—holding hands with my demon lover, my Monère lover walking beside me—it was but a momentary discomfort that quickly passed. Light or dark, skin dusted gold or alabaster white, we were still, all of us, children of the moon. And she beamed her benevolent rays down upon us as we moved through the woods with soundless ease. The direction was easy to find. Just cast your senses wide and listen for the human heartbeat. There, to the north edge of the woods.

"You do not seem to resent me," Dontaine said, and though he hadn't addressed his comment specifically, it was clear to whom he was speaking. For a moment, our moonlit harmony faltered.

"You are of the light, I am from the dark," Halcyon answered. His words flowed smooth and gentle, restoring the rhythm, continuing the harmony. "You dwell among the living, I among the dead. I cannot often be here. We both love the same woman, and are loved by her. She is not one who opens her heart lightly, or to those undeserving. And I am not so petty as to demand that she love only me. We are of different worlds. That she opens her heart to include me is already a gift beyond measure. No, I do not resent you. I am grateful to you. It eases me to know that you shall look after her during the times I cannot. That you will be with her in the times I cannot be. You treasure her as I do and will guard her well, keep her alive for us all."

Though he was dead, and that organ of life, his heart, dead within him also, love flowed from Halcyon in abundance, in wise generosity, in a river of plentitude.

"My lord," Dontaine said, bowing his head down in a

deep gesture of respect. "You have my promise. I shall guard her with my life."

Halcyon smiled and stopped at the treeline where the forest ended and a wild-grassed meadow began. The cab was parked along the roadside twenty yards distant. He raised my hand, pressed a kiss there.

"*Mea ena*," Halcyon murmured tenderly. "Stay safe for me." Then he was gone, striding across the meadow. We watched until the cab drove away. An odd sight to see—the ruler of Hell being driven away in a taxi.

"He called you his wife."

My heart tumbled a bit at the word Dontaine used—*wife*. I substituted it for something I was much more comfortable with. "I agreed to be his mate. To have it publicly acknowledged at High Court this next session."

"And me?" Dontaine asked.

Halcyon had given his blessing and his assurance that I could not pass the demon darkness inside me to Dontaine through sex.

Dontaine had given his word that he would protect me with his life, with his blood, whatever I desired of him. So generous were the men that I loved. How could I be any less so?

I took his hand—so different it was from the one I had just held, with nails blunt and short, skin pale, palm callused—a warrior's hand. Yet they both felt right in mine. With our fingers clasped together, I turned toward home with lightness in my heart and a smile on my face.

"Dontaine, do you happen to know what a condom is?"

He shook his head.

"Let me tell you about them."

THREE

I AWOKE TO bright daylight with a wolf's painful howl still echoing in my ear. An animal's call normally wouldn't wake me from a sound slumber. We were surrounded by a vast acreage of woods and swampland, after all. But it hadn't been an anonymous cry I had heard. It had been Wiley's, the Mixed Blood boy no older than fourteen or fifteen who had grown up wild in the swamp. His howl had vibrated with rage and fear, its sound like that of a wild animal caught in a trap.

I threw on jeans and T-shirt, secured my daggers, one silver, the other not, and crept down the long-winding staircase, avoiding all the creaky spots until I reached the front door. The others slept on undisturbed, and I did not call them because the sunlight that fell softly upon my skin would burn theirs. An hour under its rays would redden their skin. Four hours under it, and they would die. But not I. My one-quarter mixed human heritage ensured that while I had all the Monère's strengths, I had none of their weaknesses. Besides, with the sun high in the sky, I had nothing to fear. The most dangerous threats to me—another Monère or demon dead—were all tucked away in darkness, caught up in their dreams. I wondered for a moment if demons dreamed. Wondered if I hadn't dreamed, myself, imagining that cry. Then it came again. The long, mournful howl of a wolf in distress. Wiley.

I ran east, from where the sound drifted, and covered the distance quickly in loping bounds and unchecked speed. I found him by his heartbeat, pounding rapidly, half-hidden behind a fallen tree trunk, his wrists and ankles bound by ropes. He grew tense when he saw me, and twisted wildly, making muffled sounds under the gag tied over his mouth.

"Shhh, Wiley. It's okay, it's just me," I said, trying to calm him, but he only struggled harder. I frowned as I approached him, and wondered if human hunters had done this? If so, why? The Mixed Blood boy was dressed in clothes I had bought for him, wearing at least the trappings of civilization. He was not half-naked or as obviously wild as he had been when we had first found him. His hair had even been trimmed. By Tersa, no doubt. Why, then, would someone have tied him up like this? And how had a human managed it even? For that matter, why had mere ropes held him? He was more than human strong, young though he was. Then part of the puzzle became clear when he twisted and I caught sight of the silver handcuffs half-hidden beneath the thick rope. Silver weakened the Monère. Made them only human strong.

Not humans. Other Monère, I realized too late.

Something struck me on the back of the head.

Pain. Splinters of white. Then nothing as darkness swallowed me.

～～

WHEN I AWOKE, it was to a raging storm. Not just the one in my head, where I had been struck a painful blow, but a real one. A blinding bolt of lightning split the sky, followed almost immediately by a booming crash of thunder. It was almost as if the heavenly gods were having a temper tantrum, a scary one. Fat raindrops pelted the metal roof of the car I was in, and thick sheets of rain hurled itself against the windows. The noise from that was almost as nauseating as the deafening thunder had been.

I was laid out on the backseat of a car, with metal restraints biting into my wrists. Ropes tied my feet together. Fucking great discoveries, along with the headache. I didn't know how much time had elapsed, or if the handcuffs were silver or dark demon metal. The first I could break. Maybe even the second now. If I was bound with the latter, I would find out soon enough.

Two men—two Monère—were in the front seats. I knew this not by how they dressed, because oddly enough they were dressed like humans—less formal. They risked daylight casually, also like humans. From the back they looked like two ordinary men. But I felt their presence, their power, with that unique sensing we had of like to like. The driver was the stronger of the two, with his dark hair cut short and layered in a contemporary fashion. The one beside him emanated less power, felt younger, actually, in a way I couldn't explain, although both looked like big men from the back.

Wiley. What had they done with him? With that thought, and a simple flexing of my wrists, I broke free of the handcuffs—only silver, I saw. The ropes around my ankles snapped like threads, and I was reaching for the driver with mayhem and maybe murder on my mind, depending on the answers I beat out of him, when the other man turned and looked at me.

He was a boy, or rather a young man around my age, in his early twenties. A beautiful one at that, with a long and lean face cut with high cheekbones, framed dramatically by a curtain of dark, longish hair. He looked model pretty, like he should have been gracing the cover of a fashion magazine or maybe flirting with giggling girls in college. Not kidnapping a woman.

Soft brown eyes stared at me, startled, arresting my forward lunge. Something about those eyes, or maybe the young power I felt emanating from him . . . Whatever it was, something about the innocence I saw there checked my murderous intent.

"Dad, she's awake."

Now "Dad" I would have gladly pounded on. He would have been an equal match for me. But not the boy. I opened the door and jumped from the car. Because of the blinding sheets of rain, the vehicle had slowed enough to make the maneuver less dangerous than it might have been at a higher speed. I landed on my feet running, drenched in an instant. There was just flat land and the highway cutting through it, no other cars ahead or behind. The sun had just set, with only a few rays of lingering light, stealing my biggest advantages from me—daylight and human witnesses.

True night would fall soon, making it much more likely for them to pursue me. Like a bad thought, I heard the car screech to a stop and the doors open. Yup, they were coming after me. But then I fully expected they would. My capture during the daytime had to have been carefully planned—keeping to the shade until they snatched me, and then suffering the bite of the sun, which they had to have felt discomfort from, even through the tinted windows of the car.

I ran all-out into the nearby woods, the silver handcuffs still hanging from my wrists. I'd only broken the chain between them. I tore the separate pieces of metal off me and flung them away. A quick glance down my side told me

they had taken my daggers. No weapons. But that was
okay. My strength was weapon enough.

They closed the distance between us, moving faster than
I was because they tapped into their animal selves—used it
to fuel their strength while still in their upright forms, to
enhance their senses, increase their speed. I could have
done something similar had I not worried that attempting it
would bring that tiny demon piece in me out to the fore. It
shouldn't, but the boy's face . . . His soft doe eyes flashed
in my memory's eye and I knew I couldn't take the chance.
I didn't know the parameters or triggers of what I held inside of me well enough to risk it. So I ran unaided. And
they inevitably caught up to me as I hit what had probably
once been a mild trickling river, but was now a frothing
mass of seething water that had almost overswelled its
banks. It was more than twenty feet across, something I
could have probably jumped. Probably. But I was loathe to
do so. The current was strong, and my swimming skills
lousy. I turned, ran parallel down along the bank, looking
for a narrower point to jump across.

The father tackled me. I rammed an elbow back into his
face and kicked free, springing to my feet, which brought
me face-to-face with the boy. Maybe it was the pretty face
or the innocence I'd glimpsed in those eyes even though
they were no longer that soft, melting brown but a sharp
piercing gray now, the eyes of his beast. For whatever silly
reason, I hesitated to strike him. Fool, I. Because I saw
then what I hadn't seen before in the car—a black gun hol-
stered at his side, a dagger strapped to his waist, bracelet-
bands circling his wrists, protecting his forearms, what
warriors of old might have worn centuries ago. He was
someone trained in the art of combat, and I should have
taken him out, because that very modern gun he wore
tipped the advantage over to their side. But he didn't reach

for the gun or jump me as he could have. We froze there for a second, in arm's reach of each other.

"Don't run," he said with his hands splayed harmlessly out in front of him. "We won't hurt you."

It was his words that broke the spell. He lied. They'd already hurt me. They'd knocked me unconscious, and the blow had not been light. They'd snatched me from my home. Taken me from my people.

I turned and kicked his father—he'd been gathering himself up off the ground—and knocked him back down. I saw surprise flash in the big guy's eyes.

What? Had he thought the elbow I'd rammed into him had been an accident, that the daggers I'd worn had been only a pretty fashion statement? Had he thought I'd just stand there and let them recapture me like a silly, helpless female?

I darted past him, running upstream. Less than a dozen feet away, a hand caught my arm, and I knew it was the boy who gripped me. Doe eyes or not, I had to get out of there. Big daddy was not far behind him. I turned, struck out at him, and just met air. I struck again, but it was like shadow boxing. A slight shift, a subtle turn of his body, and he slipped out of reach. Each time I turned to flee, his hand grasped me again. Son of a bitch. I had to get in closer to him. Close enough to hit him, make him go down, shake him off me so I could escape. I spun back around into him, and my arm, which he had a solid grip on, unexpectedly twisted back and captured his in turn.

My touch seemed to shock him still. As if the feel of my body flush against his scattered all his thoughts, rendered useless all his training. I kneed him in the groin, saw the pain flash in his eyes. Saw him go down, and turned to run. And found myself still shackled to him by that hand firmly grasping my forearm. That hand that would not let go of me.

We tussled on the ground along the bank, fighting each other one-handed, our other hands locking us together. We were both handicapped, and not just by the loss of one arm. We fought each other, but not with the real intent of hurting each other.

Let me tell you: You can't fight that way or you will lose. Sure enough, I suddenly felt the ground crumble beneath me, and found myself tumbling down over the edge of the bank. The lower half of my body splashed into the swift-moving water. The only thing that kept me tethered was the forearm grasp we had on each other.

"Give me your other hand. I'll pull you back up," he said, reaching his free hand out to me. I almost took the offered hand. It was the sight of his father coming up the bank beside him that made me change my mind and reminded me once more: *Enemies. They're your enemies.*

I let go of him, and with a powerful levered twist, broke free of his grasp. Had he latched onto me with both hands, I wouldn't have been able to do that. But it was only a one-handed grip, his other hand stretched out to me. In a one-handed hold, you always have a weak link—the thumb. A hard, concentrated twist there at that point, and it gave as I knew it would. With nothing tethering me anymore, I fell into the raging water.

The cold shocked a gasp out of me. I had a moment to see the boy jump into the water after me, no hesitation. A moment to worry about him, wonder if he could swim. Wonder if he would float, loaded down as he was with weapons and clothes and those heavy metal armbands. And then the water took me, pulled me under. Washed all thoughts away as I sank down into the icy cold depths.

It was deep, deeper than my feet could touch. And it kept me sucked down for an interminably long time, sweeping me along in its powerful current. I bobbed up, broke the surface, and gasped in air. Tried to doggy paddle—my version

of swimming—in an attempt to keep my head above water.
It would have been adequate in a placid swimming pool.
Not so in fast-moving white-water rapids. I bashed up against
a rock and went down again. Hit another rock underwater
with stunning force. I hung there dazed, suspended deep in
the water for a few slow-ticking minutes, letting the current
take me where it willed, until the need for air tickled my
throat. I felt my feet scrape against bottom and pushed up,
broke the surface, took in sweet air.

"Here, my lady!"

I turned and saw the boy cutting through the water toward me with strong, powerful strokes. This time I was
willing to be rescued by him. Would have waited for him
had I been able to, but he was too distant, over twenty terribly long feet away, and I was too weak a swimmer to stay
afloat for that long. The current pulled me down under
again, but this time I fought it. When I surfaced again, he
was closer, his eyes that sharp, fierce gray.

"Hold on," he cried.

I tried to. Kicking to stay afloat, I reached for him. Before he could grasp me, our course shifted. We rounded a
bend—God, how swiftly we traveled—and I smashed up
against another big boulder and went down. I felt the pain
reverberate throughout my entire body, felt all the breath
whoosh out of me, and tried to grab onto the damn rock.
But the slippery, mossy surface was impossible to hold on
to, and the current sped me away in an underwater tumble.
Dazed and disoriented, I released my last few bubbles of
air, watched which direction they floated, and followed
them up, kicking and moving my arms sluggishly until I
broke the surface.

I sucked in air, blinked wildly to clear my vision, and felt
a hand grab ahold of one of my flailing arms. "Gotcha!"

Sweeter words, I'd never heard.

An arm came around the front of me, pulling me back

against a hip, floating me up in the water in a lifeguard's grip. "Just hang on," he said.

I took him at his word. My hands clamped down on that arm, holding him securely to me. It uncomfortably pressed the thick metal wristbands he wore into the tender flesh below my breast, but comfort didn't matter so much as keeping us together. If he lost me again, I would drown.

I felt his body surge forward as he scissor-kicked, moving us slowly through the water while the current tried to tear me away—how strong it was. I was like a deadweight, something he struggled to pull along.

"What can I do?" I asked.

"Can you kick?"

I didn't answer him, just proceeded to do so. And it helped, gave added momentum to his one-handed strokes. He moved us across the frothy water at an angle diagonal to the current. Our progress was sluggish compared to how fast we were being swept downriver, but inch by inch, we cut across the stream. Miles passed by before we finally reach the river's edge.

I felt his body twist, reach up for something, and we came to a jarring halt. The force of the water suddenly increased twentyfold, pulling my body past him, trying to tear me from his grasp. But he didn't let go, and neither did I, even when I was swept beneath the water. I held onto that arm, felt the water rushing over me, heard the frothy force of it beating above me in that odd quiet-loudness that comes when you're completely submerged.

I was no longer sandwiched between his hip and arm. Just held by his hand that gripped my shirt, nothing more substantial than that. It was really my hold now on his arm that kept us anchored together. If I let go, my T-shirt would likely rip and I would be pulled back into the rapids once more.

I didn't let go. Not even when time passed and I still

remained underwater, unable to breathe. His arm strained
and trembled. Slowly, with hard and painful exertion, he
hauled me out of the water. I took in an explosive breath as
soon as my mouth broke the surface, gulped in both air and
water, and started to cough.

"Grab the branch!" he yelled.

I blinked the water from my eyes, still coughing water
from my lungs, and saw his strained face, his arms bulging
with the effort of hanging onto me, a wet and heavy deadweight still caught in the river's powerful grip. He was
hanging onto the trunk of a fallen tree half-toppled into the
river, his white fingers buried into the thick bark. A thick
branch jutted out a foot in front of me. I reached out and
grabbed it.

"Both hands," he shouted, "use both hands. Pull yourself up!"

I was loath to release him, to give up that security. What
if the branch broke?

"Quickly," he gritted, teeth clenched. "I can't hold on
much longer."

I saw the truth in his eyes, in his trembling arms. I let go
of him and grabbed the branch with both hands. It held.

I pulled myself halfway out of the water. But getting the
rest of me out was like pulling myself out of quicksand.
The swift current tugged insistently at me like a jealous
lover, reluctant to give me up.

One great, heaving, yanking assist from the boy, and
one leg lifted free of the water. I swung it over the tree
trunk, and pulled the rest of my body slowly, painfully up.
Once out of the water's sucking grasp, I moved quickly.
Scooting down the trunk, I started the process of hauling
my rescuer out. Freed of his burden—me—he made a
much quicker and more graceful job of heaving himself up
and out.

I crawled backward until we were on solid ground, and then simply let myself fall off the trunk onto the wonderful still earth, feeling like one giant black-and-blue aching bruise, which was probably the case.

I felt him lower down beside me and gave myself a moment to rest. A moment before I decided what to do next to my rescuer: thank him or kick him in the balls again. He might have just saved my life, but he'd been the reason for its peril in the first place. I hadn't forgotten that.

The tingling sense of others—other Monère—stole across my senses and forestalled my decision. I staggered to my feet, and saw the boy rise to his also, silver dagger in hand. His holster was empty, the gun apparently lost. Which sucked, really, because we were outnumbered. I counted ten men closing in on us. Ten rogues, if I were not mistaken, Monère warriors cast out by their Queens, often banding together as bandits. Four of them had swords, the rest were just armed with daggers.

It was not just the worn clothes and hodgepodge assembly of their weapons that made me think of them as rogues. Nor the older feel of their strength, their power. It was the furtiveness of their movements, the meanness in their eyes, the disillusioned hardness in them, and the hungry, gleaming avarice that filled them when they spotted me, felt me. Queen.

"Friends of yours?" I asked.

"No," the boy said. "Yours?"

"Nope."

"Stay behind me."

"Next to you would be better. Even up the odds a little more," I said, coming to stand beside him, making it five to two instead of ten to one. More even odds, as I said.

Stubborn boy that he was, he stepped protectively forward, putting himself between me and the men.

"Milady, you seem to be lost," said a gray-haired warrior. He seemed to be not only the oldest but the most powerful among them. Their leader, I presumed.

I wanted to say, *Not lost, so much as kidnapped*, but didn't do anything so foolish. In cases like this, a lie usually served much better than the truth. Or in this case, a half-lie. "I fell into the river and was separated from the rest of my men. They should be along shortly."

"Good thing we sensed you then." The man smiled, and it made my flesh crawl. "We will protect you until your men come." Substitute *snatch and keep* instead of *protect*, and you would have their real intent. His words were helpful and benign, but his actions were not. They surrounded us in a semicircle, the river at our back, leaving us no place to run.

"Stay back," the boy warned them.

A gesture from the leader and his men sprang. They rushed the boy, all powerful warriors, experienced fighters. But he held them, unbelievably. Kept them from me.

The boy fought unlike any other warrior I'd ever seen. He fought as if he were moving in a lethal flowing dance, dipping and spinning to unheard music. He dropped to the ground and whirled with his dagger in a slashing sweep, making it look beautiful as he sliced across the lower legs of the five men engaging him to his left. Then he rolled to meet the men converging from the right, dancing with them in a wicked ballet of blades. The men slashed and thrust with brute force and chilling savagery while he dodged with grace and serenity, moving with a superior ease none of the other rogues had—that none of my men even possessed. They thrust, he parried, blocking and striking unexpectedly with his wide wrist guards, using them as both weapons and defense, whatever opportunity afforded him. Even the two rogues with long swords he danced with. He fought them off, and turned back to meet the other group.

It was an exquisite display of skill, of valiant heart, but numbers and weapons do count and usually prevail. The odds were overwhelmingly against him. He had injured some of the men, but had not taken any out. And the five he'd pushed back pressed back in immediately as soon as he turned his attention away. They circled behind him, waiting for their moment to strike.

I stepped away from the boy's protection and engaged their interest, smiling, opening my arms to them, my message plain: *You want me, come get me.*

With eager, lustful gleams in their eyes they did.

"No!" the boy shouted, somehow aware of my actions even as he fought. "Come back, my lady."

I could not obey him. Could not stand there and do nothing as they cut him down, which they eventually would. My palms throbbed, my power awakening as I called upon it. In a hot, flowing rush, it came at my beckoning, a living force pulled from the center of me, spilling down my arms, into my hands, into my Goddess's Tears—the moles that were the size and color of large pearls embedded deep in my palms.

A second powerful throb, like a living pulse of power, and a sword flew from a surprised bandit's hand into my right hand. Another pulsing pull, and I stripped a silver dagger from another rogue, drawing it into my left hand. The two unarmed men fell back, startled, and let the three others come at me.

I rushed forward to meet the trio, putting more distance between me and the boy, giving me swinging room for the sword, which I used with far less grace than my young protector but much more ruthlessly. I'd been captured before by a band of outlaw rogues. I would not willingly be taken captive again; I knew what my fate would be under their hands. While they fought to take me alive, I was under no such restriction.

I met the sword-bearing warrior first. Our blades met in a harsh metallic clash, and I saw surprise in his eyes at my strength, more than he had expected. Knocking his sword aside with my own, I plunged the dagger deep into his belly, angled upward. A hard swipe left and he collapsed on the ground, his great vessels severed. Not a killing blow, but one that took him out of commission until he healed.

His two armed companions roared and came at me with daggers in hand. I slashed out with the sword. They leaped back, then pounced, springing at me as the sword passed them by. I let the flow of it spin me completely around, and buried the dagger gripped in my other hand into the side of a very surprised rogue. I felt it break through a rib, puncture his lung. But these were seasoned warriors. Injured as he was, he still swiped at me with his dagger. I leaped away, bloody blade in hand, and found two others coming at me, one with a sword he must have snatched from the other fallen rogue.

A new man entered the fray. Big Daddy had finally caught up. He was an older, bearded version of his son, with the same warrior bracelets around his wrists, armed with a dagger and a similar gun-in-holster setup. Of course, he just used the dagger, not the gun. Gee, why carry it at all?

He stepped between us, and with a few simple blows and elegant dagger thrusts, he took the two men down cleanly and easily. The remaining bandit, unarmed, turned and ran.

"Glad you could join us," I said. "I imagine your son could use your help."

"Stay here." He turned to go.

"Here." I tossed him my sword. He caught it, and without a hitch in stride, entered the fray.

I did as he said, I stayed there. Not because he'd told me to, but to watch the two of them for a moment. In battle, they were breathtaking to behold, moving as a unit, complementing one another. It was fighting as I'd never seen before, like poetry in motion. And the way the father wielded the sword . . . it made what I'd done with it as merely hacking away—all I knew to do. In his hands, though, the sword sang. A lethal song, but a mesmerizing one, whirring through the air in the hands of a master.

Surprisingly, the dad left the sword-wielding bandit leader engaged with his son instead of taking him on as he could have. Dad fought the two dagger-armed rogues and the other swordsman, although fought implied an even match. It wasn't. He took two of them down as easily as drawing in breath—and just as quick—leaving a last trembling rogue holding a shaking sword to face him.

The son held his own more easily now, facing just two bandits instead of five. But held was the proper term. They were evenly matched. The boy kept his opponents away from him, agilely dancing away from their blows, but he did not cut any of them down.

I began a backward retreat. The boy was fine now. I could leave and should, before the battle was over and it was too late to slip away. I'd fought beside the boy, given the father my sword, but that didn't make them my friends. Just my temporary allies until the threat of the bandits was neutralized.

As before, the boy seemed aware of my movements, even faced away from me as he was and engaged in battle. "Don't," he said, turning his head slightly to look at me.

One bare moment of inattention, and the bandit leader's sword slipped past the boy's guard and ran him through.

I cried out—not the boy, he was silent—and leaped for them, moving fast. But not as fast as the father. The big man threw his dagger, burying the blade in his opponent's throat, taking him out. Then he turned, and with one powerful downstroke, cut off the leader's arm—the arm holding the sword that had run his son through. With fast-flowing economy, the downstroke turned into a side slash, slicing open the last remaining bandit in a ruby splash of blood. Three simple moves and the battle was over.

He stepped in front of his fallen son, sword in hand, but did nothing more. Just watched as the wounded bandits dragged themselves away.

The bandit leader cautiously stooped down and retrieved his severed limb and weapon. "Don't come back here again," he snarled, retreating. His men, those that were able to stand, threw their fallen comrades over their shoulders and followed him.

I ran to the boy's side, dropped down beside him, muttering, "Stupid, stupid, stupid!"

"I know," the boy said, his voice strained with pain. "I let him past my guard."

"Not you," I snapped. "Me. For coming back to you." His hand was pressed over the wound in front. I laid my hand over the back exit wound, which was spilling out blood like a dam with a high-pressured leak. The moment my palm came in contact with blood and flesh, that deep cycle of energy within me came up and out, called forth by the pain of another, easing it as my mole tingled and warmed, searching out the depths of his injury. Miraculously, it had punctured cleanly through, missing his intestines and other vital organs. Lucky son of a bitch. Of course, he'd probably have been able to heal those wounds as well. He was a Full Blood Monère, after all. What the hell was I doing?

"You took the pain away. Are you a healer?" the boy asked. My face softened when I looked down into his. Young, so young, even though he was taller than I by a good five inches.

"Not really." Not in the usual way. I could heal, yes, but through sex. And that wasn't called for here. Injured though the boy was, he would heal without my intervention. But I was trained as a nurse; there were other commonsense things you could do, like decrease the loss of blood.

"Give me part of your shirt or something to staunch the blood with," I snapped at the father, who was gazing down at me with curious attention. Without a word, he ripped off a shirt sleeve and handed it to me. I folded it into a compress and gently pressed it against the rear exit wound. He tore off his other sleeve, and I used it for the entry wound.

"Why didn't you use your damn gun?" I demanded.

"They had no guns. It would not have been an equal fight," the big man said.

"It wasn't an equal fight once you got here," I snapped back.

I sacrificed my own two sleeves, tore them into strips, and bound them into one long piece, tying it around his waist to hold the two compresses in place.

Sitting back, I glared up at the big man. He still held the sword I'd given him. "Two questions," I said, my tone a rock-hard contrast to the softness with which I'd spoken to his son. "What did you do with the Mixed Blood boy you had tied up near my home?" With Wiley. The wild fear and anger on his face when I last saw him flashed again in my mind's eye.

"I knocked him out then uncuffed him."

So Wiley should be fine. Just angry and frightened after he awakened, but essentially unharmed.

"What is your second question?" he asked.

Oh, that was an easy and obvious one. And you could say my tone was more than a touch hostile. "What the fuck do you want with me?"

The man laid down the sword, away from me, I noticed, and crouched down so that we were more of an equal height. It was his injured son, however, who answered me.

"My lady, please. My brother, he needs a Lady of Light. I beg of you, please save him before it's too late."

FOUR

WE WERE BACK once more in the car, but I was sitting up, free. No silver handcuffs. I'd have felt better if I had been restrained but, nope. I was here of my own free will. By my own stupid volition. We were crossing out of my Louisiana territory into the bordering state of Texas, and I was sitting there doing nothing about it.

The rogues, it seemed, resided along the fringe of my territory. And they were not the only rogues who plagued me. Father and son were rogues as well, something that came as almost a shock to me. I hadn't thought of them as such. They were dressed better and seemed, I don't know, somehow honorable . . . even though they'd knocked me unconscious and taken me from my people. Which went to say just how screwed up my judgment was . . . *continued* to be. Maybe I could blame it on being hit in the head. *It just knocked the sense right out of me, you know?*

I don't think that was going to go over too well with my guys when I got back home. *If* I got back home. I was trusting the word of two rogues—that they would return me

safely back after my look-see, even if I decided not to help
Dante, the reason for this all. How stupid was that? Very
stupid, because I believed them. That was why I was here,
playing the nice, sedate passenger.

We would be there in twenty-five minutes, they had said,
and were accurate almost down to the minute. The little
hand of the clock had just ticked up to eight when we turned
into the driveway of a neat little home just off of County
Road 257, fifteen minutes past the WELCOME TO TEXAS
sign. It was a rural setting, looking totally normal and feeling that way, too, if you were just a human, which I was not.

A wave of power, of need, coming from the house
punched me like a blow to the stomach, so strong and fierce
it was. I gasped, sitting there in the car, more than a little
shaken. "Christ, what the hell is that?"

Quentin, the boy, turned around in his seat, said with
sorrow in his eyes, "That's Dante, my brother."

Holy crap. "How old is your brother, exactly?"

"We're twins. He's twenty, same as me."

"Twins, huh?" And a whole year younger than me. How
thrilling.

"We're not identical."

"No kidding," I said. "You feel nothing alike."

"No, we don't," Quentin said sadly. "He's older than me
by six minutes, which is why I was spared his fate."

Lunara asseros, Nolan, the father, had called it, or lunar
craving. Also known as Moon Madness, so named because
those who had it were often driven mad by their unfulfilled
need for lunar light. It was why I was here, and what I was
supposed to cure, a rare affliction that could strike down a
warrior. Not all. Usually just the strongest or the first born.
Rare because it occurred only if a Monère warrior never
Basked, never was exposed to the moon's essential light
pouring into them. Rare because almost every Monère
Basked at least once in their lifetime. Unless you were born

rogues, as these two boys had been, and had never known a Queen's light.

What happens to those afflicted? I had asked.

If they do not receive the light that their Monère body craves in time . . . that their thinking mind needs to survive . . . then they burn out, go mad. Become nothing more than a ravening beast that must be put down and destroyed or he will go on to kill others.

I'd asked how long Dante had been ill.

Thirty-six hours now, had been the answer. That was a long time.

A brown-haired woman with warm brown eyes, standing half a head shorter than I, rushed out of the back door and hurried to the car. Her hair was coiled in a simple bun, and a gold ring adorned her left hand.

"Thank the Goddess," she said fervently. "You brought a Queen."

"My mother, Hannah Morell," Quentin said, introducing us. "Mother, this is Mona Lisa. She's come to help Dante."

I didn't quibble over his choice of words. Didn't say that they'd kidnapped me. I stepped out of the car and I saw the surprise register in Hannah's eyes when she saw that I was not restrained.

"And you've come of your own volition." She sank down to her knees, tears in her eyes. "Thank you, gracious lady, thank you."

"You're welcome. Please get up." I gestured awkwardly for her to rise, flustered at having her kneeling like that. "And I only promised to take a look at him," I clarified.

"Quentin is hurt, Mother. A sword ran him through." Nolan opened the passenger door and gently lifted Quentin into his arms. "He needs your healing touch."

I glanced back at the small woman rising to her feet. "You're a healer?"

"Yes, milady."

I turned with exasperation to father and son. "If you dun-derheads had told me that in the first place instead of knock-ing me out, I'd have come with you voluntarily. God, I'd do just about anything to get a healer for my people."

"Save my son," Hannah said passionately, "and I will serve you."

"You will be our healer?"

"Yes. My word, by the holy Goddess of Light."

"Okay, good, good," I said, immensely cheered and vastly more motivated now . . . until another powerful wave of that vibrant want, that stunning need, hit me, stealing my breath away. I swayed for a moment, then caught my breath and bal-ance and followed Nolan and Quentin into the house.

It felt odd entering their home. Odd because the real reason I was being brought here was to have sex with their son. That's right, sex. Not Basking, because we drew down the moon's rays only during a full moon—that was several weeks away, and from what I'd felt, I didn't think the boy could wait that long. But Basking wasn't the only way Queens gave off light. Sex—pleasure—also made us glow.

Nolan laid Quentin down on a sofa in the family room next to the kitchen. Leaving him in Hannah's care, he led me down the hall to his other son. "He's in the study," he told me.

I followed him, trepidation fluttering inside me like wild butterflies. I don't know what I expected to see when he opened the door and cautiously entered. Maybe someone looking like Quentin, only more drawn and haggard, sit-ting in a chair, shaking with need. I should have known bet-ter. I should have known from the feel of his power that he would be nothing like what I expected. That he would be nothing at all like his brother.

My first thought was that this was not a boy. I would have called him a man, like I was a woman and not a girl despite my years, had he been a rational being. But he was not. There was nothing rational in those eyes. And what odd eyes he had, a blue so pale they were almost translucent. They were eyes that I had never seen before, but felt somehow as if I had. Those eyes sent a chill racing through me, as if a ghost had just tripped and fallen on my grave.

He was shackled at both wrists by a three-foot length of silver chain attached to the wall, allowing him to stand and move about. And he was doing that, straining against the taut length when I stepped in, his body quivering, his pale eyes fixed upon me with unthinking hunger. Making me thankful for the chains that restrained him, otherwise he would have been on me like a famished beast.

He had his mother's brown hair, but lighter in color, honey brown. That was the only soft thing about him. His hair was an even longer length than his brother's, pulled back in a ponytail that may have once been neat, but was far from that now. Hanks of hair, freed from the hair tie, hung about his face. Unkempt stubble shadowed his chin, and an earring, if you could call it that, punctured—not pierced, but punctured—his left ear. I'd never seen a Monère with an earring before. Probably because our bodies healed so quickly. But this man-boy creature had one. Not the neat, needle-thin hole you normally saw, but a much bigger one. A crude, hand-hammered gold bar almost pencil thick was punched through the earlobe. Much more primitive, like what you'd see among native tribes in Africa maybe. And that was pretty much a good word to describe him—primitive. Primal. Dangerous.

Whereas his brother was model pretty, Dante was like his famous namesake, invoking images of Hell. Cruelty and harshness marked his face, and all he wore were dirty, torn pants. His chest and feet were bare, showing his starved leanness. It was as if every ounce of fat had been consumed from his body, honing him down to nothing but hard striations of bunched muscles. He was like a cutting blade of power, hard and austere. I could literally count his ribs, see the hard muscles fanning over them. His chest was soaked with sweat, and the smell of it was sickly, not a healthy scent. Just as the look in his eyes was not a healthy hunger, but an unthinking, overpowering one—like that of a rabid dog foaming with madness and the need to tear out your throat.

The sorrow that had been in Quentin's voice was heard in his father's now. "Dante. Son," he said softly, trying to bring Dante back to himself. "I've brought a Queen to help you. Mona Lisa. She'll give you the light you need from her, if you let her."

A rumbling growl started deep in Dante's chest and rose up into his throat. With no warning he lunged at his father. The chains jerked him to a halt, snapping him abruptly back. He prowled back and forth restlessly against the restraining length like the wild creature he had become.

The sadness I'd first heard in his brother, then in his father, was a pervasive thing. It seeped into me. Sadness at the waste, at the loss. Sadness because I thought it was too late to save him. But still I had to try. Taking a deep breath, I stepped forward until I stood only two arms' lengths away from him.

"Dante," I said softy, and knew somehow that he was as intensely aware of my presence as I was of his, even though his gaze was locked with his father's, a steady growl rumbling from his throat. I called his name again but his attention did not waver from the other man.

"Nolan, back up to the door. Don't leave, but give us some room."

Nolan did as I asked, moving back until I could no longer see him, and his presence no longer pressed so strongly upon us—until all I could see was just the tortured, wild creature that was his son. The growling stopped and those odd blue eyes suddenly turned and met mine. The impact reverberated through my entire body. Such fierceness, such intensity. There was something very frightening about those eyes. Was there anything still rational left in there?

"Dante." Though my heart beat rapidly, my voice was as calm and gentle as the freshly fallen night. "Do you understand what I'm saying? Can you speak?"

He stood still but not at ease. Every muscle in his body was tense, quiveringly taut. I took one step closer to him, and slowly lifted my hand out, a hand that shook slightly.

"Dante." His name fell from my lips like a soft melody as I touched him. As I laid my hand lightly on his chest.

He groaned, a harsh, guttural sound like an animal in great pain. The sound startled me, and I jerked my hand back. He went wild at the loss, snarling and lunging powerfully forward, jerked to a rattling halt by the chains. Only the fleece lining beneath the shackles kept his skin from tearing.

I fell back a step, I couldn't help it. Even knowing that the silver chains rendered him only human strong, there was such anger to him, such menace, I could not help but be frightened. My heart pounded and the trembling of my hand spread to my entire body.

"I'm sorry," I said, turning so I could see Nolan from the corner of my eyes. "I can't. Not with him like this. Even if I were crazy enough to try it . . ." And I would have tried it, had Dante shown even a modicum of reasoning, of understanding—making me wonder who the crazy one among us really was. "It would not do any good. We shine only in pleasure." And I doubted I'd be able to feel that with Dante, as wild and violent and dangerous as he was.

The big man didn't say anything, and his silence and sorrow weighed down upon me like a heavy stone. And why should it not? I had just essentially passed a death sentence on his son. One that he would have to carry out. But the tall, formidable warrior didn't protest, didn't try to insist, holding to his word . . . that the choice would be mine.

Because he did, I swallowed and voiced the other option I had considered. "If your other son, Quentin . . . if I glowed with him here in this room, would it help? Could Dante absorb my light if we were close to him but not touching?"

Hope flared in the big man's eyes. "Yes, it should. Proximity is all that is needed in Basking. It should be the same with this, too." This being sex.

"Okay," I said, taking a deep breath. "Let's give it a try."

We didn't have to call him. Every word we said was clearly heard by everyone in the household—one of the downfalls of possessing such acute hearing: no privacy, unless we deliberately tuned down our senses. Quentin appeared in the doorway, dressed in clean clothes and no longer smelling of blood.

"You're healed?" I asked as our eyes met in that intense awareness of two people who knew they would soon be intimate with each other.

Quentin nodded.

"Do you have a condom?"

Uncertainty passed across that pretty face. *Young. So young*, cried a voice inside me. Yeah, but he was the lesser of two evils. I sure as hell was not going to fuck his father, a married man.

Ironically enough, it was the married man's wife who appeared with a familiar square foil packet in her hand. She pressed what I had requested into Quentin's hand and left when she caught sight of my flaming face and Dante's wild, animalistic state.

With condom in hand, Quentin stepped into the room and came toward me. His brother went ballistic. Dante lunged, flung himself out. Not his upper body, but his lower one, his feet flying out in a half circle. With the added length that gave him, that of his entire body and arms stretched out to their fullest, it was enough to reach me. His feet swept across my knees, knocking me down. I fell and he rolled over me, a fluid, seething mass, coming quickly to his feet. Hands clamped down on me and he pushed me behind him, crouching in front of me, growling viciously at Nolan and Quentin, who had rushed forward in alarm.

"Stop!" I said. "Don't come any closer. It's all right. It's all right," I repeated as father and son halted their headlong rush. "Dante's just trying to protect me . . . I think." The last two words were muttered prayerlike, flung up heavenward by my racing heart.

Whatever Dante was doing, it was compelled by his most primal instincts. And the need to protect a Queen was a real hard-wired one instilled in all warriors. I was betting my safety—and his—on it.

He had latched his left hand onto my wrist, leaving his right hand free to fight with. And he'd put me behind him, a protective gesture as well as a possessive one, setting himself between me and the other men.

"Back up," I said as calmly as I could. "He has me, and hasn't hurt me so far. Let's see what he does."

Nolan and Quentin moved back to the door and stopped there, watching us, making me realize what I had said: *Let's see what he does*. I hadn't meant it literally. Not really. At least, not in Quentin's case.

"Quentin, if you could, um, leave. The less people in the room, the better," I said to soften my request. "I'll be fine with your father. Just . . . leave the condom." My face flushed fire-engine red as Quentin slid the precious foil packet across the floor to me. When he slipped quietly from the room, the coiled tension in Dante's body revved down a notch. Down to a watchful battle readiness instead of a ready-to-erupt-and-tear-out-our-throats state. He backed us up as far as we could go, until we came up against the wall. Then his attention turned to me.

Oh boy.

Intensity was a nice thing in a would-be lover. It told

you they were paying attention to you. But not to this degree—this raw, overwhelming amount. This much of it was more scary than exciting . . . but a spark of sanity had crept into that blue sea of madness. Those fierce, pale eyes swept over me, examining every detail as if I were a two-headed alien suddenly plopped down in front of him. He studied me as if he felt the same thing I did: like he should know me but didn't. I had the feeling that if he could have drank me down with those pale, eerie eyes of his, I would have been drained completely dry and left like parched, cracked earth.

He raised a hand slowly as if *I* were the wild creature that had to be gentled, and swept it just above my skin as if he could feel my force, my presence, my aphidy—that unique, attractive force and fragrance inherent to all Queens. It had flared out wildly, reaching for him the first time his hungry power had hit me. I had clamped down on it tightly, desperately contained it. It vibrated my skin now where he ran his hand over it, stroking my invisible power, buzzing and prickling where his hand wrapped around my wrist. A small pulse of power escaped from me and jumped to him against my will, as if our energies wanted to blend, merge, come together—something I'd never experienced before with another man.

As startled as I, he dropped my wrist and we faced each other, inches apart, both of us breathing heavily, our bodies quivering and tense. He was behaving himself as much as I was, keeping his power controlled on a tight leash, not letting it pummel me as it had before. He was sane enough not to want to scare me away, I realized. Comforting. But if we were to get intimate, I wanted—*needed*—to know that he was rational enough to control himself, to not hurt me. He was bound by silver. I was stronger than him, I could protect myself. But still . . . something in me could not help but fear him.

Strong though I was, when a woman opened her body to a man, she was vulnerable to him in ways only another woman could understand. Before I let loose my aphidy, before I had sex with him, I had to trust him enough to let go of the tight rein of my control. That was the only way I'd be able to glow. And I didn't know if I could do that with him.

He was such a raw mass of seething pain. I sensed it, and that part of me that had always been drawn to pain was drawn to him now because of it. I didn't try to resist it. Lifting my hand, I laid it again on his bare chest. Once again, the small pulse of power jumped between us. His face twisted, as if my touch pained him, but he did not groan as he had before—the sound that had startled me, made me jerk back away from him. He clenched his teeth, swallowed down the sound, and shuddered from my touch.

Just my palm laid flat against his chest with my Goddess's Tears pressing into his skin, and something between us connected like a current flowing out of me to him. A circuit that cycled back to me. My pearly moles flared to life and did what they usually did around pain. My palm began to tingle, my hand grew warm, and my power, drawn forth by the suffering of another, spilled out of me and seeped into his flesh in a wide, assessing sweep, easing the pain.

God. Such agony he was in. What control it had taken on his part simply not to lash out at me in reaction to that pain. "Dante, can you say something? Anything?"

"Touch me more." The words came out hoarse and guttural, as if they'd been wrenched from him.

I looked into his eyes and saw that tiny spark of sanity firm, grow stronger with our physical connection. "Thank God," I whispered. Looking into his eyes, feeling him through my palm, reading him, I knew that we'd pulled him back—both he and I together—from that brink of madness he'd been teetering on. I knew that he would not hurt me, that I could save him. That I *wanted* to save him.

Not just for the healer he would gain me. But for himself. For the valiant warrior that he was, the fierce will inside of him that had tenaciously pulled him back from the encroaching madness.

I stuffed the condom in my pocket, freeing my other hand, and laid it across his forehead, pushing my disquiet aside to just concentrate on him, the poor suffering creature before me. My palm flushed and tingled as that pain-easing power of mine spilled into him, soothing the jagged edges of his mind and body. His eyes closed and his jaw clenched. Wetness spiked his lashes.

"It's okay. You can groan if you need to. It just startled me that first time," I murmured. But he didn't, and I was glad he didn't. I still felt uneasy around him. "I'm taking away some of the pain, removing the symptom. Not curing the disease," I told him.

His lashes lifted, dark wet crescents. "How can we cure it?" He spoke with less strain, but his voice still sounded rusty, sore.

I hesitated, then answered him with his own words. "Touch me."

His right hand lifted slowly, hesitantly, the chains clinking with his movement. It came to rest cautiously on my shoulder. "Your shirt is wet," he said. But it was his body that shook as I brought my other hand to his face and traced both hands down his cheeks, his neck, moving to his shoulders, pausing there a moment, then drifting down his arms, back up. Smoothing across his chest in gentle, tingling sweeps.

"I fell in a river," I said, explaining why my shirt was wet.

Chains rattled as his left hand came up to rest on my other shoulder. He began an echoing refrain of my motions, gliding them down my arms. Back up.

"When you touched me that first time, I knew I could

not let you go." His voice was a raw and husky murmur. "Don't leave me."

"I won't," I promised, even though my heart sped up in disquiet at his words. The thought of being held by him, captured by him . . . I shook off the unease. "I won't leave you unless you bite me. That is the only thing that will make me go," I said, continuing my ministrations, learning his body, easing his pain. I tried to lose myself in the pleasure of touching him, my hands drifting down his abdomen, sweeping up his sides, skimming lightly up and down his back.

"I won't bite you," he said in that ragged voice of his.

"No biting. No blood. All other things you may do." Meeting Nolan's eyes over Dante's shoulder, I gestured for him to leave and he slipped from the room, closing the door softly behind him. Taking that mental step, committing myself wholly to this, I swept a hand lightly over his groin, finding him long and hard, swollen full.

His teeth ground together audibly, and his body tensed to rock hardness. His skin stretched taut over the sharp blades of his cheekbones, and his pale blue eyes glittered down at me. I looked away, finding it easier to touch him, be with him, if I did not look into those eerie, familiar but unfamiliar eyes.

"This is the cure," I said softly, taking the verbal step. "Touch me. Make love to me."

His hands gripped my shoulders tightly before he consciously eased his grip. And that one moment of force, that hint of strength, drew my breath in.

"Don't be afraid," he said, alarmed, almost panicking, lifting his hands away.

"I'm not." Warmth spilled across my cheeks in an embarrassed blush. "It was . . . nice," I admitted softly. "I liked that firmness, the hint of your strength. Touch me more."

I felt him heat at my words, but he stood there in an

agony of stillness, fear that I would be frightened into leaving battling with his desire to do as I said—to touch me more.

I took his hands in both of mine, and some of that frightened tension left him as we connected once more. Until I slid them under my wet T-shirt and laid his hands against my bare skin. Then tension roared back into him again. Simmered between us as I swept my hands over his hips and slid them down his buttocks. He sucked in his breath, expelled it out when I continued on my journey, sweeping my palms down the back of his cloth-covered thighs.

He trembled as if a fever shook him, his cheeks slashed red. Breathing hard, his hands drifted slowly up my torso. The metal of his right restraint bumped up against my side, and I winced. In pain this time, not pleasure. His hands stilled. "You're hurt."

"Bruised a bit. There were some big rocks in that river."

"Let me see." He waited until I nodded, then drew up my T-shirt. And hissed.

"That bad, huh?" I swallowed. "Best to take the T-shirt off so you can see where to touch, and where not to touch." I smiled as I said it, but inside I was not smiling. As my shirt was lifted over my head and tossed away, inside I was cringing. I was built modestly on top. Neat and compact were the best words to describe me. And the vivid purple and red bruises discoloring my left side and right arm did not help make me any more attractive. Despite my bold actions with him, I was far from confident when it came to sex. The men I'd been with had loved me, and I them. Dante hardly knew me. And his vision of me was not colored by love. My turn to tremble, to feel horribly vulnerable. I could not meet his eyes. Did not want to see what expression filled them.

If only Monères glowed from embarrassment. How easily then it would have been to cure him.

"Take off your pants." A brief pause. Then he added, "Please," like it was a word he was not used to saying.

Well, heck. Why don't we just make it harder? But I nodded, and despite the trepidation filling me, undid the button, pushed down the zipper, and stepped out of my wet jeans and underwear, completely bare to him now. Still, I could not lift my eyes, even when he removed his own pants. He folded them neatly—an odd thing to do in this situation, I thought—and laid them on the floor. Then taking my hands, he drew me down to sit across his thighs as he leaned back against the wall.

"You'll be more comfortable this way. And I'll be less likely to hurt you," he said. And it put me in control, as much as a woman could be in control when you made love with a man. It touched me, the gesture. The thoughtfulness behind it. The heavy chains, though, clinking and rattling with each move were distracting and annoying, setting my already jumpy nerves even more on edge.

"Let me remove the chains," I said, reaching for his shackles.

"No," he said sharply, pulling his wrists out of my reach. "It's not safe. *I'm* not safe yet. Leave them on."

I mentally dug a hole and buried the last of my unease in it. *Yes*, I thought, *he's a man worth saving.* But instead of making me feel better, it made me feel worse. Never had I felt the burden of my own pleasure so keenly. My initiation into sex had been a painful thing. With humans. Humans that Monère are not compatible with because we're of a different chemistry, a different race. It wasn't until I came across another Monère, across Gryphon, that I had found the joy and pleasure that could be had in being intimate with a man.

I'd never had a man's life—a virgin, to boot—dependent on my glowing in pleasure before. Of him going mad and being executed by his own father if I didn't. It wasn't so much his lack of lovemaking skills I was doubting as much as I was questioning my own adequacy. A woman is harder to stir up and please than a man. Pure, unalterable fact. And right now, bruised and unsettled among strangers, bare skin to bare skin with someone I felt I should know but didn't, I did not feel up to the burdensome task that pleasure had suddenly become.

Dante was calmer, saner now, after I'd eased his pain. Maybe we could wait until we returned to Belle Vista and Dontaine was there to help us. I knew that I could glow with Dontaine.

"What is your name?" Dante demanded in a gritty voice.

"Mona Lisa."

"Mona Lisa," he repeated. And while his next words were said in a soft whisper, they were tinged with strain. "Can you . . . touch me? It's starting to hurt again."

My faint hope died. Nope, we weren't going to be able to wait.

I shifted up on my knees and laid a hand on his chest, another on his forehead. Praying while I did so. *Please. Help me be enough for him.*

He closed his eyes, relaxing beneath my tingling touch.

As the pain seeped out of him, my touch changed from soothing to caressing, stroking the slight swell of his chest, trailing down the bristly side of his face to trace his slightly chapped lips. Such a smooth-rough contrast. Like what he was—dangerous pleasure. I leaned even closer until our lips were just a breath apart. "Dante," I whispered, brushing my mouth against his. "Come dance with me."

We kissed and it was a sweet, light thing. A mingling of breath, of scent. A simple pleasing of our senses.

At first his lips were soft and yielding, pliant. As if he'd never kissed anyone before, and perhaps he hadn't. As if he were just absorbing the feel of me. Then they firmed, moved across mine in a light caress, brushing across my lips, easing back, coming back at a different angle. He danced with me as I had asked him to. With his mouth, with his lips, *only* his lips, closed and gentle-rough against mine. He kissed me now as an active participant, with pleased discovery, with growing delight. With quickly learned skill, and slowly budding pleasure. Finding what he liked. What I liked. Building that slight, fragile connection between us with soft caresses, gentle touches. Until I yearned for more than just the feel of his lips brushing against mine. Until I yearned for the taste of him, too.

My tongue swept lightly across his lips. His eyes, still closed, twitched with surprise. I smiled and did it again. A light, deliberate wet stroke across the seam of his mouth. "Open for me," I whispered.

He did. Our mouths mated again with our lips open, and I tasted him. A light sweep in his mouth, a gentle foray, retreating then. I did it again—gentle probe in, a teasing flicker of my tongue against the tip of his. When I retreated this time, he followed, delving into my mouth with a light stroke of his own. Another, and another. Tasting me as I tasted him. Teasing my tongue as I'd teased his, a sure and quick learner. And all the while our mouths and tongues danced with each other, my hands moved over him. A sweep over his wide shoulders. A caressing stroke down the muscles of his arms. He did not have the thickness and breadth of chest and shoulders that he would have in another century. He had the sweet, budding slenderness of youth still yet, with more. The muscles carving his body marked his entry into manhood, and his claim on a warrior's body, strength, and will. That will now was focused on finding my pleasure.

We were playing a more intimate version of Simon Says. He did as I did, went where I went. His hands lifted, touched me, across the shoulders, feathering over my collarbones. He sighed into my mouth with pure unadulterated delight at the raw pleasure of touching me, tangling our tongues together in a wet, intimate caress. He sipped upon me, nibbled on my lower lip.

When I tensed and drew in a breath as his teeth skimmed across my flesh, he said in a gritty whisper, "No biting, no blood. I remember. But all other things I may do, yes?"

"Yes."

He smiled and watched me with half-closed eyes. The hard intent gleam, his rough stubble, the primitive ear piercing, and the darkness I sensed in him tangled up with this gentleness—it all sent a tremor shooting through me. Because playing with him was like playing with a keg of dynamite. Safe until it blew up on you. And that darkness that dwelled within me—that had been a part of me even before I took in the demon essence—was both scared and thrillingly turned on by that perilous pleasure.

With deliberate lightness, he drew his hands slowly down my breasts, learning their shape, their feel, watching my re-action to his touch. Helpless tremors shook me as his fingers skimmed over my nipples. They pebbled in response and those hooded eyes lowered down to them in fascination. His fingers returned to circle the pouting hardness that he'd drawn forth, rimming the brown areolas, brushing softly over the sensitive tips. He watched me respond, his piercing eyes lifting back up to mine, and I was helpless to look away as the control suddenly shifted from me to him.

"You like this?"

I nodded, unable to speak with the rough pads of his fin-gers brushing over my nipples. A light swirling stroke, then a firmer caress. His fingers traced down the slight swell of my breasts. Drifted down my belly. He splayed his hands across my waist, my hips, down my thighs, back up again. With just the tips of his fingers, as if he were a blind man reading braille, reading *me*, he ran those sensitive rough pads around to the back of me and bent his head down.

Again I had the sense that he was reading me, *learning* me, as he moved his mouth inch by inch closer until his lips brushed my nipple.

My hands tightened on his arms. Tightened more as he drew that sensitive tip into his mouth and I felt wetness and warmth. And pleasure. Oh my God, so much pleasure. He played with that nipple the same way he had kissed me, with slow, deliberate intent, with loving thoroughness, with pleased discovery.

I leaned into him, increasing the pressure, asking for more, and he gave it to me. A firmer lick, a harder suction, the dangerous tease and scrape of his teeth across the budded tip while his hands cupped my bottom, kneading the rounded flesh in a firm, caressing grip.

He drew me to him and our naked flesh met. Our bodies pressed together and he was unable to hold back the groan that welled up in him, that seemed to come from his very soul. It came tumbling out of his mouth as he released my tender bud and buried his face against me. His stubble scraped across my erect nipple and it felt good, so good. I moaned softly and moved against him, increasing the friction against the rough abrasiveness of his beard, twisting like a cat in his lap, purring with delight.

Our breath came faster, and yet we still held to our individual control. The time had come to loosen it, and I was frightened and scared and excited and impatient. Sex—ultimate pleasure—was about losing control, not keeping it, and I felt eagerness stir within me. My power knew that it would soon be freed.

Stretching sideways, I grabbed my pants and dug the foil packet out of the pocket. Gripping the condom in my hand, I prayed that it would be all right. That we would be okay in the storm I was about to unleash.

"I'm going to loosen my power now," I told him. "I have to let go of my control, but you can't. You have to stay in control." My next words were delivered with a wry smile. "I'll try to be gentle." Something a man would normally say. "But it's probably going to hit us hard."

I felt it like an eager wave, ready to fall, to crash down.

"What do you mean?"

"Just remember. No biting, no blood. Or I will leave you."

His pale eyes darkened at that threat. "No biting, no blood. My word on it."

Trusting in him, I let go of the tight rein I had over myself. We had a moment of quiet, of breathless silence. Then the presence that was within me, the power and attraction that made me Queen, that drew all males to me, emerged, set free. It came roaring out in a dazzling gush of power. And spilled out and onto him.

"Shit," he said. His hands clamped down tight around me as it hit him, and then his own power rose up to meet mine so that we were suddenly drowning in biting energy, awash with primitive vital urges. Becoming nothing more than what we instinctively needed. I felt his hunger, his cry for the moon's light. And within me was pulled forth my own need, my own personal craving. Not the demon urge for blood that I had feared, but the urge that was buried in all Monère women—the need to feel life growing in them. It flared up hot and hard within me, and spilled out onto him. Every hard-wired instinct in us propelled us together in that unthinking need to mate. To bear forth life.

With a growl, his mouth came back upon me. He drew in my nipple, sucking hard with primitive drive, and that forceful sucking built the need in me even greater until it became almost pain. *Give me a child! Give me a baby!*

As if he heard my body's cry, his finger pushed into me and found me wet, moist and ready. Warm fertile ground. He shifted, laid me down on the floor, and came over me, covering me, braced on his arms. His pale blue eyes were wild, his body trembling with need, but he held back, poised there at my gate. "Say yes," he gritted.

A split moment to decide. An endless cycle of time to let the foil packet spill out of my hand, to fall onto the floor, released. "Yes," I breathed.

He thrust forward, missed the entrance, and we both cried out in painful frustration. I reached down, took ahold of him, and guided him where we both wanted him to go. He thrust forward again and penetrated me, filled me up, brought forth my light. And my light brought out his—a weak, pale glimmer of my own, as if he were a dying battery, almost completely drained.

He drew out, surged into me. And it was suddenly not enough. I was the one who went wild, becoming nothing more than a creature of instinctive need, twisting beneath the hard male body thrusting into me. Writhing against him, rising up to him, my legs wrapped around him to help him slam into me. *More, more, more!* my body demanded. And he gave it to me with grunting force. He thrust deep, he thrust hard, spilling his seed into me in a harsh, choking climax. Then I was coming, too.

Power crystallized within me and exploded out of me. Light spilled out, illuminating me, blindingly intense. I felt him drink in my light, not a passive process, absorbing it, but actually *pulling* it into him with the force of his own need, like a physical hand hauling in a rope, and I was that rope. He glowed, suddenly bright like a fire ignited, and my light lessened for one shaking, shuddering moment that passed so quickly I could almost believe it didn't happen, *would* have believed it had I not felt it so keenly. A momentary blast, then the light that lit us up, was emitted from us, became normal once more.

He watched me as ecstasy filled us both. Watched me as I shattered beneath him. Watched me still. "Again," he said and moved. And with surprise, I felt him still hard within me.

How could that be? I'd felt him come. Had felt the pulsing jets of his release shooting within me. Had felt the wetness of his spilled seed mixing with my own juice, trickling
out of me. But the hard, smooth length moving within me,
washing me anew with sharp, edgy sensations was undeniable. One stroke. Two. A fluttered heartbeat. A skipped
breath. And then he sank himself down deep inside me like
a sword thrusting home all the way into its sheath. And with
us connected like that, he rolled us on the floor until we
came up against the wall.

He shifted around until he sat propped up against it with
me sitting on his lap and him still deep inside of me, thick
and throbbing. In this new position, he began moving in me.
A slow, languorous stroke, deep and fine. In this new position, his hands, freed, moved over me also, stroking me on
the outside as he stroked me on the inside. Lazy, thorough.
But whereas he moved inside me with firm hard pressure,
along my skin he touched me with but the barest pressure.
Deep strokes within, light tantalizing strokes without. His
fingertips trailed almost ticklishly light over my skin, sensi-
tizing it even more until I became screamingly aware of
everything he did to me. Everywhere he touched me, inside
and out.

Those grazing fingertips crisscrossed a devilish path down
my back, arching me into him as he leaned forward until his
breath fell with teasing, tantalizing puffs upon my breasts.
Until my nipples hardened into pebbles, puckered up under
the warm current of air moving over them. Inside, my sheath
tightened in corresponding reaction, in parallel anticipation,
gripping his thick stalk even more tightly, even more sweetly,
as he did what I'd asked him to do—as he danced with me. As
he danced *within* me. As he played me with his hands, with
his breath, with his hard male organ. As he finally touched
the spear points of my breasts, not with his soft lips but with
his rough bristles, I gasped in shock, in surprise, in pure

seething pleasure. Jerked against him. Bucked against him below as he rubbed that sandpapery roughness over me, scraped it over my peaks, drawing forth such an abrasive cascade of pleasure, of sweet, moaning sensation.

Light finger strokes down my back, over my buttocks. A hard, bristly rub across my breasts. While inside me he moved in a sure, lazy rhythm as he tilted his head back and watched with heavy-lidded eyes. Watched what he did to me. Watched the feelings he drew out of me. Watched my reactions to his every move, his every light and rough caress. And all while he felt what he did to me inside. In the quivering spasms that rippled my internal walls. In the wet sucking grip of my hungry sheath squeezing down on him with more and more tightness as he slowly built up the pleasure, the wracking tension once again.

He made love to me like his father and brother fought. With sure grace, with natural athleticism, with extraordinary physicality, as if his body had moved this way a million times before. No fumbling, no hesitation.

He's a virgin. A virgin, a voice inside of me screamed. Had to be. But he played me like a master violinist played a beloved Stradivarius. With familiarity. With a skilled touch. With an exploring, swiveling plunge of his hips that drew forth a muttered gasp, a deep moan from me. That lit me up once more with a soft, illuminating glow.

A slow withdrawal. Another leisurely swivel-stroke in, that had me mewling and grasping his arms in breathless pleasure and hardening demand. It was wonderful and not enough. I rose to my knees, fisted my hands in his hair. Tightened around him even more, and rocked against him with hard, surging moves that brought forth his own light again. That made his breath catch and hold, and his eyes gleam even fiercer.

"No," he said, his voice so harsh it was almost a growl. "Let me learn you. See what pleases you."

"Everything you do pleases me."

"Then let me do it more."

"I don't know if I can take more."

"You can." And unvoiced—*You will.* Those odd bright eyes of his demanded it, holding me still, almost in thrall as he began to move in me again. Screamingly slow. Agonizingly gentle. So that I felt every hard slip and slide of him in and out of me while I trembled and held obediently still, poised over him.

When he was assured of my compliance, when I ceded control back to him and harsh primitive triumph glittered in those warrior eyes, he rewarded me by leaning forward and brushing his bristly beard across my eager pouting nipple, then taking it into his mouth.

Just wetness, warmth, nothing else. And I gasped, swallowed back a moan of need. *Please.*

As if he heard my silent plea, he gave me the suction I needed. A hard sweet pull that zinged from my breast down to my womb as if the two separate organs were connected somehow. So that what was done to one affected the other. So that the light sucking, tugging pull of his mouth upon me was felt not only by my nipple, but deep inside me also, in that part of me that cried out to be filled by him again. Not just by his hard, throbbing length, but what it ultimately thirsted for—the wetness of his seed.

I trembled and shook and twisted against him. And wound even tighter within when his light, tracing fingers accidentally grazed over my sensitive rear rim as he trailed his way from one cheek to the other. He groaned as I unconsciously clenched around him.

His fingers moved back to trace around my anal pucker, both of us groaning as he did so. I was shaking, wound up so tight as he played with me there for an endless moment. Then his other hand moved in front, drifted down through my silky triangle and explored me there where we were joined. He moved those light, grazing fingertips along my stretched outer lips, and I tightened even more, cried out, jerked against him when he traced over my hard, swollen nub. Like an explorer finding treasure, he returned to the spot, traced over that tiny sensitive part of my body where so many nerves screamed. His two hands traced over me, one in front, one in back. And I drew tense, tremblingly tight, like a bow drawn back by an expert archer, my light spilling out from me, his light mixing with mine, making the room glow.

Those dancing fingers suddenly stopped. Stilled all movement of hands, but not of body. His body arched up with sudden thrusting force, plunging up into mine, filling me with his hard, spearing length once, twice. Three savoring strokes in that suspended, taut stillness, that spiraling tightness. Then those fingers moved once more, pressed down firmly over those two spots he had found, one in front, one in back. And it was this, that sudden pressing firmness in those twin spots along with the rough-frictioned drive of him deep inside me that gave me what I needed. Flicked the ignition switch. Made me blast off.

I cried as I came apart again. As my second climax roared through me in a hot, convulsive rush. And as I shook and shuddered, my light bursting from me, he drove into me again and again in a slow, steady rhythm, unhurried, as if he had all the time in the world to fuck me as he drank down my light, as he *pulled* it into himself, dimming my radiance for one brief instant while brightening his own. Then, as my twitching convulsions lessened, his pace quickened. His driving thrusts into me grew even more forceful, stronger. Deeper. His right hand moved down my leg and caressed my foot with the pleasing strength with which he had gripped my shoulders. With that same strong firmness and pressure, his thumb pressed down deep and hard into my sole. He pushed there, right in the center of my foot, and ripped another wash of splintering sensations through me so intense that it was frightening. With his other hand he squeezed my swollen clitoris while he speared himself through my spasming tightness, seating himself home deep inside of me. I came a third time, explosively. Crying out. Coming apart. Splintering into a million sundering pieces. I collapsed on top of him, drained, limp, literally shocked with pleasure, and felt him come inside of me again. Felt the powerful jetting of his own release.

And as he drank down my light, I drank up his seed.

We lay there, chests heaving, bodies and worlds torn apart and slowly coming back together, our lights fading. One last glimmer and we no longer glowed. The light of our pleasure vanished, and I felt the wetness of his seed ooze out, trickle down my thighs.

My eyes fell upon the innocent foil packet, unopened, unused, lying there abandoned on the floor. And the cold light of reality set in.

Oh my God. Oh my God. What have I done?

FIVE

I SCRAMBLED UP and off of him, and frantically threw on my clothes while that refrain ran over and over in my mind. *Oh my God. Oh my God. Oh my God! What have I done?*

"What's wrong?" Dante demanded, and I realized that I'd been muttering the words out loud. I shook my head and stumbled to the door, desperate to get away, my instinctive unease of him twining with fear of what I'd just done. Behind me chains rattled, jerked harshly as he came up against the restraining length of them. "What did I do wrong?"

I glanced back, saw his face, harsh and wild, the muscles of his body bunched tight as he strained against the chains, trying to come after me. His body glistened—the sweat of his malady mixing with the sweat of the sexual exertion that had healed him. His male organ, semihard, was wet with our combined essence, with my fluid and his ejaculated seed that swam even now in me. That hard male body, that fierce, frightening face, the smell of sex thick and pungent in the air—I saw it all, smelled it all, and had to get away. Had to leave. Him. Everything. What I had done.

I slammed out of the room, past the startled faces of his brother, his father. Then I was outside in the dark and starry night. A cool, cleansing breeze drifted over me like a soothing hand, easing some of the panic, some of the madness that had gripped me for a second. Our mother moon, whose light we held within us, glimmered serenely down from above, her soft lunar rays falling upon me like the hand of a Madonna soothing her restless child. A comparison that reminded me starkly of my dilemma. That I may have just gotten myself pregnant . . . *knowingly*. That was the hard part to swallow.

I found a large, flat rock a short distance away from the house and sat there, my hand drifting down to cover my belly, the gesture part protective, part horrified. Sounds drifted from the house and I ignored it, shut it out, lost in my own world, my own tormenting reflections.

A baby. How could I have done that? Risked that?

How could I have not? a voice within me demanded. That dominant part of me that was woman. That was Monère.

The odds were against my getting pregnant because the Monère are not a fertile people. It's hard for our women to get pregnant. But the man whose seed lay wet and pungent within me came from a line that had proven obviously potent. Not just one son, but two. Twins.

Shit.

I sat there, lost and alone, for a countless space of time. I don't know how many minutes passed before the crunching of footsteps on fallen leaves alerted me to another's presence. Sounds that were deliberately made to give me warning of their approach. Not that I needed it. Even lost in my thoughts as I was, I would have felt him. Dante. The possible father of my child . . . or not.

It was with this new and stunning realization in my eyes

that I rose to my feet and turned to face the young man I'd just had sex with: If I became pregnant, I might not even know who the father of my child was. Dante or Amber. I'd slept with Amber several days ago, right after Basking.

Dante had showered, shaved, and dressed. His wet hair was slicked back and the grizzly beard gone from his face, allowing me to see the rough, stark beauty of his angles. But even groomed and dressed in the trappings of civilization, nothing could change those eyes. Those pale blue eyes that shimmered with wildness and aggression barely contained. The madness in them was gone, but not even sanity could soften the instinctive fright that coursed through my body like a shocking jolt when I looked into those formidable eyes. Eyes that I could have *sworn* I knew. He was un-chained, free, and fear suddenly thudded within me, coursed in a riot through my blood.

He stopped twenty feet away and spread his hands in front of him to show he was unarmed, that he meant no harm. But my heartbeat did not lessen its rapid-fire stac-cato. When he took a step forward, I took a step back. I couldn't help myself.

Something moved in his eyes. Hurt, pain. Reciprocal wariness, perhaps. His eyes dropped down to my hands that I had unconsciously lifted to ward him off, to keep him back, and his eyes narrowed. Something in him grew very still.

Suddenly aware of what I'd done, I made myself drop my hands back to my sides. "Are you well now?"

"Yeah." But he spoke as if he were troubled, distracted, making no move to draw closer to me. With effort, he brought his attention back to me. "What about you? Are you well? Did I hurt you?"

"No," I said, as gently as I could with all the adrenaline coursing in me.

"Then what's wrong?"

"I may be pregnant." My whisper vibrated with the horror I was feeling. "And I just realized, if I am, I may never know for sure who the father is."

His attention centered even more sharply on me. "You have another lover?"

"More than one." A choked sound came out of me that was half-sob, half-laugh. "But only one before you who could get me with child." Not Halcyon, my demon dead lover. Not Gryphon, whose child I had wanted in remembrance of him. Not Dontaine, with whom I had lain, but not in a way that could result in a child. "Just Amber. Or you."

Something flared in those eyes for a moment before he dropped his gaze. His hands curled into fists, and tension seeped into his body before he consciously released it with a slow, deep breath.

"Thank you for saving me," he said, his rough voice deliberately gentle, oddly formal. "And my deep regrets for any discomfort I may have caused you with my fumbling. It was not meant intentionally."

Frightened though I was of him, I pushed aside my distress to soothe his. "You didn't cause me any discomfort. Nor was there any fumbling on your part. You brought me great pleasure. Made me come three times, in fact. How can you doubt that you pleased me?" I said, shaking my head. "Was that your first time?"

He cast me an odd look but nodded.

"Well, let's just say you show a true natural talent," I said with a wobbly smile.

"Then why did you run from me?"

My smile disappeared. "Because we didn't use the condom. It was right there in my hand. Then your need flared up my own and I felt this terrible, gripping urge to bear life, to have a baby. It came out of nowhere, ambushed me, drowned me in it, until I felt as if I would literally *die* if I didn't feel your seed jetting into me. The condom was right there in my hand, and I deliberately dropped it, let it go. How could I have done that? I don't even know myself anymore, who I am, what I'm becoming."

"Would being pregnant be so bad if that is what your body craves?"

"You don't understand." And I couldn't explain it to him. "It could be disastrous. Not for me, but for the baby. And I knowingly risked it."

Even more distressing, I thought I was going crazy. I felt as if I should recognize Dante. That even though I'd never laid eyes on him before, my body knew him in some way . . . and feared him.

"Do I know you?" I felt like an idiot asking him that question, but was compelled to ask it anyway.

He stilled. Froze in a way that made him seem as if he were not real, not living. Then he moved, released a breath. He cast me a searing, searching gaze. Then without a word he turned and walked swiftly away—as if a ghost had suddenly sprung up before him and he was fleeing it.

Only when he was gone did my heart slow down.

God, I thought. *Who the hell are you? How do I know you?* And most important of all: *Why do I fear you?*

S I X

EVENTUALLY, I WANDERED back to the house. Dante was nowhere to be seen, deliberately avoiding me, it seemed, to my relief. After a shower, some clean clothes borrowed from Hannah, and one soothing cup of chamomile tea to settle my frazzled nerves, I called home. The phone at Belle Vista rang only once before it was picked up, as if someone had been standing there waiting for it to ring.

"Hello," said a voice abruptly.

"Tomas?" I wasn't sure if that was who I was speaking to. It sounded like him, but sharper, crisp, without his usual soft twang and easy way of speaking.

"Mona Lisa?" The shocking loudness of his voice was heard clearly by everyone in the room, which happened to be the entire Morell family. All but Dante.

I winced. "Yeah, it's me, Tomas. Is Dontaine there?"

"No. He and everybody else are out looking for you. Where are you?"

"In the next state. In Texas. I'm okay. I, uh, found a healer, and I'm bringing her and her family back with me.

But it might take a little while for them to pack up everything, and then hours more for us to drive home. I'm going to try to make it back before sunrise, but don't worry if I don't."

There was just the jagged sound of his breathing for a few long seconds. Then his voice sounded in my ear again, softer. But it was a harsh softness. "Worry? Why should we worry? Wiley woke the entire house up and they tracked your steps back to the woods. They found the scent of two strange men there and signs of a struggle." His restraint slipped then. *"What the hell happened, Mona Lisa?"*

Oh crap. I could imagine the panic and uproar that had followed. "Listen, I'll explain everything when I get back home, I promise." Hopefully by then everyone would have calmed down some. *Please let it be so.* As it was, my raw nerves couldn't take Tomas's distress any longer. I felt oddly fragile, like a ceramic doll that would crack with any additional pressure. "Call off the search, Tomas. Tell everybody that I'm okay and that I'll be back soon. I'm going to hang up now."

"Don't!" Tomas yelled, panic in his voice. "Don't hang up! Tell me where you—"

Gently, I disconnected.

"Was that your lover?" Quentin asked. He seemed the only one capable of speaking in the sudden silence. His mother and father looked shocked, as if what they had heard was not what they had been expecting to hear. Their surprise surprised me. *What was the big freakin' deal here?*

"No, that was Tomas, one of my guards."

The big man, Nolan, unglued his tongue. "You allow a guard to speak to you like that?"

"He's upset," I said, shrugging. "I think it would be best if we left here as soon as possible, so my people back home don't freak out any more than they already have. How long will it take for you guys to pack?"

"Hannah's things are ready," Nolan said, looking at me in an odd manner.

"Good. What about the rest of you?"

"We're rogue males," Nolan said, "who kidnapped you."

Ah. So this was the reason for their shock.

"I know," I said. "To save your son. It's not the first time I've had a run-in with outlaw rogues, or been kidnapped by them. Some have become my dearest friends."

"Oh, milady." Hannah's voice quavered. "You wish *all* of us to come with you?"

"Of course. What did you think? That I'd just take you and leave the rest of your family behind?"

"Yes," Nolan said. "That's exactly what we thought."

They thought I'd take the woman, the valuable healer, and cast aside the men who loved her. "No, I'd never separate a family."

"It was the reason we fled," Hannah said, her voice trembling. "Because our Queen refused to let Nolan and I marry, even when it was known I was growing heavy with his child."

"I thought it was customary for fertile couples to marry?" In the hopes that they would breed more offspring. Dontaine had explained some of it to me.

"That is the usual custom, if they both wish it, and we did," Hannah said. "But our Queen denied us this."

"Why?"

"Because she desired Nolan for her own bed."

Husband and wife looked at me questioningly. It took me a second to figure out what they were asking, without actually saying it.

"Oh! No, I'd never . . . He's a married man!" I squawked, and felt myself blushing. I took a deep breath and untangled my suddenly clumsy tongue. "You have my *word* that I will never ask Nolan to sleep with me or any other woman.

I respect the bonds of matrimony, and appreciate those who honor them."

"And our sons?" Hannah asked.

"I wouldn't require it of them, either," I assured them. But my words actually seemed to distress rather than please Nolan and Hannah.

"Milady, apart from myself, my sons are the last living descendants of Lacedaemon," Nolan said, seeming to expect some sort of reaction from me. What, exactly, I had no idea.

"I'm sorry. I grew up among humans. My knowledge of Monère history is almost zilch. I only became aware that people like us existed several months ago."

"In human Greek history, Lacedaemon was the son of Zeus and Taÿgete," Nolan explained. "He was the founder of the city of Lacedaemon, more commonly known among humans as Sparta."

"Oh, well, Sparta. Sure, I've heard of that." Who hadn't? The ancient Greek city famous for its military—the strict training and the superior soldiers it raised. And Nolan and his sons were descended from this line. I guess that explained their unusual fighting skills.

"Lacedaemon was a Full Blood Monère who came from an ancient bloodline of supreme warriors. He fathered several Mixed Blood sons. Instead of abandoning them, he built a city-state for them and taught them some of his fighting skills. Most of the citizens of Sparta had some Monère blood running in them."

The concept was mind boggling. "Those fierce Spartans were Monère *Mixed Bloods*?"

"Alters your view of history, doesn't it?" Quentin said with a slight smile.

"Greatness runs in my sons' blood," Nolan said. No bragging, just a statement of fact. "They would be worthy of you."

It hit me then what they wanted and why they were so distressed. They wanted their sons *in* my bed. Not out of it.

Oh, cripes!

I struggled with what to say and finally settled on the truth. "Frankly, your sons can do much better than a Mixed Blood Queen. You know I'm a Mixed Blood, right?"

Nolan nodded.

"With their lineage and fighting skills, they can probably have their pick of Queens. Just not me. My bed is full, more than full. And not just by Monère, but demon dead. I guess you should probably know that I've . . . um, agreed to be Halcyon's mate."

Nolan paled, making me notice only then what I should have noticed before. That his skin was not the pure lily-white of most Monères. That all of them, even Hannah, were a light brown shade. "You're tanned," I said. "You can walk in daylight?"

"Like any other Monère can for limited amounts of time," Nolan answered. "The few minutes of sun exposure every day—driving my sons to school, picking them up, and then driving to my business—results inevitably in darkened skin after several months' time." He shrugged and returned to the subject at hand. "The Halcyon you mention. Do you mean the High Prince of Hell?"

"Yup, that Halcyon. So you see." And I think they did now. "It would be in your sons' best interests to seek another Queen's bed." *Any* other Queen's bed. I chewed my lip and continued. "It is my hope that you and Hannah will choose to make your home with me. And that I can serve as your sons' reentry into Monère society. They should be ready to . . . I mean, I saw boys younger than them seeking positions with Queens." The main position hopefully being over or under her in bed, though I could scarcely say that to them. But that was the reality of our Monère society. Virgin boys . . . I winced at that, wondering if I had just hurt Dante's chances of being selected . . . were taken into a Queen's bed at a young and tender age. An arrangement that bene-fited both parties. The budding warrior gained power from mating with a Queen, and the Queen gained a sexual play-mate she was not afraid of, a man just coming into his power, indulging herself with him until that power grew too threatening for her, or she tired of him and cast him from her bed.

"My sons are two years past the age of maturity when most young men would seek to intimately serve a Queen," Nolan said. "They are, as you say, ready to go into service."

"Oh, well, good. The next Council meeting is coming right up in nine days. They can . . ." Offer themselves up? "Sign up then at the Service Fair. If they want to, that is." I blushed, unable to look at Quentin. "I was just thinking that the sooner for them, the better."

Nolan nodded. "You are correct, milady. Indeed. The sooner for them, the better."

I took a breath, willed the blush to fade away. "Yes, well, um . . . all I ask is that you come and give me a try for a few days. If you're not happy settling in my territory, you can seek a position with another Queen of your choosing at the coming fair, and I will do my best to aid you in that en-deavor. I know it's not your usual Monère arrangement—a Mixed Blood Queen and a Demon Prince." I smiled weakly. Actually, that didn't sound attractive at all. I hesi-tated. "If you and Hannah would rather not join me be-cause of this, if you'd just rather continue on as you have been doing, I'll understand."

"You humble yourself for no reason. You give my sons a chance I never thought they'd have, and myself a privilege I'd never thought to know again." Nolan dropped to his knees and Hannah and Quentin knelt beside him.

"It would be a great honor to serve you, my Queen."

SEVEN

IT TOOK LESS than an hour to gather up their things. Thankfully, most of their stuff had already been packed. They'd been planning to leave anyway. Hannah cooked a steak for Dante, and had him eat it and drink something before we left. He hadn't taken the time earlier for sustenance when he had rushed out to see me. When asked if I cared for some food, I hastily muttered that I would grab a hamburger on the road, and quickly fled the kitchen.

We were ready to go in short order. One of the two vehicles they had, a Honda Ridgeline truck, had thick mats and bulky gym bags loaded in the open flatbed, along with the other packed household stuff. I slid into the front passenger seat and turned to gaze curiously at the unusual items. The truck was surprisingly roomy inside—as roomy as a regular car. Nolan took the wheel while Hannah sat in back. Quentin drove the other car, following us, with Dante seated beside him. I was grateful they hadn't put Dante and me together.

When asked what all the mats in back were for, I was told that it was equipment from the self-defense school they'd operated in their little town. That was how Nolan and his sons had made their living.

"We taught the use of sword, dagger, and firearms, as well," Nolan told me as I blissfully devoured a hamburger we'd gotten at a drive-through. I discovered that fast food tasted especially good when you hadn't had any in a long while. "We even held special classes for the local police," he added.

I chewed and washed down a mouthful of the steamy burger with a cool sip of Sprite. "Cops?"

Nolan smiled, probably at the way I'd said the word. "Yes, cops. They made up over a quarter of my client base, good customers actually. Hannah also offered her healing services to the local community."

"You healed humans?" I said with surprise.

"In a much more subtle way, milady," she said, nodding. "My talent is limited with non-Monère. More diagnosis, pointing out what is wrong, and the easing of some of their pain. Sometimes boosting their own natural healing. I give them herbal infusions to drink while I examine them, and they believe that it is the herbal tea that helps them."

"You seem to have made a comfortable life here," I observed. "Why were you planning to leave?"

"We knew we could no longer stay after we brought you here," Nolan answered.

A germ of an idea was sprouting in my mind. I tried it on, out loud. "Nolan. How would you like to open up a similar school in my Louisiana territory?"

Nolan glanced askance at me. "For humans?"

"Yes, and some Mixed Bloods I have under my care."

"I am yours to command, milady."

I waved his perfunctory comment aside, and continued, warming up to my idea. "The expense and income would be yours to manage. And any profit would be yours to keep like before, other than a ten percent cut—the tithing portion I owe High Court from all my businesses. Would you like to do this?"

He seemed astounded and uncertain. "Yes, of course, milady. But that is not how things are usually done."

"The usual way being that the Queen owns everything, everybody works for her for free, and she provides for their needs. A feudal way of operating that really should change. And maybe can, beginning with you."

"But I will not be contributing much to you under those terms," Nolan said, troubled.

"You will be contributing more than you know. You will be showing my people another way to live, a more independent way. And one of the Mixed Bloods you will be training will be my brother. Teach him how to protect himself, and you will have served me invaluably. Besides, you're contributing a *healer* to our community."

Regardless, Nolan insisted that I take twenty percent of the profits. Ten percent for the tithe, the other ten percent for myself. In addition to that, he said, "I would extend my services in the training of your men, as well."

"That's very generous," I said, pleased with the offer. "I'll introduce you to Dontaine, my master of arms. See what he says."

Nolan asked me who the drill master was, and the length and frequency and routine of practice for my warriors. To my shame, I was unable to answer him.

"I'm sorry. I don't know as much as I should about that."

"You don't practice with your men?"

"No."

"You should," Nolan said. "You fight well, but your swordplay is crude."

Nothing like the truth to make you wince. "I haven't had much practice," I said in my own defense.

"You will now" was his ominous reply. I had a feeling that whoever the drill master had been before, Nolan was the new one now, at least for me, if he had anything to say about it.

Dawn was just beginning to break when we finally pulled into the long driveway leading up to the house. We rounded a curve, then Belle Vista, the grand plantation home, was rising before us. But lovely though the building was, it was the people streaming down the steps that truly lifted my heart. My family, my people. And Amber was here! My big, craggy giant. My Warrior Lord, my love. Happiness swelled my heart.

That happiness faltered a bit, though, when I saw the harshness on his face. And Amber's was not the only grim, tight-lipped expression I saw as we pulled up. Dontaine, tall, fair, and handsome, stood beside Amber, looking like a thundercloud ready to burst and rain down on us. Flanking them were my guards: Aquila, the former rogue who had kidnapped me, now one of my most trusted men; and loyal, plain Tomas, on whom I had hung up the phone. He was looking as angry as I'd ever seen him. The four of them were an intimidating wall—fully armed with swords, daggers, and aggressive stances. Behind them, kept safely back, was my younger brother, Thaddeus. His dark straight hair and almond eyes, so like mine, grew big with relief as he caught sight of me. Next to him were Jamie and Tersa, the brother and sister of my heart, the other Mixed Bloods in my care. Their mother, Rosemary, a Full Blood Monère woman, stood tall among them. And beside them, guarding them, was Chami, my chameleon, my deadly assassin.

"It's all right," I said stepping out of the car. "Everything's o—"

The rest of my words were cut off as Amber grabbed me in a crushing embrace. Good thing my bruises were gone, healed with the first orgasm Dante had given me, or I would have been yelping in pain and upsetting my men even more.

"Are you hurt?" Amber demanded, holding me at arm's length to look me over from head to toe with a keen, razor-sharp inspection.

I was able to answer him honestly, "No, I'm not hurt. I'm fine."

Car doors opened and shut, and Dante and Quentin came to stand beside their father; the truck separated them from my men. Hannah remained in the car per her husband's quietly murmured command.

"This is the healer and her family that I told you about," I said, made nervous by my men's continued tension.

"'Tis the same scent from the forest," Dontaine said. "The *intruders*." The snarled pronouncement had my men drawing their weapons.

"Stand down," I said sharply. "They are not armed and they offer you no violence."

"They wear guns," Amber rumbled dangerously.

And so they did, in harnesses hidden beneath the light jackets they wore. I'd totally forgotten about them. How stupid of me. Thankfully, Nolan and his sons were smarter than I. They made no move to draw their guns. Just stood there, a solid wall of three.

"Your Queen thinks you dead, Nolan," Amber said, his eyes fixed on the big warrior.

"The only way I could have ever left her," Nolan replied. "It has been long since I have seen you. You are no longer Amber, but Lord Amber now," he said, noting the medallion chain the other man wore, and the greater feel of his power.

"Did you take Mona Lisa from us?" Amber asked.

"I did," Nolan answered.

"Why?"

"My son Dante was afflicted with *Lunara asseros*."

A ripple of reaction, felt more than seen from my men.
Amber's gaze traveled over the two young men, coming to
rest on Dante without having to be told which one he was.
No need to. His stronger presence, greater than that of his
brother, and my scent which he still carried, identified him
readily. Amber studied him carefully, and was examined
with equal intensity in turn.

Abruptly Amber resheathed his sword. The tension lessened palpably as the rest of my men put away their weapons.
They may not have entirely forgiven Nolan, but at least they
understood his actions better now.

"You have a family, Nolan," Amber said.

"Yes, I have been richly blessed." At Nolan's calling,
Hannah stepped out of the car and went to her husband's
side. "This is my wife, Hannah," Nolan said proudly. "And
my two sons, Dante and Quentin."

"Welcome." Amber inclined his head formally to them
all, then his eyes returned to Nolan. "Welcome back into the
fold, brother." The two big men stepped around the truck
and embraced each other in that rough, back-slapping way
of powerful men.

You couldn't help comparing the two of them. Nolan
stood around six two, but Amber topped him by at least
a good four inches. Nolan was big, but Amber was even
bigger.

As if a silent signal had been given, the others rushed
down to me, and I was wrapped in teary embraces. I returned hugs, spoke reassuringly to Rosemary, Tersa, Jamie,
and Thaddeus. Even apologized to Tomas for hanging up
on him the way I had.

Daylight streamed softly over us, and while I enjoyed
the feel of the sun's warmth upon my skin, I knew that it
had to be uncomfortable for the rest of them.

"Grab what you need," I instructed Nolan and his family. "You'll sleep here tonight until we can settle you into a place of your own."

Hannah grabbed a satchel smelling of medicinal herbs, and a second light tote. Nolan and the boys each took two bags from the car. The heavier, longer one contained their weapons. The second, smaller bag was filled, no doubt, with lesser necessities like clothing. I mentally rolled my eyes and shooed everyone into the house.

If a house could give a sigh, Belle Vista did as we walked through her grand doors—of happiness, of contentment, of joy. I was back where I belonged with my people. And like a good Queen, I had brought back even more people to fill her hallways with.

EIGHT

I SLEPT IN Amber's arms that day. No scolding, no questions. Just sweet, blessed sleep. As soon as he wrapped me in the comfort of his big embrace, with his slow-beating heart thudding gently beneath my ear blocking out all other sounds in the house, I drifted off to sleep.

My eyes fluttered open as dusk began to fall. Wide awake and refreshed, I left Amber still sleeping, drifted silently down the stairs, and slipped out the front door. A few last, lingering rays of sunlight still defiantly painted the remnants of the day, as if to say, *Do not hasten me on my way.* I walked across green grass so lush that it cushioned each footfall, drinking in the magnificent hues of sunset, the vibrant splashes of color thrown upon the rich canvas of the sky.

It wasn't until he spoke that I became aware that another watched the ebbing day as I did. "It's beautiful, isn't it?" His voice came from the trees lining the eastern edge of the lawn.

"Dontaine," I said with surprise and pleasure, and walked

across the carpet of grass to where my master of arms sat against a tree, half-hidden in its shadows. Sunset's last faint light fell across the leaves to dapple his skin with purple-pink hues.

"You can walk in daylight?" I asked.

"Like any other Monère," Dontaine replied in a voice carefully devoid of emotion, his eyes lifted to the setting sun. "Not like you, without any pain, any burning. It stings my skin still."

I sat on the ground beside him and said softly, "I'm sorry."

"For what? That I did not receive your gift, your immunity from the sunlight through our mating? Or for walking so carelessly out of the house like this, without any guards? Without anyone aware of where you go. Or are you apologizing for doing that very same thing yesterday, twenty-four hours ago, allowing yourself to be snatched from us, leaving the entire household in a state of frenzied panic?"

His voice was deceptively calm. But his eyes . . . his eyes, when he turned them to me, were far from calm. He was furious in a way that was even more frightening than if he had screamed and yelled. Contained fury.

I flushed with shame, with guilt, with knowing that I was wrong. "Dontaine, I'm very sorry for that."

"Sorry doesn't cut it, as you humans say!" He lashed out at me with the biting edge of his emotions unleashed, and I flinched, wisely shut up as he pressed his lips tightly together, holding back the hot torrent of words just waiting to spill out. Somehow he managed to swallow them down. His next words came out in a hoarse, strained whisper. "I promised him that I would guard you with my life."

"Who?"

"Halcyon, your Demon Prince. Remember?"

His caustic tone made me wince. "Dontaine, please. Stop."

"I *can't*! It eats at me so. He entrusted you to me, to watch over you when he could not. And hours later, not even a *day* later, you are gone. Stolen from us while we slept." He looked at me with tormented eyes, a painful mix of guilt and anguish filling them. "And I was not here. I do not live in this house. How can I watch over you if I do not even *live* here?"

"Dontaine . . ." My voice trailed away. What could I say after all?

"I am your master of arms by your decree. And your lover by the generosity of your heart. Let me stay here with you, Mona Lisa."

The open vulnerability in that proud face hurt me more than any scalding anger ever could. I gave beneath the gentle force of it with a yielding sigh. "All right. Yes. You can stay here at the house."

"In Gryphon's room, next to yours," he said. "I've spoken to Amber and have his agreement. He wishes it, too."

Ah, so that was why Amber had held back on the tongue lashing. He knew Dontaine would deliver it to me with far more effective results. And that, loaded down with guilt, it would be hard for me to deny Dontaine this request.

My men were learning how to handle me.

But at the thought of someone moving into Gryphon's quarters, my heart twinged painfully. *He's dead but not really gone,* I told myself. Just moved to another realm. And it would hurt my new lover more were I not to let him use that empty room.

I nodded my consent.

"Thank you," Dontaine said in a soft rush of relief, and brushed trembling lips across mine. I felt his weariness then, beating down upon him as we touched, as that electric spark of sensation jumped between us almost sluggishly.

"Did you sleep?" I asked, pulling back.

He shook his head and smiled sadly. "How could I when

no one else was watching? When someone could lure you out? Or you could simply wake early, before others, and wander out as you just did."

"I'm used to taking care of myself, Dontaine."

"You did not even scan your surroundings. You were not aware I was outside with you until I spoke."

I flushed. "Very careless of me, I know. I just feel . . . safe here."

"And we can make it so, if you will allow us. With but a few simple measures."

I'd refused it before when he had suggested it. "There's no need, with three warriors living in the house. Four now with you."

"There is *every* need when they are all sleeping and you are not." Some of the bite leaked back into his voice. "Please, do not hinder me in my duty. A simple rotating watch, that is all I ask."

"Not much, just moving into the house and setting up a watch guard," I grumbled, but pecked a light, affectionate kiss on his lips. "Very well. Anything else you might want to ask for while I am in the mood to give in to any and all requests?"

"Not at the moment. But I'm sure I shall think of something later when I am less fatigued."

"Silly me, then, for wanting you to get some rest. Come on." I pulled my weary master of arms to his feet. "You need to sleep."

"Lie with me?"

"Hah. See? You've already thought of something more to ask for," I teased gently as we walked back to the house.

"Just rest beside me for a while. Until the others awake," he asked softly as we made our way to the guest room on the lower floor.

"Sure."

Of all the things he had asked for, that was the easiest to grant.

I LAY QUIETLY in Dontaine's arms as he drifted off to sleep, finding a different sort of comfort with him. The comfort of bringing my warrior rest, easing his soul temporarily from the burden of my care entrusted to him by Halcyon and by his own heavy mantle of responsibility as my master of arms. He'd tiptoed around me. They all had these past few weeks after I'd returned to them once the storm of my grief over Gryphon's death had broken and passed. But I was stronger now, less fragile, and they were treating me as such, making demands once more.

"You eat that, now. All of it," Rosemary said at dinner that night, after all had risen to break fast, even Dontaine, who had managed to catch an hour of sleep. Rosemary had been a cook at High Court. She had left her coveted position there to follow me out to this hot and humid southern clime because of her Mixed Blood children, Jamie and Tersa, because she knew I would do my best to protect them. *At least you'll try,* she'd said. *No one else will do even that.*

She was a natural, caring mother. And let me tell you, that was a rare thing among the Monère, at least toward their Mixed Blood offspring, which were often looked upon as little more than garbage to be gotten rid of.

She turned the brunt of her mothering nature on me now. "Eat," she said, and I did. Not a hard thing to do when the food was so delicious. Tender roasted lamb with mashed potato, rich gravy, and the light salad greens that I enjoyed. Rosemary had taken over the general management of the household upon our arrival here. Good thing, because I wouldn't have known what to do or who to ask to do it. Though she no longer cooked, she oversaw the kitchen, her first love, with a keen, critical eye.

I ate to please her and myself, and because it was wisest not to go against her in this matter that fell in her domain— a domain over which she ruthlessly presided, and which basically stretched to include any and all sundry matters pertaining to the household. Not only did I fear her tongue lashing, which could be quite blunt and biting, but one tended to fear her physically as well. She was huge, both in height, almost six feet tall, and in girth. She was built like an Amazon, with strong, capable hands that could wring a squawking chicken's neck with one easy twist. I'd seen her do it once.

Only when I cleaned my plate, the last one to finish, did she release us from the table. Hard to believe that cheerful, freckled Jamie, reed tall and slender, and tiny, petite Tersa, walking beside me, had come from her massive body.

"Is Wiley all right?" I asked Tersa now. Wiley was actually short for Wild Boy—what I had called the feral Mixed Blood that the previous Queen had left behind as a snarling welcome present for me. He'd been half-starved and completely wild, having grown up in the swamps, abandoned there by his Monère mother.

Wiley, who was no older than thirteen or fourteen, had bonded with the tiny Tersa, trusting her as he trusted no one else.

"He was upset but unhurt," Tersa said in that soft way she had of speaking. "He led us to where you were taken in the forest and did his best to tell us what happened." Meaning that he had come to the house, dragged Tersa out into the woods, and the others had followed.

"He can talk?" I asked with lifted brow.

"A few words that I taught him. He learns quickly," Tersa said with a smile. That was one of the changes the wild boy had wrought in her, those smiles. "He showed us what happened, mostly through gestures. Then he left. He didn't stay."

"He'll be back," I assured her. He was drawn as irresistibly to quiet, solemn Tersa as she was to him.

"I know," she said with simple confidence, and quietly slipped away.

Our guests, the Morells, following behind us, watched our small byplay with interest. I sensed curiosity from Quentin, watchfulness from Dante, and puzzlement from Nolan and Hannah. Couldn't blame them. The dynamics in this household were puzzling even to me, always shifting as we all tried to find the harmony that was necessary for a happy home. And that was what I was trying to make this, a happy home for all of us . . . adding one more to the mix this morning— Dontaine. Rested and fed, he was much more cheerful, eager to see to the new arrangements we had agreed upon.

As good a time as any to debrief him on the past day's events, and to talk to him about Nolan. Amber and the rest of my guards needed to be debriefed also.

Our meeting took place in the front parlor, and if Hannah was unsettled by all the male testosterone squeezing the large room small, she didn't show it. I guess she was used to it, having spent the last twenty years being the sole woman in a household of men. She sat serenely as I explained to my guys what I should have explained the previous day but had been too tired to. I told them about the snatch, my breaking free, falling into the river, and the fight with the other group of outlaw rogues.

"They were in our territory?" Dontaine asked, frowning.

"Yes, near the border fringing Texas," I said.

"I'll bring some men and see to them tonight," he said curtly.

"Have they bothered us or disturbed any humans?"

"Not that I am aware of."

"Then there is no need to."

"They are rogues," Dontaine said. As if that statement said it all.

"Who have harmed no one," I returned.

"They threatened you."

"Because I literally washed up in their laps. Who could blame them? If they've harmed no one, we will offer them no harm in turn. Besides, I doubt they're still there."

Nolan concurred with me. "They will have left the area by now."

"I should have been aware of them," Dontaine said, revealing the core of his frustration. What really ate at him.

"Do you perform regular sweeps of your outer area?" Nolan asked.

Dontaine eyed the bigger man with arrogance. "Every fortnight."

"If you like, I'll be happy to come along with you on your next patrol. Show you what to look for."

Pride warred with need for a moment. Practicability won out. "Your assistance would be most welcome," Dontaine said stiffly.

As good a lead as any for what I had to say next. Keeping my fingers crossed, I told them how Nolan had supported himself operating his self-defense school, and that I had asked him to set one up locally. "He will not just run the place, but own it, keeping all the profit as before, except for a twenty percent portion. Ten percent of that will go toward High Court's per annum tithe."

This didn't just surprise everyone, it shocked them. They looked at me as if I had suddenly sprouted two heads.

"Why would you do this, Mona Lisa?" It was Amber who asked. Amber who ruled the western Mississippi part of my territory for me. He seemed truly curious, wanting to know my reasoning.

"Because Nolan and his family have managed to support themselves for over twenty years this way. Why should I strip them of this hard-earned independence and expect them to go back to being wholly dependent on me for everything they eat and drink and wear? What does it hurt me to let them continue on as they have, and share a little in their profit?"

"You wish them to remain separate from our community?" Chami, my chameleon, asked. He was six feet tall, with a lean, wiry build like a greyhound. With his almost boyish slenderness and curly brown hair, one could be fooled into thinking that he was just an average guard and not very powerful, at that. But that would have been a sore miscalculation. He was a chameleon, old both in years and experience, able to blend in with his environment, become invisible. And even more deadly, he was able to mute his presence so that he could creep up silently on his target, unseen, unfelt, until he killed you. The perfect assassin. At the moment, though, with his violet eyes as puzzled as the rest of his fellow guards, he looked little older than Nolan's twenty-year-old sons.

"No, Chami. They will be full members of our community, sharing in the benefits and responsibilities."

"What particular responsibilities, milady?" Tomas asked, his voice once more flowing with that easy Southern twang. With his wheat-colored hair and light brown eyes, he was the plainest looking among my men. Sweet, honest, loyal Tomas. Plain only in looks, not in his presence, which reflected his long span of years and accumulated power. All the guards here in this room, my most trusted men, were older in years, strong in power. The type usually discarded by their Queens. Or killed by them.

Instead of answering Tomas's question, I asked one of my own. "Do any of you besides Amber know Nolan?"

"I know *of* him," Chami answered. "He is reputed to be a great warrior, a most gifted fighter."

"I saw him fight once long ago. They say none can best

him with a sword," said Aquila, speaking in his usual precise and clipped manner. Everything about Aquila was neat and tidy, including his thin mustache and Vandyke beard. His gentlemanly appearance was odd only if you knew what he'd been before. Not just an outlaw rogue, but a rogue bandit serving under the infamous Sandoor. The confusion cleared up, though, once you knew what Aquila had been prior to becoming an outcast rogue—not only a warrior, but a man of business, a profession much more suited to his precise and tidy nature. Aquila and my brother, Thaddeus, had overseen all my business affairs in my absence. Were still continuing to do so, actually.

"I've seen them fight, also," I said. Had in fact briefly fought Quentin, though I thought it prudent not to bring that up just now. "And I'm impressed. Nolan has graciously offered his help in training our men. Dontaine, the guards' training falls under your province, right?"

Dontaine nodded.

"I'll leave it to you then to see how best to use them."

"Them? His sons also?" Something flickered in Dontaine's eyes, and I wondered for a moment if he might be jealous or threatened by Quentin and Dante. Or rather more specifically, by Dante.

"I misspoke. Just Nolan. Quentin and Dante will be—" I still didn't know quite how to say it. "—seeking positions with other Queens at the next Service Fair."

Something eased in Dontaine and I knew then that he *had* felt threatened by my intimacy with Dante, and wanted to laugh . . . or maybe cry. If Dontaine knew how much I feared Dante—instinctively, unreasonably, something I'd been able to hide thus far—he would not have wasted any time at all worrying.

"Do the men have practice tonight?" I asked.

"We train every night." Something I would have known had I been paying any attention, which I obviously hadn't.

"Fine. His sons can join the other guards in practice, and you can assess Nolan's skill and see how best you would like to work with him. If you do not wish to involve Nolan in the men's training, I will abide by your decision, Dontaine. Hannah's healing talent alone is more than enough contribution to our people." That was a fact no one could dispute.

Dontaine inclined his head, pleased that I was leaving the final decision in his hands, and seemingly reassured by it.

"I will be happy to accept the assistance of one of whom everyone, including my Queen, speaks so highly," Dontaine said, confirming that any reticence he had felt resided with the young virile sons, not the married father. "Will you come watch practice tonight?" he asked me. "The men and I would be pleased to see you there."

There was only a brief pause before I nodded. Curiosity to see how Nolan and his sons fared against my guards won out over my instinctive need to avoid Dante.

TRAINING, I FOUND out, took place in the twilight hours just before dawn, after the men had finished their patrols and other duties.

Amber had to leave before then, and return to the small slice of my territory that he ruled on my behalf. He'd left there abruptly when he had learned of my disappearance.

"I will return and make sure that Nolan does not bring you more profit with his single twenty percent than I do with all of my businesses that you have entrusted me with," Amber said with a tiny smile.

My giant had made a joke, I realized, and felt tears prick my eyes.

"Why do you cry?" Amber asked, lifting my face gently to his.

"Because you're leaving."

"Do you wish me to stay?"

Yes, stay with me always. "No, go back to your people."

"They are *your* people, Mona Lisa, as am I. You do not have to wait for me to return here. You could come down and acquaint yourself with the businesses and people in that part of your territory."

I shook my head. "No, I can't go back to that place. Not yet." It was where Gryphon had been killed and bad memories still lingered there for me. To turn our thoughts away from that, I brought up what I had been considering for quite some time now.

"I will be petitioning the Queen Mother to make the Mississippi portion of my territory officially yours, Amber. Your rule, separate from mine."

Amber stilled. "There is no need to do that," he said. But he was wrong.

"There is every need. You are my backup for our people. I want to know that there's someplace safe for them to go if anything should happen to me."

"Nothing will happen to you," Amber said gruffly.

But so much already had, I thought sadly.

He stroked a gentle hand down my melancholy face. "Dontaine is now by your side. I am pleased that you are allowing him to take up residence in the house."

"You don't mind?" But my real question was: How did he feel about my taking Dontaine as a new lover? We had not spoken of it yet.

"No, I do not mind," Amber said softly. "He is a good man and a strong warrior."

"And Halcyon. Did Dontaine tell you of my arrangement with him?"

Amber's eyes darkened with the mixed feelings he had always had about the Demon Prince. "I know of what you have agreed upon."

"Do you approve of that as well?"

"It is not for me to approve or disapprove," Amber said neutrally.

Smacking his thick arm, I glared up at my giant. "Don't give me that bullshit. Tell me what you think."

His eyes crinkled as he grinned down at me. Amused, I think, more by the girly way I'd hit him than my unladylike language. "Very well. I believe that the protection Halcyon offers by his public claim of you will be a good thing. Hurting you will risk his wrath. But I also think your relationship with the Demon Prince is a dangerous thing. Not just because you are a way to get to Halcyon, but because of the nature of demons themselves. They are blood drinkers, Mona Lisa."

He hardly needed to tell me that. I was achingly aware of that fact.

"And they are dead, truly dead, while you are of the living."

Not entirely true anymore. And one of the reasons why I wanted Amber safe and far away from me.

"Many Monères will be outraged by your union," Amber continued. "And they will fear you even more because of this alliance."

"Does it matter? You just said that hurting me will be risking Halcyon's wrath."

"That only means they will not risk doing so openly. They will be more devious if they choose to move against you."

"Well. Isn't that a thrilling thought?" I said dryly.

"Why could Halcyon not simply be with you discreetly?" Amber asked. "Why must he lay so public a claim on you?"

"He has to," I told him softly, "for my protection."

"You are in danger?" Amber's face darkened.

I am the danger, I thought.

"Not from anything that you or anybody here can protect me from," I told him. "Things are changing in me, Amber.

Having Halcyon publicly claim me as his mate is more like a necessary diversion." And would become even more so as the changes occurring in me became more apparent. "It will keep me safe."

"I am not the one being ambiguous now," Amber rumbled.

"It's a demon matter," I said solemnly, with utmost seriousness. "If I speak of it to anyone, I risk my life as well as the one I tell. Just know that whatever happens, none of it is Halcyon's fault. It's mine, through something I did."

"Mona Lisa—"

"Please, do not press me on this matter."

Tight furrows of frustration cut deep into that dear, craggy face. I traced over them with a finger, trying to smooth them away. When that didn't work, I drew his head down to me and, stretching up on tippytoes, kissed him.

"Don't be mad at me," I whispered against his lips.

He kissed me tenderly back, his voice deep and rough. "I am not mad. Just concerned."

"I'm safe for now. I promise." *For now* being the operative words here. Couldn't promise about later. Only time would tell.

"Are you happy ruling?" I asked, needing to know.

Amber's harsh face gentled. "Yes, I enjoy it. I like the challenge, making the decisions, bearing the responsibilities. But I hate being apart from you. You have given me a bittersweet gift, my love."

"Most things in life are." I gave him one last kiss. "Go on." Stepping back away from him, I wrapped my arms around my waist so I would not cling to him, beg him not to go. "I'll see you soon."

"Soon," he promised, and left.

NINE

To occupy myself, and because I had skirted my duties as Queen long enough, I spent the next five hours with Rosemary, trailing behind her, learning not just her routine but that of the other various staff she introduced me to. We went over the household accounts. Then, even more tediously, and therefore good penance serving, we went over her first love, the kitchen, an empire unto its own.

Rosemary was delighted with my interest, the first time I had shown any, and enthusiastically flooded me with details. As big and as intimidating as her physical self was, inside she was a warm and caring person who ruled over her domain with a blunt tongue and a benevolent iron hand. Belle Vista sparkled under her care, from the spotless mantel in the dining room to the huge chandelier dominating the foyer, all two hundred dangling crystals gleaming with proud and pristine glitter.

"You've done a wonderful job, Rosemary. Thank you

for stepping in like you did. I wouldn't have known what to do without you."

Rosemary waved her hands dismissively. "Mostly a matter of training good staff."

"And seeing to a thousand details, and making a million important decisions. You've made this a wonderful home for us all."

"Thank you, milady. But you are the heart of it, around which we all gather."

Her words panged me. Brought tears to my eyes. "Oh, Rosemary. I've been a lousy heart." Sadness and guilt over Amber swamped me—how I kept him apart from me. More guilt over how I had neglected everything and everyone these past several weeks . . . with not one word of complaint uttered from my people.

"You've a grand heart, milady. It is a privilege for me and my children to serve you."

At the mention of Jamie and Tersa, concern for them snaked into me. I gripped the hands of the woman who had spread her love so generously in a blanket that enveloped not just her own Mixed Blood children but the young Mixed Blood Queen she had taken under her wing as well. She'd been more of a mother to me in the short time I'd known her than my real one would ever be.

"Things are changing, Rosemary. Beyond what I can control."

"That is the nature of life, ever changing," Rosemary said with kindly wisdom.

"Where are Jamie and Tersa?"

"I sent Tersa with a couple of girls to help settle Healer Hannah and her family into the house down the road. Jamie is outside working on the lawn."

"I thought they were studying for their GED."

"They sat for it last month. The results should be in soon."

Life had continued on around me, it seemed. I was glad. "And college?"

"They've applied to several local ones."

"What did they list as their previous education?" I asked, curious because there was no formal schooling among the Monère—not enough children for that. Jamie and Tersa had been tutored at High Court by a Learned One in reading, writing, and basic math.

"Home study. 'Twas what your brother, Thaddeus, advised. He and Aquila procured all the records and recommendations needed. Very resourceful, the two of them are," said the former cook with a twinkle in her eyes.

Thaddeus and Aquila, my unofficial business managers. They were slotted next for a visit. But that was for another night. I'd tortured myself enough already tonight. On to another part of my Queenly duties. A much more fun part.

"The guards will begin their training practice soon. I'd like you, Jamie, and Tersa to come watch it with me."

"Now why ever would you want us to be doing that?" Rosemary asked, resting her big hands on her ample hips.

"Hannah's husband is setting up a self-defense school in the local community."

"Among humans?" she asked, eyebrows rising high on her ruddy face.

"Uh-huh. That's how they made their living before. Once Nolan gets his school up and running, I'd like Jamie and Tersa to train there with him. You have to see how well Nolan and his sons fight. They're incredible."

"Milady, Jamie and Tersa have already been taught some basic knife work by Chami, and a good teacher he's been to them. But my children are Mixed Bloods. Their strength will never be more than human strong, and my Jamie is never going to be a guard. I do not see the use in more training."

"Nolan doesn't just teach self-defense. He also instructs in weapons training. Guns," I told her. "Guns are a good equalizer for those with lesser strength. I need to know that Jamie and Tersa can protect themselves."

"Well, why didn't you say that sooner," Rosemary said. "Learning how to shoot a gun sounds like a grand idea, mi-lady."

TEN

EVEN WITH ROSEMARY, Jamie, and Tersa accompany-
ing me, I felt awkward. Like a stranger intruding. It was
a feeling that grew even heavier as we made our way onto
the practice grounds, the same circle where, once a month
when the moon rode full and high in the midnight sky, all
my people gathered to Bask.

Men were scattered around, stretching, conversing, sharp-
ening their weapons. I glimpsed Nolan and his sons, and the
familiar faces of Dontaine, Chami, Tomas, and Aquila. The
rest of them, however, were strangers to me. Their easy chat-
ter died away as the men became aware of us.

What an odd lot we must have looked, a Mixed Blood
Queen accompanied by her Mixed Blood waifs. Rosemary
was the only Full Blood among us.

"I hope you weren't waiting for us," I said as Dontaine
came forward to greet us.

"Not at all." Catching my hand in a courtly gesture, he
placed it upon his arm, and led me into the woodland

clearing with as much pride and formality as if we were being presented at High Court.

"The men are just warming up," Dontaine said. "They're excited, knowing that you would be here tonight, watching them."

If they were excited, they did not show it. A sea of male faces—there must have been over a hundred of them—turned to us. Hushed silence rang the air. It was as if the silent echoes of an unheard bell had tolled, calling them to attention. As if now that the Queen and her civilian entourage had arrived, all the guards had to watch what they said and did. Gone was the easy camaraderie with which they had spoken and interacted, vanished completely like smoke whisked away by a strong wind.

I swallowed. Gestured toward them. "Continue on, please."

They simply stared back at me, unmoving. Making me wonder if I shouldn't have said, "At ease, men," instead. Maybe they would have understood that better.

"This is Rufus, my drill master," Dontaine said, stopping before a short, barrel-chested man with hair gone completely gray, denoting his advanced age, over two hundred years old—that was when our hair started to whiten. His was a face I remembered seeing the night they had come to my rescue after I had been captured by Mona Louisa, the former blond bitch ruler here. She hadn't been too thrilled with me taking over her territory, and had tried to get it back by eliminating me.

"I remember you." With a pleased smile, I took the drill master's hand, clasping it with gratitude. The gesture seemed to surprise him. "You and your men helped rescue Prince Halcyon and me. I never got the chance to thank you for it afterward."

Rufus blushed beet-red. Slipping his hand from mine, he mumbled, "'Twas my duty and honor, milady."

I smiled. "An awkward one, I imagine. Having to save your new Queen from your old Queen."

Someone snickered, and like that, the easiness of the night was restored. The men moved about, making quips and snide comments about those who had fought that night. And how well or how lousy each had fared.

"Skewered like a kebab" was one comment that floated to my ear. I didn't know if the man was referring to himself or to his opponent.

Rufus nodded to me with an appreciative light in his eyes that seemed to say, *Well done, milady.*

Turning to his men, he called out, "All right, you lazy louts. Fall into your drill groups. I want the new lads with the other boys. Nolan, I'm putting you with the senior group."

The men fell into three formations shaped much like a whale—smaller at the head and tail. The end groups consisted of the young boys and senior warriors, respectively, with the bloated middle group being the largest: warriors older than the teenage boys in the first group, but younger and less seasoned than the senior group, which was comprised entirely of my contribution of men—Chami, Aquila, Tomas, and Nolan. The power emanating from the four of them was richer, stronger, like the heady scent of sweet wine squeezed from grapes fully ripened and matured. Without my additions, Dontaine and Rufus would have been the only two powerful warriors here. Two to my four. And that was without counting my two strongest, my Warrior Lords—Gryphon, who had become demon dead, and Amber, who ruled my Mississippi slice.

No wonder some of the other Queens had feared me. I could almost see their reasoning. If I surrounded myself with such strong men, so many of them, what did that speak of my own power, my own abilities?

Therein lay the key difference between me and other Queens. I did not fear my men being stronger than I. Did

not see them as threats to watch out for, competitors to cut
down. I saw them as friends, allies, lovers. Men who wanted
to protect me, not hurt me.

The men broke up into pairs, spreading out, and soon
the clash of metal filled the air as they commenced sword
practice. Rosemary, Tersa, and Jamie's eyes were fixed on
the senior group, watching Nolan. My own eyes drifted to the
younger group, which had yet to begin their practice. They
stood waiting for the crusty drill master to make his way
down to them. There were eight of them, ranging from
what looked to be as young as twelve to as old as seventeen, perhaps. The addition of Quentin and Dante was, in
my opinion, like throwing in lions with the lambs. But I understood Rufus's reasoning. They had to start from the bottom. It was responsible, wise even, I realized as Rufus
passed out wooden swords to the boys. He wanted to see
how Dante and Quentin fared with practice weapons before
letting them drill with real swords as the other men did.

Quentin was paired up with a younger boy who looked
to be about sixteen. Dante was matched with the oldest lad,
the boy whose age I had pegged around seventeen. He was
as tall as Dante but far more slender, as if his body mass
had yet to catch up with his height growth. Dante was built
much more solidly. And aside from the physical difference,
there was a confidence to the way Dante moved that set
him apart even more markedly. As if he was older than
them not only in age—a few scant years in difference—but
in experience.

As if Dante felt my eyes upon him, he turned. Our gazes
met, and a shiver of apprehension skittered down my spine
like the trailing footprints of a ghost. Without breaking eye
contact, he stabbed the blunt tip of the wooden sword into
the ground and took off his jacket. Metal bracelets hugged
his forearms, different, darker than what his brother and

father had worn, made from an unusual burgundy-colored alloy. They were as primitive an adornment on him as the gold bar piercing his ear. With the jacket stripped away, he took up his sword and turned back to his practice partner with a cool nod.

A quick glance at the others showed that neither Quentin nor Nolan wore their wrist guards. Just Dante. Then all thoughts scattered as I watched Dante fight. He stood with relaxed poise, countering the other boy's blows easily, blocking his strikes with minimal effort. One, two, three countering hits. Then, as he had with me, he took control. Two powerful forward lunges like a cobra suddenly striking, and the boy was on the ground, his weapon knocked from his hand, Dante's wooden sword tip pointed at his heart. Quentin disarmed his opponent almost as quickly, though with less coiled violence.

A quiet word from Rufus, and Quentin and Dante moved to the middle group. Wooden swords were traded for real swords, and a pair of young guards were broken apart, one paired with Quentin, the other with Dante.

By outward appearance, they were more evenly matched. I knew better, though. I'd seen Quentin fight before, had caught a glimpse of Dante's ability just now, and was both frightened and eager to see more.

What else can you do? I wondered. *How well do you fight with a real weapon? Show me.*

He did. Again, those few testing strikes and parries, feeling out his opponent. Then he took control, setting the pace, increasing the tempo and the force of the blows. Whereas Quentin fought with flowing grace, like a song, a dance, poetry in motion, Dante fought with brute cutting force. He fought as if the man before him was not a sparring partner but an enemy in truth. He moved with the same fluid grace as his twin, but whereas Quentin was like cool, clear water, Dante was like the raging rapids. Savage, lethal, deadly. As I watched him fight, something inside me whispered, *I know you. I've met you before.*

In no time, Dante disarmed his opponent, his sword, this time, stopped a bare inch from his neck. My own neck tingled in a memory flash of pain, here and then gone, distracting me, pounding my heart, so that I hardly noticed when Quentin defeated his partner.

Rufus grunted, narrowed his eyes, and walked Dante and Quentin down the line of sparring men to a pair all the way at the other end, men older in age, whose power thrummed greater than the Morell brothers. But it wasn't power Rufus was trying to match up, so much as weapons' skill.

The two men broke apart, and eyed the brothers curiously.

"Want us to have a go at these two young lads here, Rufus?" asked the bigger of the two guards, grinning. He had dark curly hair and was as tall as Dante but an entire width larger, outweighing the "young lads," as he called them, by almost a hundred pounds. His arms were massive and his thighs were well on their way to becoming tree trunks. If one were to judge someone's age by the feel of their power—not always an accurate gauge, granted—I'd have guessed him at close to seventy or eighty years old.

"Aye, Marcus." Rufus nodded. "And no holding back. I be wanting you and Jayden here to show me whether or not I should be moving these two young 'uns up to the next group."

It was a statement guaranteed to wipe the grin off of Marcus's face, and Jayden's as well. Jayden stood slightly shorter, just shy of six feet, and was built along less bulky lines than his bullish partner. But he, too, felt older in years.

Rufus's words snapped the two of them to full attention. Because what the drill master was really implying was that the two "young 'uns" were better than they were. Good enough, perhaps, to practice with the senior men.

They paired off in grim silence, Dante with Marcus, Quentin with Jayden. Once their swords engaged, there was no holding back as per Rufus's instructions. It was fighting that was almost frightening to behold. Whirling movements, dangerous flashing steel. Rufus came at Dante with full slashing force, and Dante smiled as if finally set free, his sword singing in turn, an eager, intent look in those pale eyes.

Metal clashed against metal, the usual sounds. Then came the sound of something new, something that caught everyone's attention. A lighter, higher resonance. Almost a clinking chime as Dante caught Marcus's sword against his metal bracelet, deflecting the blow in a most unexpected manner. Dante's sword darted forward and Marcus leaped back. The burly warrior gazed down at the neat cut that gaped open his shirt front, exposing the muscled slabs of his belly. The white skin itself was uncut.

"Neat trick." Marcus grinned, teeth bared, his dark eyes lighting up with the pleasure of a worthy challenge. "Let's see you do that again, boy." He lunged forward, a big bear of a man, his full power and weight behind the thrust. The high chiming clink sounded again as Dante deflected the blade past him with his right wrist guard. A quick turn and twist like the steps of a ballet, a lethal one, and Dante was suddenly behind Marcus, the edge of his own sword stopped a hair's breadth away from the thick neck.

Complete silence for one long moment, then big, bullish Marcus dropped his weapon. "And I'm dead." He turned around slowly, unarmed. "Witch's tit," Marcus said, grinning. "That's some real nice moves you've got there, Dante boy. Course, you'd be minus a hand now, if your aim with those fancy cuffs was off by a tad."

"True," said Dante, lowering his sword. "Lucky, I guess."

"Lucky, my balls," muttered Jayden. He and Quentin had stopped their fighting to watch the other two. As had all the rest of the men the moment that first clinking chime had sounded in the air.

"You fight like the Lacedaemons of old," said Chami, my chameleon. He was tall and boyishly slender, but his voice held the chill of death, stilling everyone. "You are descended from that line?" He asked the question of Nolan, with whom he had been sparring.

"Yes," Nolan replied, eyeing the smaller man warily. "It is not common knowledge among the other Queens I served. But Queen Mona Lisa knows of my lineage."

He'd only told me in a bid for his sons, casting it out as enticement for me to take them into my bed. Or maybe Nolan hadn't tried to hide it from me simply because I'd already seen the unusual, distinctive manner in which they fought.

"Of all the Queens, she is one you should have kept this knowledge from," Chami said. His words puzzled me as much as they did Nolan.

"Why do you say this, Chameleo?" Nolan asked, calling Chami by his full name. A name that stated what Chami was, and what he did. Chameleon. Assassin.

"You do not know, do you?" Chami asked.

"Explain yourself, chameleon."

Chami turned his gaze back to me. "Mona Lisa. If you will please show him your hands."

Feeling something almost like dread well up in me, I lifted my hands and turned my palms out to him. When Nolan caught sight of the pearl-like moles nestled in my palms, his sun-darkened face whitened, became ash pale. He looked from me to his son. To Dante, who watched us with his pale blue eyes glittering and gleaming like shards of ice melting beneath the sun's brilliant light.

Chami quoted the following words in an almost singsong

manner, reciting them like an old familiar song. "*With pale eyes touched by the faint color of the sky, the fierce son of Barrabus slew our heart, our hope, our Warrior Queen.*"

Hearing that name, Barrabus, something tingled to life within me. It was a name I'd never heard before. By the same token, deep in the soul of me, I knew and recognized it somehow.

The charged tension between Chami and Nolan suddenly grew thicker, more threatening. Reacting to that incipient promise of violence, Tomas and Aquila moved swiftly in front of me, as did Dontaine, though he looked as confused as everyone else. It was like watching a play that had suddenly, unexpectedly, veered away from its usual dialogue and storyline. Only Nolan looked as if he understood it. And Dante. From whom men were protecting me—as if he were some horrible threat.

"Chami," I said, trembling from something right there, hovering on the cusp of my awareness, tickling my memory, but still just beyond reach. "Explain this. What's going on?"

It was Dante who answered. The words he spoke were almost lyrical, and his voice, fully recovered now, was smooth and rich, a sharp contrast to the harsh stillness of his face, the bitter fierceness of his glittering eyes. "Long ago on another planet, in another world, in a time of great strife among our people, there rose a Queen named Mona Lyra. She bore the marks of the moon's blessing in her hands. The Moon Goddess's tears, they were called, given to her by a mother crying over the blood being shed by her children, one against another, crystallized and captured in a woman's hands, giving her great gifts and powers as healer and fighter both. A Warrior Queen."

The first time I'd met Gryphon, he had spoken of such women in the past bearing the same marks as I. Women who had been both blessed and cursed by their gifts, I remembered.

"What does that have to do with you?" I asked. "With us?"

"Damian, the son of Barrabus, was a warrior with eyes of silver touched by the sky." Dante smiled, a humorless gesture, as I looked at his eyes, noted their color. "He slew Mona Lyra, killed the last Warrior Queen, and was cursed for it, he and his descendants. By the sword they would live and die. Damned, in an endless cycle of life and death, never ending. Reborn each time into an ever diminishing line of those who carried his blood. His curse was to see his line die slowly out, killing his heart as surely as he had cut down theirs. Lacedaemon was one of his descendants." The line from which Dante and his family descended. The line that had been cursed.

I pushed passed Aquila and Tomas, and if my hands shook and my heart beat rapidly, it did not show in my steady voice. "You speak of legends, Dante. Of people that may or may not have existed. It's just a story. It has nothing to do with us."

"You are wrong," Dante said, speaking as softly and gently as the breeze that blew across our skin. "I remember killing you."

ELEVEN

WITH DANTE'S WORDS, over a hundred swords were suddenly raised up against him. The promise of violence hummed in the air and was reflected in Dante's silver-blue eyes. All it would take to ignite it would be for him to lift his blade, the sword that was currently gripped loosely in his hand, the sharp tip resting on the ground.

Something flickered in his eyes, and I knew he was going to do it.

There was power in the ground where we stood. Hundreds, perhaps thousands, of times before, a Queen had called down the moon's light here, and her people had Basked in the glowing rays. It was a sacred circle of light, of power. Of blood spilled on the ground in practice. Of challenges called and met here.

I'd stood here once and called down those lunar rays. Drawn down those butterflies of renewing light. And that once had made this place mine. It recognized me, accepted me, embraced me. This place, this clearing, was mine even more than the house where we slept and ate. *This* was my place of power.

I called upon it now, drew upon it deliberately, and the land answered me, wrapped me up in invisible strands of past and present power. All the authority that was mine, given to me, *claimed* by me, filled my voice as it rang out sharply in the suddenly still night. "Hold! Stand down, everyone."

There were times when I felt like I was stumbling around in the dark. As if I had tripped and fallen, and a crown had accidentally tumbled down on top of my head. Oftentimes, I felt as if I didn't know what the hell I was doing, that I was not worthy. But all that confusion, indecisiveness, and inadequacy fell away. Here and now, in this moment, with the power and authority of this sacred ground thrumming through me, I was Queen as I had never been before. And I knew what was in my men's heart. Every single one of them, even Dante's. Especially his.

"Dante." I held his gaze. Let him see the understanding in my eyes. "It's not going to work. I'm not going to kill you. Drop the sword."

A flicker in his eyes—surprise, wariness—as I began to walk toward him. He stood alone. All others had fallen back, encircling us.

"It would be foolish of me to drop my only weapon," Dante said, his tone easy, reasonable. I was not fooled by it.

"And you are not a foolish man," I said as I shortened the distance between us. "So why would you reveal yourself like that here in my circle of power, surrounded by over a hundred of my men, all armed? Bad odds, even for you."

"I was discovered, not revealed."

"You revealed yourself deliberately," I corrected. "Why would you do that unless you wanted me to strike you down through my men."

I turned to fasten my gaze upon my guards, each and

every one of them. "No one here is to lift a hand against Dante or his family, or you will be foresworn by me and cast out of my court. That is my command as your Queen."

As I drew uncomfortably closer to Dante, Dontaine dared speak. "Mona Lisa. My Queen, please—"

"He will not hurt me."

"How can you say that and believe it?" Dante said, his calm façade dropping away. "I *killed* you before."

"If you wanted to hurt me, you could have done so before now. You had ample opportunity." He hadn't known me at first, when he had been stricken by the light-craving madness. Only when I had healed him and he had sought me out afterward. When I had lifted my hands up to him in an unconscious gesture to keep him away. He'd seen my moles then.

I stopped before him, unarmed. Sure of him, sure of myself. "If you wish to hurt me, you can do so now and none of my men will stop you."

He did nothing. A most telling inaction.

"Dante." My hand reached out slowly to rest upon his hand, the one gripping his sword. "I know what is in your heart. I will not give the order for your death as you intend."

His hand spasmed beneath my light touch. "You should if you are merciful. It might end the curse. Satisfy it. My life for yours."

"Or begin it anew. Please, Dante."

His fingers opened and his sword fell to the ground.

I raised my voice to the others. "Sheathe your swords, men."

They did as I commanded.

I pulled Dante away from the temptation of his dropped weapon, and he came docilely along, looking confused, baffled. I drew him to his father, who watched us with shattered eyes.

"Milady," Nolan said, dropping to his knees, his head bent to the ground. "Thank you for your mercy. I had not realized. My family and I will leave here immediately."

"There is no need to go," I told Nolan. "And every need to stay."

"For what possible reason would you want my family and I to stay here with you?" Dante asked. His hand was still clasped in mine, and he gazed down at our joined hands with almost a bewildered blankness.

"For the reason fate crossed our paths once more," I said. "For a second chance. This time as friends instead of foes."

Dante dragged his eyes back up to mine. In a low, deep voice, he asked, "Do you remember me?"

"Not clearly, but some part of me does. Enough to be afraid of you," I said honestly.

"Not as much as you should," Dante said. But he left his hand in mine.

"We were enemies once, long ago," I said. "And could have been again. First, when your father and brother snatched me. Then just now, when you made our past known." And what a past it was. One that had taken place over four million years ago, in another world. But I could not doubt it, not when my soul recognized his.

"We're different people now," I told him. "We've made different choices. If there is a way to end your curse, I believe that this is the way—to live a different life and not repeat the same mistakes of our past."

"You have no memories of before, do you?" Dante asked.

"No. Do you?"

"Some. Flashes of it. You may feel differently when you remember."

"Then I'd rather not" was my reply. "Remember it, that is. Whatever was then, now is a new time, a new life." I looked at Nolan. "What I offered you before still stands. You and Hannah are welcome to stay here. Your sons also, until they go to seek service with another Queen. My sponsorship still holds, nothing on that has changed. If in the next week you and Hannah decide to seek another position elsewhere, you may do so at the next Service Fair with my full blessing. All I ask is that you stay here for a little while. Give us a try until then."

Nolan glanced at Dante, and some silent communication passed between father and son.

Nolan nodded. "We'll stay, milady."

I felt both relieved and nervous at his agreement. Just a handful of days, I thought, after which time husband and wife would hopefully stay, and the two sons depart. What could happen in that short span of time?

TWELVE

I HAD MY first dream of that long-ago time when I lay down to sleep that day. We were in the midst of battle. So much blood, I thought. And even worse than what coated my hands . . . so many lives I'd taken. Mostly innocent in the fact that they were merely following orders, their Queen's. And therein lay the most guilt—with the ones who had decided this war, been eager for it. Blood had been spilled, but not theirs. Not yet. Their blood, now . . . I would not feel so guilty about theirs. Only then would this madness stop. And only then would the healing begin. But the healer part of me wondered if the lives I saved before and after would ever balance out the blood-drenched scales of now.

A cry drew my attention, a voice that I knew. I cut down the one I was battling and turned, bloody blade in hand, to see Shel, one of my last few remaining strong warriors, run through by a sword. A heart wound, I saw, as the blade was pulled from him and he toppled to the ground almost gently. Incapacitating, but not fatal. Not yet.

As the one who had bested my warrior lifted his sword for the killing blow, the beheading one, I lifted my hand and threw a punch of power from where I stood, making him stagger back away from Shel.

He turned and looked at me, and I recognized him through the feel of his powerful presence and from his red-brown warrior bracelets that gleamed darkly against his wrists. Barrabus. Mona Ella's warlord general himself. A warrior of great renown who had killed two dear to me in the last battle—Ewart and Trey, my strongest fighters. It was odd seeing his features in this dream, and recognizing the same likeness in his son, Dante, whom I'd come to know intimately in another lifetime.

"Here, Barrabus. To me!" I called.

With a fierce smile, he plowed his way toward me, sending those who tried to stop him hurtling away. Our blades met and I fought him as he deserved. With sword, with skill. With brute strength. He was a fearsome fighter, a most gifted swordsman who moved with swift, cutting grace.

"Draw your dagger," I commanded as the sword blades caught and held for a moment, interlocked. I tangled my foot behind him and shoved. He rolled backward, surprised at my strength, and sprang to his feet with the dagger I'd asked him to draw clutched in hand. He waited there, poised, ready.

"You do not draw yours," he said.

I held up my left hand. The Goddess Tear in the center of my palm pulsed and thrummed with power. "I have something much deadlier than a dagger. But that you ask and wait for me to draw my weapon speaks of the warrior you are. An honorable one. You are on the wrong side, Barrabus, serving a Queen who has no honor."

Something passed in his eyes. Silent acknowledgment of what I said. "She is my Queen."

"Because you gave me a chance, I will give you one in return. I ask you to join me. Serve me instead."

"I have sworn my oath to Mona Ella. I cannot switch allegiance here on this field of battle." Regret filled his dark blue eyes and was reflected in my own, I knew, because in another time, a peaceful one, we would have likely been friends.

"Then do not hold yourself back because you do not think me as equally armed as yourself. Because I will not hold myself back."

"As you say, milady."

Our swords clashed together again, and his dagger came at me. With a thought, a pulse of power, I blocked it, stopping his knife with my invisible energy shield emitting from my pearly mole. We held there for a moment, at an impasse. Then with a grunt, using his greater height and weight, he pushed against me. Feeling myself start to slowly give beneath his denser, heavier mass, I spun to the side. His sword struck me a glancing blow as he went sailing past me, slicing open my left arm. I lunged after him, my own blade stabbing forward in turn. In an unexpected maneuver, one I'd heard about but had never seen, he turned and deflected my thrusting sword with his wrist bracelet, using it as I had used the pulsing power in my left hand—as a shield. Then he used it as an offensive weapon, striking a side blow with the hard metal into my right side, knocking the breath from me. Caught unawares, with my shielding hand down, his dagger plunged into my chest and pierced my heart.

What I did next was without thought, just instinct. The sword dropped from my hand and I lifted my palm against his chest. I had a moment to feel his heart beat once, a thud of life. Then my Goddess Tear flared. Obliterating power shot from my hand and took out his heart in an aching, throbbing burst of heat. A moment to feel pain even sharper than that caused by his plunging knife—a healer's pain when she turned the use of her gift to take lives instead of saving them—and Barrabus was gone in a flash of light. A puff of ashes.

I woke up gasping, my hands clutching my chest where the knife had stabbed me. I felt a presence besides me and rolled away with a startled cry.

"Mona Lisa, it's just a dream." It was Dontaine, I realized, looking into his handsome, worried face. Dontaine. Not Barrabus. I glanced down at myself and lifted my hands away from my chest, expecting to see blood. No liquid redness, though, gushed out, and the flesh beneath was unmarred, uncut. But my palms, my Goddess's Tears . . . I looked down at them with horror and felt them throb in aching remembrance.

My eyes shot to Dontaine's bare chest, searched it frantically, a visual inspection only. I dared not touch him. "Are you okay? Did I hurt you?"

"I'm fine. You were just dreaming," he said. Drawing me into his arms, he held me close. His heart beat reassuringly beneath my ear.

"Oh God, Dontaine. I remembered . . ."

"What?"

"I remember killing Barrabus."

The fierce son of Barrabus slew our heart, our hope, our Warrior Queen.

I'd killed Barrabus, Dante's ancestral father, in a past that suddenly seemed not so distant. A past that felt as if it had only just happened.

Dontaine drew back to look at me, his eyes shuttered. "You were saying his name."

"Whose?"

"Barrabus's."

"I took out his heart with my Goddess's Tears," I said

and hugged myself, more to keep my dangerous hands away from Dontaine than because of the sudden cold filling me.

"So it's true. Those stories of Barrabus, of Mona Lyra. You are her, returned," Dontaine said softly.

"I don't know. It's the first time I've ever dreamed"—or more accurately, *remembered*—"something from that time."

"So Dante truly is this Damian. Cursed for killing you long ago."

"I don't know." A shiver ran through my body. "I just know that I recognize him somehow, that we've met before." *Not in this lifetime, but another.* A concept I had a hard time wrapping my mind around, even though my heart believed it to be true.

The woman in my dreams had felt older, harder, her soul much darker than mine. So heart sore and body weary. Was that me? Was I her? Or were we different people now? Different people capable of making different choices? *In another time, a peaceful one, we would have likely been friends,* had been my thought of Barrabus. Might it be true now for his descendant, for Dante? Or were we destined to be enemies once more?

So many chances we'd already had of being that again— enemies. But I had saved Dante, brought him back from the brink of madness. He'd drunk down my life-giving light and had spilled his seed into me in turn.

We had not been lovers before, that I instinctively knew. Already so much was different from the past now. We'd shared our bodies generously with each other before we'd known who we were, who we had been. I remember his gaze falling on my palms as I'd held up my hands to ward him off after I had fled outside after making love, fleeing from what I'd done and had allowed him to do. I remembered the stunned look in his eyes, his distracted manner. That odd way he had looked at me when I had asked him: *Do I know you?* He'd known who I was, had had a chance to kill me then, to harm me again, but he hadn't. In turn, I had held back my men's swords, stopped them from killing him and his family.

Blood, once shed, was a hard stain to ever wash clean again. I'd learned that long, long ago.

God, I'd killed his father! And his father had killed those who had meant much to me, would have killed Shel had I not intervened. Innocent lives lost on both sides, caught up in a war not of their making. We had a second chance now. A fragile peace.

No more bloodshed, I prayed. *Please. No more of that senseless wasting of lives.*

Dontaine murmured my name, drawing me away from my thoughts. "Mona Lisa. You're shivering. Come here, let me hold you." The same thing he'd said to me when he'd asked to share my bed and I had hesitated, too upset, too distracted to want sex. *Let me hold you. I just want to give you comfort . . . and to receive it,* he'd said with an open and vulnerable smile on his first day here in this house as resident, not guest. I'd let him join me in bed, fallen asleep held by him, and had awoken with my Goddess's Tears throbbing after dreaming of using them in a most horrible manner.

I looked at them now, those pearly moles. I glanced from them to Dontaine's beautiful unmarred chest, remembered the throbbing power that had ached in my hands when I had awoken, the energy I had felt there waiting to be released . . . and felt a wave of nausea rise up in me.

"I'm sorry, Dontaine, could you go back to your room? I need to be alone right now." *So I don't accidentally hurt you. Or kill you.* And because my thoughts were on another man, on Dante. Not on the man beside me in bed.

Guilt churned with worry and a fresh dose of horror upon this newest revelation . . . what those innocent-looking moles in my hands were capable of. Death. Destruction.

Dontaine slid out of the bed and picked up his clothes,

not bothering to put them on. "If you need me, you know where I am," he said with a smile that was gesture only. A thin shield to cover the hurt I had inflicted by asking him to leave. Of all my lovers, he was the one I rejected the most.

Another apology formed on my lips. But what could you say, over and over again, besides sorry? Perhaps a suggestion to look for love elsewhere? "Dontaine . . ."

"Hush," he said, stopping the words from being said. "Try to go back to sleep." With that quiet urging, he left.

Sleep, however, was the last thing I wanted to do now. As I'd told Dante before, I'd really rather not remember. So instead of risking another dream, another memory, I lay there in that big bed staring up at the ceiling, trapped by Dontaine's knowing presence next door. If I got up and slipped out of the house, he would know and follow me, and I did not want to see him, talk to him so soon while I still felt so raw. I might have been better protected, but my freedom was curtailed, and it felt stifling.

So I lay there, still and alone, and despite myself, played and replayed that little snippet of memory endlessly. Truth or mere dream, a fabrication of my mind? Only one person could tell me. And with that thought, my mind circled back to Dante.

I had believed myself unarmed when I had walked up to him. No sword, my dagger sheathed. But in Dante's eyes, I had been armed in the deadliest of manners. And he'd let me touch him.

Who are you? Who am I? And why have we come together again?

Last time we had, it had ended with my death. And as I had just discovered, I did not want to die yet. So soon, so young, with no afterlife ahead of me . . . triggering another thought. Was I really young, merely twenty-one years old? Or did my previous life, and the long stretch in between, make me an ancient hag? And regarding that long stretch of time in between, had I lived other lives before and not remembered them?

I gazed down at my moles as if they could provide me with an answer. And in their fashion, they did. The Goddess's Tears and their incumbent gifts had not been seen since the time of the Great Exodus when the Monère had fled their dying planet. So, no. Chances were that I hadn't lived other unremembered lives in between. Just before . . . and now.

Dante. His name was a soft whisper in my mind. *I have a lot of questions to ask you.* I wondered briefly if he would answer them. If he could? Or would it be better if he did not?

You may feel differently when you remember.

My flesh prickled with goose bumps and I shivered again.

For the next several long hours, as sunset inched slowly closer, the most tantalizing, morbid question of all teased my mind.

How did you kill me? How did I die?

THIRTEEN

A S DAYLIGHT EBBED, the house finally stirred and I
was freed from the prison of my room. Thaddeus hadn't
returned yet; the space where he normally parked his car was
still empty. I wanted to talk to him, tell him what I'd learned.
Perhaps comfort myself with his presence. He was not
aware yet of the revelations of the night before because he
ran on a different time schedule than the rest of us did. The
normal human cycle: sleeping at night, going to school during the day.

After school, in deference to our flip-flopped habits,
Thaddeus usually studied at the library, doing his homework
there so as not to disturb the rest of the sleeping household.
And probably not wanting to be inhibited by us either, restricted by the need to be quiet. He returned to the house
when the brilliant hues of sunset began to paint the sky.

Chami, Thaddeus's unofficial guardian, hadn't liked the
idea at all. If it were up to him and the other men, Thaddeus and I would have been guarded at all times, Thaddeus
because he was the men's hope for a different future. My

brother was the only male who could call down the moon's light, who could Bask, something before now only Queens could do. They had wanted to put a guard around him 24/7. Both Thaddeus and I had balked at the idea. Thaddeus had argued that instead of protecting him, it would point him out as a target. His greatest safety lay in secrecy, in letting no others know of his gift. In treating him like a normal Mixed Blood. And trust me, they were not guarded around the clock. Far from it.

I'd backed Thaddeus because I had promised to try to give my brother as normal a life as possible . . . and because had I allowed the men this twenty-four-hour watch, the next person they would have imposed it on would have been me. Same blood that we were, we both were used to our freedom, and did not wish it restricted so.

Chami had finally relented, agreeing that Thaddeus would probably be safer among humans. In general, humans were much more peaceful and civilized than Monères were. In general, though, as I found out, did not take into account the high school teenage subspecies *homo sapien idiotae*. Schoolyard bullies.

Thaddeus made himself scarce that evening after returning home. And I saw why in multihued blue-and-purple glory when he slid quietly into his chair at dinner that night. He was sporting not only a black eye, but a bloody nose— one that had stopped bleeding not too long ago. The faint iron-rich scent of fresh blood clinging to him was unmistakable.

"Thaddeus, what in Hellfire happened to you?" Chami demanded, beating me to the question by a nanosecond.

I repeated the question. My version of it. "Yeah, what the fuck happened to you?"

I'd invited the Morells to join us for dinner, with thoughts of having them get to know us better. All thoughts of polite table talk, however, went flying out the window as

I gazed at the livid bruises that swelled up Thaddeus's left eye and puffed up his nose like a bumpy balloon.

Thaddeus sighed.

What had he hoped, I wondered? That we would just ignore the black-and-blues and pretend that someone hadn't used his face as a punching bag?

"I got into a fight after school."

That much was obvious. We waited, but nothing more was forthcoming. I was sorry about focusing everyone's attention on him, but the fury, the trembling *outrage* that rose up in me demanded answers now! Not later.

"With who?" I asked in as calm a voice as I could manage, which was not very calm at all.

"With three other guys from school," Thaddeus muttered into his plate.

"Three other seniors?"

He nodded. His eyes were cast down so he didn't see the heat flash through my eyes. Three seniors! Eighteen-year-old boys who were probably taller than I, and way bigger than Thaddeus. He'd basically skipped a grade, and was not only a year younger than the other seniors in his class—he'd only turned seventeen a couple of weeks ago—but he was much smaller in size and of slighter build, making him look years younger than his age. His predominant Monère blood made him mature more slowly, so that while all his classmates had already hit puberty, cruised long past it, he was only just starting to enter it. Only just beginning to hit that fast spurt in physical growth and supernatural strength. He had almost a Full Blood's strength, but he'd suppressed that part of him through denial.

Thaddeus had grown up thinking himself human. When his sharper senses and supernatural strength had started to emerge, he'd thought he was going crazy. He'd imposed an unconscious blanket of control over that part of himself, so that his greater Monère strength flared only when that control cracked, usually during times of anxiety and stress. Still . . . being ganged up on by three boys much bigger than you . . . that had to count as one of those times of stress.

"Tell me that they look worse than you do," I said. "Make me feel better about this."

My little brother shook his head.

"Why didn't you wipe the floor with them, Thaddeus? You could have if you'd wanted to."

His answer surprised me, and made me close my eyes and grind my teeth.

"This sudden spurting strength is so new, Lisa." He was the only one who called me by just my human name. "I was afraid of hurting them if I fought back."

If I fought back. Meaning that he hadn't. He'd just stood there, or lay curled up on the ground, letting them beat on him without fighting back. *Shit.*

"I was worried that . . . I don't know . . . that I might even kill them without meaning to," he mumbled. "I didn't start it."

"I know that, Thaddeus." He didn't have to tell me that; I knew my brother. Even in the short time we'd known each other, I knew he was not the kind of kid to go around looking for trouble.

"Why were they picking on you?" I asked.

"Why else? I'm smarter than they are and much smaller." It obviously bothered him, his short stature and skinny build. "I'm helping a girl out in calculus who's failing the class. Her jock boyfriend didn't like the time we were spending together. He and his football buddies decided to let me know just how unhappy they were today after school."

A girl, I thought, gritting my teeth. Of course it had to involve a girl. A jock boyfriend usually implied a pretty cheerleader-type girlfriend. A popular blond ditz who, if she stayed true to stereotype, was stupid enough to fail calculus but smart enough to latch onto some brainy guy and use him to help her pass the course. And who better than the new kid, someone desperate to fit in, make some friends? I wondered if Thaddeus had a crush on this girl. I wondered if maybe it wasn't just the Neanderthal boyfriend and his two buddies I should beat up but the girlfriend as well—the real instigator of this mess.

I took a deep breath, determined to act responsibly, both as Queen and as older sister. I would not give in to my primitive urges, which were screaming for vengeance.

"I'll talk to your principal, Mr. Camden," I said, not knowing what else to do.

"No!" Thaddeus said with horror. "If you do, you'll make it *impossible* for me at school."

"He's right, my lady," Quentin said, speaking up from where he sat with his family down at the other end of the long table. Speaking to Thaddeus he said, "Dante and I just went through what you're going through now. High school can really suck if you have some guys gunning for you. My brother and I taught at my dad's self-defense school. We'd be happy to work with you. Get you used to your new strength, show you how to defend yourself. Make you more comfortable with how much strength to safely use against human opponents."

"You two went to high school?" Thaddeus asked. "During the daytime?"

It surprised me, also.

"Sure, most of the time in school is spent indoors. We only went out during gym, only a forty-minute period. A few guys used to pick on me because of my looks. Called me a girly girl, said I was gay, things like that."

"What did you do?" Thaddeus asked.

"I ignored them, but they kept bothering me until one day I fought back and knocked them on their asses. They left me alone after that."

And therein lay the answer to Thaddeus's dilemma. He had to stand up for himself. If someone else did it for him, it would only make him look weak, and the bullies would continue to pick on him.

Thaddeus looked to me with eager excitement. He obviously wanted to accept the help Quentin was offering, help given by someone who knew exactly what he was going through. It had been my original plan to enroll Thaddeus in Nolan's self-defense school—a school that might never be now.

My own safety I might be willing to risk. But the real question was: Did I trust Dante near my brother? Because the help Quentin had offered had included Dante. *We'd be happy to work with you.*

"That's generous of you, Quentin. Thaddeus, would you like to train with them during this next week while they're here?" Anything longer than that was not guaranteed. Come the next Council powwow, the twin Morell boys were likely flying this coop.

My brother nodded enthusiastically. "Yeah, that sounds great."

"Then I would be very grateful for your help," I said to Quentin, accepting the offer.

Quentin smiled at Thaddeus and me. Dante did not. His pale, hooded eyes gleamed at me. Opaque, inscrutable.

"Great," Quentin said. "We can begin tonight."

FOURTEEN

THEY DID INDEED begin that very night, right after supper. Not in the clearing, which was deep in the woods, but on the lawn behind the house. Another smooth move on pretty boy Quentin's part—choosing a spot where it would be easy for everyone to keep a discreet and not so discreet eye on them. Aquila and Tomas chose to do their watching from the kitchen window, which overlooked the back lawn, while Nolan and Hannah more tactfully sipped tea in the parlor, affording them a nice side view of things.

I was much more blatant about it. Come on, now. This was my baby brother. And not just him but Jamie, who had volunteered his help as the human Thaddeus could practice on. With Jamie's Mixed Blood strength, he was essentially just that—only human strong. His sister, Tersa, had silently come outside with the rest of us to watch. The rest of us being Chami and me. Chami was ostensibly acting as my guard. His true charge, though, was Thaddeus.

Dontaine had gone out with his men to attend to their regular duties, though he had wanted to stay. I had seen it in his eyes, in the tightening of his jaw. But with Chami, Tomas, and Aquila watching over me, he'd had no reason to linger.

Quentin was a good teacher, keeping things low key and casual. He demonstrated the move first with his brother, Dante, who acted in the role of aggressor. A simple maneuver of blocking Dante's slow punch, grabbing his wrist, and sweeping him over a fast, tripping foot, using his opponent's own momentum to send him flying. Quentin and Dante went through the moves in slow motion two more times, calling out the steps—punch, block, grab, sweep, and trip. Like a dance.

Then Quentin had Thaddeus practice it on him.

"You don't have to worry if your strength flares up with me," Quentin told my brother. "Try to keep it at human level, though. I'll let you know if you start using too much force."

He put Thaddeus through the steps three more times until he was more comfortable with it, keeping the moves slow and deliberate.

"You learn the steps first," Quentin said, "then you worry about speed and strength." Though he did work on the latter. He didn't automatically just go flying past Thaddeus when my brother pulled on his wrist. He made him exert enough strength to accomplish the maneuver on his own.

"Yes, like that," Quentin praised, and Thaddeus's face lit up with a wide smile. "You won't need to use any more strength than that when someone's really trying to hit you, putting the full force of their momentum behind their punch."

After Thaddeus performed the steps consistently two more times, he paired him up with Jamie.

"Keep it nice and slow," Quentin said, watching them both closely. "That's it. Perfect." And it was. Jamie swung at my brother, moving in slow motion. Thaddeus blocked and grabbed, and tripped him.

"I didn't hurt you, Jamie, did I?" Thaddeus asked anxiously.

"Nah, you kidding? You could grab my wrist even tighter if you wanted to. The pull was good, though. I went sailing right by you."

And so it went. Then it was Jamie's turn.

The two boys joked with each other, their eyes lit up with excitement, eager to learn. They were clearly having a blast. The rest of us were much more relaxed, seeing how well Quentin had matters in control. He used Dante only in the initial demonstration; he had no actual contact with Thaddeus and Jamie. The slow, step-by-step instruction paid off when they moved on to the next phase.

"Now we're going to practice it faster," Quentin said to the boys' cheers.

He illustrated the move at a more realistic speed with Dante. They were beautiful together, all effortless strength and lithe grace, executing the moves in perfect choreography. Two healthy young animals. One fair, the other dark. Both natural superior warriors by blood and birthright.

"And when you are comfortable with that, even faster, like this." Quentin caught his brother's punch with an easy block, a punch that came at him so swiftly it was just a fast blur. The next two movements flowed naturally—sweep and trip—and Dante went sailing past Quentin. He hit the ground in a smooth, tight roll and sprang to his feet.

"Hopefully the guy you take down will just hit the ground hard and lie there instead of doing what Dante just did," Quentin said, grinning.

"Oh, man! Can you teach us how to do that next, the roll Dante just did?" Jamie asked, eyes shining.

"Sure." Quentin smiled. He seemed to be enjoying himself as much as the boys. "That's the next thing on the plate, how to fall correctly."

Tersa stood quietly by my side throughout all this.

Nothing to give away her thoughts while she was out here, watching. Just her actions themselves—that she was here.

"Tersa, would you like to learn this stuff also?" I asked her quietly.

A hard, uncertain silence met me, an answer in itself. Yes, she wanted to learn, but was wary about the physical contact required. She had an instinctive fear of men now. Most girls would after they had been violated by a man.

"You could practice the moves on me," I offered.

All hesitance disappeared. "I would like that. Thank you, milady."

She followed behind me shyly as I took her hand and stepped out toward the others.

"We've decided to join you," I said.

Quentin smiled in welcome. It was Dante who unexpectedly protested. "Tersa is welcome. But I would ask that you just watch, milady."

"Why?" I asked, ready to argue with Dante, thinking that he didn't want Chami and the others to worry about my close proximity to him. I was wrong. That wasn't the reason at all.

His pale blue eyes moved down to my midsection then back up, a tiny eye flicker indiscernible to the others. But its impact on me was as if a giant hand had reached out and smacked me. Made me remember: *Oh yeah, I could be pregnant.*

I might have even swayed, because his hand started to lift before he checked the movement. I stepped back abruptly, knowing my face was utterly pale. He'd almost touched me . . . a near disaster. It would have sent my men spilling out of the house. I almost laughed out loud at the thought: my men rushing to me, concerned about my safety, while Dante was worried about the very same thing—keeping me safe . . . because I might be carrying his child.

"Tersa," I said when my voice was steady enough to speak. "Will you be okay practicing with your brother?"

She nodded. Glanced at Dante, back at me. "Thaddeus, too. I feel comfortable with him."

I made my lips stretch out in a smile. "Good. It's probably better if I just watch you guys then."

My mind and heart were in a tumult as I walked back to Chami. With everything that had happened, I'd forgotten that Dante and I may have created life. A tenuous possibility, but one that still guided Dante's action. Not just tonight, I suddenly realized, but also that of the two previous days: yesterday when he had revealed himself, trying that suicide stunt; and the first day, after we made love, when he'd seen my Goddess's Tears and known who I was. Was that the reason he had not killed me then? Because of that one in a million chance I was pregnant by him?

Oh, Dante, I thought. *What happens when my period comes as it undoubtedly will in a few weeks and we all know my womb is empty? Will you try to kill me then when that possibility of a child no longer holds back your hand?*

As if sensing my thoughts, Dante glanced at me. Our eyes met across the distance separating us. But I didn't know what was in his mind. What he thought, what he felt.

An explosion of movement from the forest's edge caught my attention. Movement so fast I didn't know what I was seeing for a split second. I felt another Monère's presence but didn't register whose it was. Only Tersa's happy exclamation of "Wiley!" clued me in. The wild Mixed Blood barreled straight toward her, and she had no fear, just a welcoming smile.

I had only a moment to shout, "Don't hurt him," when he hit them. Or more specifically, hit Quentin. Wiley took Quentin down in a smashing tumble of grappling limbs and vicious snarls. The sharp scent of spilled blood suddenly permeated the air—a smell that filled me with fear, especially when I saw Dante's face.

I'd never seen him look the way he did now. Even when

he had been gripped by the madness of *Lunara asseros*, he wasn't near as frightening. His eyes—those odd pale eyes—glowed with the heat of his rage . . . a murderous one. He reached for Wiley's head, not to pull him off his brother, to stop the fight, but with the clear intent of killing him. To snap his neck.

I cried, "No, Dante!" He hesitated, giving me enough time to reach the tangled fighters. To grab a hold of Wiley and shout, "Stop, Wiley, stop!" as I dragged him off of Quentin, kicking and snarling. Then Tersa was there, and with her first word—his name—and her touch, Wiley grew calm. He allowed himself to be pulled away, and submitted to Tersa's frantic patting search after pushing aside his bloody shirt.

"It's not his blood," Tersa said, looking up at me.

"No," Dante said, wrath vibrating his words. "It's my brother's blood."

I turned and saw that Quentin's neck had been cut open. Dante's hand was clamped tightly over the wound, but blood still seeped out from beneath his fingers.

"How did Wiley do that?" I asked.

"With the knife Quentin took away from him," Dante snarled, his eyes flashing with such fury, I took a step back from him. "The knife my brother had in his hands but did not use against his attacker *because you said not to hurt him*. That is why Quentin is injured and why Wiley is not dead by his hand."

Those eyes and the searing emotions contained within them were too intense for me. My gaze dropped from his, and I turned to find my chameleon suddenly there between Dante and I. "Chami, get the healer. Quickly, please."

"No need," Dante said, forestalling him. "She comes."

Hannah rushed to Quentin's side with Nolan beside her. The same heated emotion that gripped Dante seemed to grip Nolan also. The big warrior's eyes flashed with rage over his son's injury, making him a sudden fearsome threat. Something the rest of my men, who were pouring out of the house, obviously sensed as well.

Aquila and Tomas came up beside Chami, forming a solid barrier of flesh between me and the Morells, including Wiley and Tersa behind our protective wall. At the sight and scent of Nolan, Wiley began snarling again, reluctantly stopping only when Tersa hushed him. There was a tense, brittle silence with just the sound of harsh breathing. Then I felt the gentle thrum of Hannah's power as she poured her energy into Quentin's wound.

When his neck was healed, Quentin coughed, cleared his throat. "It's all right," he said. "Not the boy's fault. Father and I trapped him, tied him up, and used him to lure Mona Lisa out of the house."

It took me a second to realize that Quentin was explaining things to his brother. That he was soothing Dante, whom he had accurately pegged as the most volatile threat.

"He was watching us last night," Quentin said, his eyes on Dante. "Thought he was getting used to us, that he was coming to accept our presence, but something set him off just now."

"Me," Tersa said. "I didn't know Wiley was here watching us. I got too close to Quentin, and Wiley rushed to protect me from what he saw as a threat."

"He wasn't just protecting you," Dante corrected coldly. "He was trying to kill my brother."

"He doesn't know better," I said, pushing through my wall of men until I could see Dante. "Wiley grew up wild. He doesn't speak, doesn't understand what we're saying. He only knew that your brother and your father had hurt him once, and that Tersa, the only person he loves and trusts in this world, was suddenly within Quentin's reach."

I walked to Quentin, to where he sat on the ground flanked by his father and mother, with Dante standing like a burning flame of retribution in front of them, protecting his family. I crossed that invisible line that had suddenly sprang up between us and the Morells, walked past Dante, and knelt in front of Quentin. I took his hand and felt the strength, the calluses already formed there.

"Thank you, Quentin, for not hurting Wiley. I'm sorry you were hurt because you held yourself back, but thank you for doing so."

"No need to thank me." Quentin glanced up at his brother. "I wouldn't have wanted to hurt the kid anyway, Dante. Even if Mona Lisa hadn't said anything. Can't blame the kid for being angry at what Dad and I did to him. We were the bad guys here. The boy was trying to protect Tersa from what he saw as a threat to her." His eyes asked his brother to let it go. He did.

By small degrees, the brittle tension left Dante. The hot burning rage faded, leaving behind a chilling frost in its place. Trust me on this, it was a definite improvement.

"That was a stupid thing you did, little brother," Dante said, extending his hand down to Quentin, "allowing him to hurt you like that."

"Hey, you're only older by six lousy minutes," Quentin protested. Taking Dante's hand, he let him pull him up. We were all linked briefly for a moment—brother with brother, my hand still holding Quentin's. Then our hands unclasped, and the three-way connection broke apart.

"My apologies," I said formally.

"No apologies needed, milady," Nolan said in his deep voice. "No one is at fault. Or perhaps it is more accurate to say everyone is at fault, therefore no one person is to blame. Bring Wiley here," he instructed Tersa. "He needs to accept us."

Agreeing with the wisdom of that, Tersa tugged Wiley forward. Wiley bared his yellow teeth at his former captors, but he didn't try to break free of Tersa's hold as he could so easily have done. Wiley's three-quarters Monère heritage gave him almost full Monère strength. He was much stronger than Tersa, who was only half Monère.

"Step to the side, please, my Queen." It was a bit jarring for me to hear those words—my Queen—coming from Dante's mouth.

"What?"

"Step to the side," Dante repeated, his face set in hard, uncompromising lines. "If the boy goes ballistic again, I do not want you standing next to him."

I hesitated. If Wiley went wild again, I could help restrain him. Next to Tersa, Wiley tolerated me the most. He wouldn't intentionally hurt me. But the cold, implacable look in Dante's eyes, and that slight dipping gaze down to my waistline made me swallow back my protest and take several steps back from them. Dante retreated as I did, and Nolan nudged Hannah behind him. Behind her husband's protective bulk, the healer rolled her eyes at me and smiled, a woman wise enough to yield to her man's natural, protective urges without arguing. It was the type of wink given from one woman to other in the same situation. The thought froze the answering smile that formed on my lips. Did she see Dante as my man? Did I see him that way? And last but not least—did *he* see himself that way?

I was obeying him. Had yielded to him twice already. But what other choice did I have? All that he had asked was for me to stay safe. Until I knew if I was pregnant or not, I felt compelled to obey his wishes in this matter.

Crap. There had to be a faster way of determining whether I was pregnant, other than waiting three long weeks for my period.

Tersa's voice drew me back to the present drama. She said Wiley's name and touched his chest. Putting a hand on Quentin's arm—something that made the feral Mixed Blood growl—she did the same with Quentin.

"Quentin. Friend. Quentin is my friend." She repeated it with Nolan.

It was almost funny . . . if it wasn't so darn scary . . . to see tiny Tersa, almost birdlike in her delicacy and size, standing so fearlessly between the three males, two of them much bigger than her, all of them far stronger. *Fearless* was not a word one usually used to describe Tersa, someone who quivered uncomfortably in the presence of men, but it fit her well now. Steely determination shone in her eyes, was heard in her voice. *You will all be friends,* the rigid posture of her spine shouted.

"Friend," Quentin said with a faint smile. Moving slowly, his eyes fixed on Wiley, he picked up the small dagger lying in the grass at his feet. "Friend," he repeated, and offered the blade, hilt-first, to Wiley.

I didn't have to look at Dante to feel the sudden tension emanating off of him in waves. I held my breath—we all did—as Wiley cautiously took the knife from Quentin.

Tersa, wisely, immediately took the weapon from Wiley. His hand tensed briefly on the blade, then with a faint shudder, he yielded it up to Tersa without any further struggle.

"Say it, Wiley," she said, gentle determination lacing her words. "Quentin—friend."

Amazingly enough, he did. Wiley opened his mouth and said the first words I'd ever heard the wild boy speak. "Quentin. Friend."

Tersa had him repeat it with Nolan. When he uttered the words, "Nolan, friend," she smiled at him, blindingly bright, and it was like the sun suddenly breaking out behind dark and stormy clouds.

"Good, Wiley, good," she murmured, and led the boy away.

"She's beautiful when she smiles," Quentin murmured, earning a scowl from her brother, Jamie, who had been standing quietly next to Chami.

"And very stubborn," Jamie said, sticking out his chin. "Comes with our red Irish hair."

"She's incredibly brave," Quentin said with admiration.

"Not anymore. Not since . . ." Jamie stopped. Sighed. "But she's different when it comes to Wiley. She'll do anything to protect him. Don't hurt the boy."

"I won't," Quentin promised, eyes solemn.

And like that, the little drama was over. Mine, however, was just beginning.

FIFTEEN

Aᴌʟ I ᴄᴀɴ say is thank God for Safeway. That was one
of the wonderful things about this country. That no
matter where you went in the United States, even to the lit-
tlest rinky-dink, no-name town, you could always find the
basics like a gas station, a bank, a McDonald's. A super-
market.

It was the latter I found myself being driven to, with
Aquila as my driver. I was lucky to have only the one guard.
The rest of the men had sort of turned red when I'd baldly
announced that I had to buy some feminine products at the
grocery store. Aquila had been nominated to go with me, and
he was not a bad choice. I knew I could depend on Aquila
for discretion. Still, I felt bad about the knowledge—the
possibility—I was going to burden him with.

"Aquila," I said, when we were a short distance from the
town, "what you see and what you hear tonight, you cannot
tell anyone else."

He glanced at me curiously, but nodded readily. "As you
wish, milady."

I guess that was better than saying, "As you command, my Queen." But barely. I still squirmed over the absolute power given to me over my men, my people. The power that came with my mantle as Queen. I was more used to free will, and decided to treat his answer as that. Because he'd *chosen* to do so.

"Thank you, Aquila. And I apologize ahead of time."

"For what?"

"For making you highly uncomfortable."

He smiled, and his neat beard and small mustache shifted with the movement of his lips. I think it was the first time I'd ever seen him smile. He was one of the oldest among my men, and the most serious. Not somber like Tomas, but more proper, more severe in his demeanor.

"Being in your company can only be a pleasure," he said, as relaxed as I'd ever seen him.

"Are you happy here, Aquila?"

"Yes, milady. I am the happiest I have been in a very long time. Your guards' betrayal turned out to be a blessing for me."

Not long ago, Aquila had been a rogue bandit under Sandoor's command. My lover Gryphon had bartered himself in return for four of Mona Louisa's guards to protect me during the vulnerable time before I was officially acknowledged as Queen. It had been a poor bargain, because those guards betrayed me into the hand of outlaw rogues at the very first opportunity. Aquila had been one of the rogues. He'd had a perfect opportunity to molest me, but had held strict discipline over himself and the rest of the bandits.

"I never thanked you, Aquila."

"For what, milady?"

"For your kindness before, when I was doused with the witch's brew." An aphrodisiac that had set me on fire. "The other rogues with you would have raped me had you allowed it, I saw it in their eyes. But you . . . all I saw in your eyes was compassion. Not lust."

"I do not enjoy seeing a woman abused, much less a Queen," he said in a sad voice. How tough it must have been for him, then, because Sandoor's outlaw group of rogues had used and abused a Queen for ten long years—Sandoor's former Queen, who everyone had thought dead. It struck me now, as it had then, how different Aquila was from the rest of the bandits. Even dressed in rags, he had been a gentleman.

"I have to thank you for now, as well. For managing all the business details for me."

"That truly has been a pleasure for me," he answered, smiling. "And your brother has been wonderful assistance. Young Master Thaddeus has a natural flair for commerce."

"A gift I don't seem to have inherited," I said ruefully. That part of my responsibility was quite daunting, actually, since I knew next to nothing about money—vast amounts of it, anyway. Or how to manage it profitably. "Do you have time tomorrow to go over the financial records with me? I've shirked this part of my duty long enough. I need to familiarize myself better with my holdings."

"Of course, milady."

"Call me Mona Lisa, please. I like that better."

He dipped his head. "Mona Lisa, then. Do you have any time tomorrow, after dinner?"

"All night. Though I hope it doesn't take us that long to go over everything."

"It might be better if we pace ourselves, spread it out over several days," he said seriously.

"Several *days*?" I squeaked. "I only expected it to take one night. Cripes. How detailed are those records?"

Amusement shone briefly in his eyes, but his voice was his normal serious tone when he spoke. "I was thinking that we could look over the books of a few businesses, then go visit them. You will get a much better understanding of each place that way."

It was a smart suggestion. I nodded my agreement as we pulled into Safeway's parking lot. Pushing aside the duties of tomorrow, I concentrated on my quest for tonight.

I found my answer not in one of the aisles as I had initially thought, but from the pharmacist I happened to stop and seek advice from. It was one of those stores that had a full pharmacy, open until eight o'clock at night, according to their posted sign. Twenty minutes until closing time, I saw, glancing at the clock, with no one in line. The pharmacist was a kindly looking older man, a grandfatherly type. One you found easy to approach and ask questions of. Even difficult ones like the one I hit him with.

"Excuse me," I said, feeling my face flame with embarrassment. "Could you tell me which pregnancy test would be the best one to get here? One that's good in early detection."

He rattled off a few brands, mentioned how early they could detect pregnancy—"As early as eight days after conception"—and threw in something complicated about things called Human Chorionic Gonadotropin and false negative tests, which went completely over my head. All I retained were the brand names he recommended.

"Which aisle?" I asked.

"Aisle eighteen."

I thanked him and headed there. A quick glance at Aquila showed his face to be carefully free of all expression. He considerately stayed at the end of the empty aisle, keeping me in sight, but affording me a small measure of privacy as I looked over the home pregnancy kits. The store carried four different brands. The ones the pharmacist had recommended did indeed have the earliest detection capacity. With the other tests, you needed to be further along, at least two weeks into your pregnancy. I was already freaking out after a few days. Forget waiting two more weeks. I snatched up two brands, paid for them, and went immediately to the ladies' room.

"Wait here," I told Aquila tightly.

Yeah, I knew it was too early. Even with Amber, it would have only been four days, not eight. There was also the fact that a human pregnancy test might not work for a mostly Monère, only-one-quarter-human woman. But something in me needed to know *right now*. I needed to do something, even if that something was to pee on two plastic sticks and see if a blue line appeared in one, and a smiley face on the other.

They did. One blue line and one smiley face.

Oh shit. White dots hazed my vision. I had to put my hands against the stall walls and wait until it passed. Until I could see once more without little white dots floating in my field of vision. I took a deep breath and looked again, sure I had to be wrong.

A blue line was in the center window of the first plastic stick. Not faintly blue, but distinctly and solidly blue. A very strong *positive* blue. A smiling happy face peered up at me from the other pregnancy test.

With trembling hands, I opened up both instruction booklets and read all the tiny print, especially the parts about accuracy. I had to read them three times. If I understood it correctly, most of the inaccuracies rested with false negatives, meaning that the test read inaccurately as negative when you were actually pregnant. They recommended repeating the test when you were further along, if there was any question. False positives, on the other hand—having the test read as positive and *not* being pregnant—were very rare.

I stuck the plastic testers back in their boxes, shoved

them into the brown paper bag, and left the ladies' room. Aquila immediately came to my side and took my arm in a supporting grip. I guess I must have looked as pale and shaky as I felt.

"Do you wish to go home?" he asked—not if I was okay, or if I was pregnant or not. Just whether or not I wanted to go home. For some reason, his tact and consideration brought tears to my eyes. Me, who rarely cried. Those tears, more than anything else, really scared me. Made me wonder. *Oh my God, can I really be pregnant?*

"I need to speak to the pharmacist again," I said.

Without another word, Aquila guided me back to the pharmacist, then wandered over to a nearby aisle, pretending to browse the items there.

The pharmacist smiled when he saw me again. "Did you find what you needed?"

I nodded and took out the two boxes, opened them, and solemnly showed him the results. I should have felt a little awkward presenting him with something I had just peed on, but I was pretty much numb to all embarrassment at this point.

"What does this mean?" I asked.

"It means you're pregnant, ma'am."

"But I can't be," I said desperately. "It's too soon. Way too soon. Only a few days. Four at the most."

The pharmacist looked from me to the glaringly positive tests, then back again. "If these tests were negative, and you just told me it had only been a few days for you, I would tell you to repeat the tests in two weeks. But with not just one but two positive results, how early you are doesn't matter. It pretty much means that you should be expecting a little one nine months from now."

He glanced down at my hand, took in the lack of a wedding ring. In a compassionate, nonjudgmental tone he added, "Unless you don't want it. If that's the case, then you're early

enough that you have some other options open to you, like
Plan B."

"What's that?" I asked, carefully putting all the incrim-
inating contents back in the bag.

"Pretty much what the name says. It's an FDA-approved,
emergency contraceptive. A second chance for a woman to
prevent an unplanned pregnancy. You have to use it within
five days of intercourse, though it's most effective if taken
within the first twenty-four-hour period. And you have to be
eighteen or older. If you're younger, you'll need a doctor's
prescription for it."

"I'm twenty-one."

"Then I can offer it to you without a doctor's script.
Would you like it?"

My throat closed up. Words wouldn't come out. I nodded instead.

Tossing away the other brown bag, I left clutching a
new white one, even guiltier in its content. It was not taking life, the pharmacist had emphasized kindly, simply preventing it from taking hold in your womb.

I got into the car feeling numb and shell-shocked.

Aquila didn't speak until after we had pulled out onto
the freeway. "My first thought was that you were upset because you were not pregnant."

When I didn't say anything, he continued softly, "A
child would be celebrated by our people, milady. You
would not even have to raise it. Others would gladly do so."

I flinched. "Milady" once more, instead of "Mona Lisa."

"I cannot risk a child, Aquila." How to explain what I
could not explain. "There's something wrong with me. And
my greatest fear is that it will affect the . . ." I stopped, took
a deep breath. "I just can't."

"Before you take the pills, you should see the healer,"
Aquila said, "for your own safety. So that she will at least
know what is happening should things go wrong." The

pharmacist had listed a bunch of things. Adverse side effects, he had called them. Things like nausea, abdominal pain, fatigue, headache, menstrual changes, dizziness, breast tenderness, vomiting, and diarrhea, to list a few.

"If I'm going to be taking a life"—*preventing it*, the pharmacist had insisted, but I knew what I was doing— "then it's only right that I suffer a little discomfort."

"Mona Lisa." My name once more. Bringing another round of tears to my eyes. "You are mostly Monère. Human tests and medication may not work on you the way they are meant to. Before you put yourself through this, and risk harming yourself, you should ask the healer to determine if you are even with child first."

With child—such an old-fashioned phrase. One that made me want to weep.

"Mayhap you can even ascertain from her if this thing you believe is wrong with you will even affect a child should you carry one."

Putting aside all my fears, it made a lot of sense. I leaned back in the seat with those two destructive pills sitting like a hundred-pound weight in my lap, and nodded. "It's a good suggestion, Aquila. I'll talk to Hannah first."

The relief on his face was palpable. We didn't talk anymore. Just drove the rest of the way home with both of us lost in ponderous thought.

The pharmacist's words that the pills had to be taken in the first five days and were most effective if taken early worked like a ticking clock in my brain. Chances were, the life growing in me was seeded by Amber. But I remembered my body's sudden undeniable craving for Dante's seed. Surely my body would not hunger like that had its need already been met. If it was Dante's . . . and a part of me strongly thought that it was . . . then we were still in the first two days. A better chance for the pills to work.

"Aquila, could you find Hannah for me?" I asked as we

parked in front of Belle Vista. "See if she can speak with me now."

Seeking out Hannah proved an easy matter. Resourceful man that he was, Aquila asked Rosemary. She promptly directed us to the infirmary, which, I learned to my surprise, was set at the rear corner of the house. We returned outside and made our way around to the back.

Belle Vista, when translated, meant Beautiful View. It was a huge mansion, so big that I still had not viewed all the rooms. No surprise, then, to find Hannah and two house-maids cleaning up a large room in a separate, detached building almost hidden away in the back. It looked as if it had originally been a four-car garage. Some time in the past, though, the wide garage doors had been taken down and replaced with regular doors, and it had been converted into an infirmary. The front half of the room was set with eight cots: four lined up in neat order along one wall, another four along the opposite wall. The second half of the room was separated by curtains, which were currently drawn back, and looked to be the medicinal storage part of the infirmary, the healer's workroom—what Hannah was in the process of presently setting to order.

"Milady," Hannah said with a welcoming smile as she caught sight of me.

"Do you have a moment to speak with me?"

"Of course, Mona Lisa." Her smile faded as she noted the tension tightening my eyes as she washed and dried her hands. "Let's walk outside, shall we?" she suggested.

Aquila trailed forty feet behind us, far enough to lend us a semblance of privacy, close enough to still guard. We didn't speak until we reached a burbling stream with small boulders lining its edge, and found comfortable seats on two rocks set near each other. I opened my mouth to speak, but Hannah drew a shushing finger to her mouth and took out a necklace that had been hidden beneath her dress. It

looked like a very old piece of jewelry, a plain and simple
dark gray stone that hung from a gold chain. The stone was
the size of a robin's egg, but much less pretty. She touched
it with a gentle thrum of power, and that ugly gray stone
turned a startlingly beautiful orange color. As it started to
glow and resonate, I felt a light field of energy expand and
encircle us.

"What's that?" I asked. "What did you do?"

"It's a privacy charm," Hannah explained. What had no
doubt allowed Nolan and Quentin to come so near the
house without detection when they had snatched me. "Now
we can speak without others hearing us."

"How did you know that I needed privacy?"

"Your face, your body's tension. Tell me what troubles
you."

She was so kind, so motherly in her manner and expression that those stupid tears stung my eyes once more. "I
need to know if I'm pregnant. It's only been a few days.
Can you tell this early?"

"Sometimes, not always. May I lay my hands over your
belly, touch your skin?"

I drew up my T-shirt. She leaned forward, spread her
hands over my lower abdomen, and I felt that slight buzz of
warmth as her energy sank into me, going deep in a searching foray. It felt like forever, though it must have been only
a second or two, before she lifted her hands away.

"Yes," she said with a trembling smile, her voice thick.
"You have life growing in you."

She said something else, but I didn't hear it. A pounding
roar had filled my ears. My drumming heartbeat, I realized, and dimmed down the sound.

"Can you . . . can you tell how many days old it is?" I
asked.

Hannah shook her head. "No. Only that it is as you say,
very early in its being."

"Your hands are trembling."

She laughed. "Can you blame me when a part of me knows that it may be my grandchild I am sensing?"

Seeing my visible distress, her eyes grew somber. "You are not happy."

"No, Hannah, I am not happy. Far from it."

I opened the white pharmacy bag and took out the small purple box the pharmacist had given me. PLAN B was neatly emblazoned across the top of it.

"What is this?" Hannah asked.

"It's an emergency contraceptive. Helps rid you of an unwanted pregnancy if you take it within the first five days." I lifted my eyes. Met the healer's soft brown ones. "Hannah, if I told you that I have somehow taken demon dead essence into me, and that it was changing me, could you assure me that this demon taint . . ." I hesitated over that word, but could find none better. "Could you tell me with certainty that it would not affect my child?"

She shook her head, taking the news more calmly that I could have imagined. Making me wonder what had she seen that she could accept something like this so readily.

"No, I cannot tell you that. Nor have I ever heard of anything like it happening before. Mona Lisa, are you sure about the demon taint? That it is true fact and not something you are, perhaps, imagining?"

"I grew fangs, Hannah, in my human form, and drank down a stag's blood. It's not something I'm imagining."

"Demons cannot have children," Hannah said, frowning. "They are of the dead, and you bear new life in you."

"Halcyon said that I was becoming *Damanôen*. Demon living."

She paled, and I did not know if it was because she recognized the word, or if it was because I had mentioned the High Prince of Hell's name. It tended to have a frightening effect on people.

"What will that do to a child of mine?" I asked her.

She looked at me with eyes wide and lost. "I don't know."

"Neither do I. That's why . . . Hannah. Could you ease the pregnancy from me?"

"Kill it?" Her face lost every ounce of its color.

If she could speak the plain truth, so could I. "Yes. Could you do that for me?"

"Oh, milady," she whispered, those warm brown eyes stricken. "You do not know how hard it is for our women to get pregnant. And what it is you are asking of me. I am a healer, milady." And I was asking her to take a life.

I remembered that terrible pain that I had felt when I had killed Barrabus.

"Never mind, Hannah, I do know. And I shouldn't have asked, not when I have other means at hand." I looked down at the innocuous looking purple box. Putting it back inside the white bag, I stood up.

Hannah rose also, gripped my hand. "Milady. Please—"

I interrupted the healer's plea. I knew what she was going to ask—that I not do this. That I not abort the precious life growing in me.

"Hannah, will the medicine work on me with my Monère blood?"

"I don't know. I just don't know." She shook her head helplessly.

I wanted to say: *It's all right, Hannah.* But it wasn't. Everything was far from all right.

"The baby could be normal. It may not be affected by your demon condition," Hannah offered.

"I know. I thought of that. But what if it isn't normal, Hannah? What if it isn't? You and I both know that a demon-human-Monère offspring would be feared by all, belonging to none. It would be seen as a monster, and they would try to destroy it as such. Even if I managed to protect it from everybody, it would still be sought after, perse-cuted all its life. Either that or shunned. How can you ask me to bring a child into this world, facing such a fate?"

There was nothing she or I could say to that. With a sweep of her hand, Hannah deactivated the charm, and we walked back to the house in weighty, sorrowful silence.

SIXTEEN

I STARED AT the cup of water and the white pill laid out beside it on the desk before me. I was in my room. Alone. Aquila was downstairs, struggling with the secret I had burdened him with. I was sorry for that. I knew full well the weight of it. It was enough to crush even the most valiant heart.

He hadn't looked at me when he left, and I couldn't blame him. I could hardly look at myself either. Killing, taking an enemy's life in the heat of battle, was one thing. Taking the life of your unborn child . . . that was another completely different act. I wondered if he'd ever forgive me. I wondered if I'd ever forgive myself.

Energy slid over me, a light familiar feel. A part of my mind processed it, remembered when and where I had just recently felt it. The privacy charm. Though I couldn't see the intruder, I knew who had my arms pinned and secured behind the chair I sat in. The hands were too big to be Hannah's.

"Do you have a death wish?" a cool and dangerous voice asked.

"Dante," I whispered, though I could have shouted it and no one would have heard me. "Hannah told you."

He didn't answer me; his presence here in my room was already an answer. His energy signature—what all Monère sensed in one another, how we usually knew when another was near—was spiky, vibrant with strong emotion despite the coolness of his tone.

The feel of warm metal closing about my wrists, locking with a click, was almost anticlimactic. As soon as his hands left me, I pulled, holding back none of my greater strength. To my shock, the restraints held.

"They are not silver chains or demon chains," Dante said. "They are something that will hold even a demon . . . something my mother tells me you are becoming."

He turned me to face him then, and I saw that the calmness of his voice was terribly deceptive. The naked fury I glimpsed on his face, making it almost masklike in its ferocity, made me gasp and lean involuntarily back from him.

Danger! Danger! my body shouted. No need. I could see it clearly enough. His eyes glittered with primitive anger, hardening his otherworldly eyes to shards of pale ice. Sharp enough to cut me to pieces. The amulet he wore about his neck sparkled as if it blazed beneath the sun—a privacy charm. How he had come upon me unawares. A different one, I realized, than the one Hannah wore. The orange of this stone was speckled with black instead of being completely clear.

"Did you take them yet?" he demanded in a voice harder than even the stone he wore around his neck.

"Wh-what?"

"The *pills*," Dante spat out. I recoiled from him, almost toppling over my chair in my effort to get away. It teetered precariously for a moment on two legs, before he set it back down gently. And that gentle, deliberate maneuver, that one point of calmness in the face of the incipient violence threatening to spew over me, unnerved me even more than if he had slammed the chair back down, expressing some of the anger harshly carved on his face.

He leaned that face down into mine, and repeated slowly, calmly, dangerously, "Did you take the pills?"

I shook my head wildly, my teeth chattering beyond my control. I had never felt such awful, overwhelming fear before. "No, I d-didn't take them yet."

"Is this it?" he demanded, looking down at the opened packet. I had taken out one pill and laid it on the desk. The other still resided in its little plastic window.

"Yes, just the two pills."

"Do not lie to me," he said in a low and terrible voice that trembled with violence barely leashed. "Not now. Not when I'm like this." It was part threat, part plea, as if he was asking my help to keep him in control.

It only served to spike my fear higher.

"I'm not lying, I promise you. It was just two pills, you can read the instructions. One to take now, the second one twelve hours later."

"Mona Lisa." He closed his eyes and said my name in a swirling mix of agony and hatred. As if it meant both redemption and despair to him.

Those pale blue eyes opened again, focused on me, and I felt something wash over me as they drew me into their cold and furious depths. His eyes turned completely silver, and didn't just gleam brightly at me. They began to actually glow.

"Sleep," he said.

His words traveled from the surface of my ears down into the vortex of me, penetrating deep inside like an echoing, expanding wave sweeping to the center of my being. And I was unable to resist his command, though I tried. My eyelids lowered as if a heavy weight bore them down. And I slept.

When I came to awareness again, it was on a silent scream. Pain throbbed my neck, and I tried to put a hand there, expecting to find it hacked open, with a fountain of blood gushing from it, as in my dream. A dream that had been mine, and yet not mine. But I couldn't move. My hands were restrained behind my back, secured to the bed I was lying on.

I blinked, disoriented, ripped from the past and thrown back into the present. Had I dreamed of my death before, from that other lifetime? I couldn't remember. And was thankful for that.

Hours had past. It was daylight now, with the sun at its highest point in the sky, just past noon. I turned my head and became aware of the fact that I was in a cheap motel room. And that Dante lay beside me, asleep. He was adrift in peaceful slumber, gentle in repose. And I realized that I wasn't afraid of him like this. In sleep he was relaxed, free of all strain, all burdens of the past. He had an interesting face: not perfect, not stunningly handsome, not blindingly beautiful. An interesting face, as I said. Strong, aggressively molded with a sharp beak of a nose and a square, firm jaw. The lips, though, were soft and full—generous lips. It was a face of character. And so it should be, having lived so many lifetimes.

Dante. I whispered his name deep inside me, and felt sadness stir in me. *Have I made us enemies once more?*

As if my mind had touched him, or my emotions, he blinked his eyes open. He smiled when he saw me, a sweet, unburdened smile.

"Mona Lisa," he said in a voice that was still half caught up in dreams. Then reality and remembrance came crashing back into those eyes and I watched them cool, harden against me . . . and wanted to cry as fear renewed itself in me.

He could have killed me, came the sudden realization. At any time, he could have killed me had he wanted to . . . with his privacy charm, his forceful, compelling eyes. I hadn't known that it was possible for one Monère to compel another Monère like that. That a nondemon could wield that much power.

"Dante," I said softly. "What are you doing?"

He sat up, totally alert now, his face so different from its softness in repose. It wasn't any one detail but the entirety of it—the forcefulness of his nature, his ruthless will—that shaped and changed his features, making them harsh, unrelenting.

"I'm protecting my child."

"It might not even be yours. Chances are that it's *not*. It usually takes longer than two days for a pregnancy test to work; it needs eight days at least, usually. And that's how I found out, Dante, through a human pregnancy test."

He didn't look at me, but a muscle jumped in his jaw. Then he turned his head, and his eyes captured mine . . . no other word for it. Nothing else to define the sensation of being held by those pale eyes—as if you could not look away, even if your life depended on it.

"There is nothing more guaranteed to rouse my ire than if someone harms or threatens one of my family," he said in a very gentle voice that sent chills skittering down my spine. Barrabus's death by my hand flashed again through my mind.

"Save your breath," he said. "Nothing you say will convince me that the child growing in you is not mine."

"You . . ." I wet lips that were suddenly dry. "You can't think to hold me prisoner for nine months."

He braced his hands around me and leaned his face down into mine, dominating my vision, my world, for a moment. "There is nothing I cannot do," he said softly.

It was fear that he was right, fear at what he was determined to do—*was* doing—and my helplessness before his will that made me lash out at him suddenly, viciously.

"If that is true, then why don't you break your curse and save your dying bloodline?"

His face grew even harder, if that was possible. Became rocklike. A charged stillness fell with just the sound of our harsh breathing. Then he moved.

He did nothing more than draw back away from me, but I flinched.

He turned away from me, the muscles in his back and shoulders knotted tight. "You do not have to fear me striking you," he said.

"Just cutting off my head, right?" I said with a half-hysterical sob.

He turned, glanced sharply at me. "You remember?"

"Not really."

I remember killing your father. I remember the feel of my own death by your hand, but I don't remember how it was done. I said none of this to him, though.

"Please, Dante. What you are doing will stir not just my men, but everyone that Halcyon can rally from High Court and all the other surrounding territories to hunt you down. And not just you, but your mother, father, and brother. Please don't do this."

"My mother was aware of that possibility when she came and told me of the new life you carry. My family will have gone by now. They will be safe."

"Dante, not just Monère will be hunting us. Eventually demon dead will be tracking us also. I'm Halcyon's chosen mate. Didn't your father and mother tell you that?"

He growled, a silent emanation felt more from the vibration of his energy spiking rather than from any real audible resonance. It was even more frightening than simple sound would have been.

"You are *my* mate. You carry my child." He crawled over me, lay the entire length of his long body over mine, bracing himself on his arms. That one thoughtful gesture amidst the dominating one—sparing me the pain his full weight would have caused me with my hands handcuffed behind me the way they were—brought those annoying tears welling back up in my eyes. They overflowed, spilled down my cheeks.

His harsh face softened, and a surprisingly gentle finger brushed away the wetness. "Don't cry, *dulcaeta.*"

It was a word my inner stirring consciousness half-remembered. An endearment. It made my breath hitch. "Dante, please. Let me go."

His face hovered over mine, his eyes grave, inscrutable. "I will. If you promise to do nothing to harm the child you carry."

"What if doing nothing is the greatest harm?"

"How can allowing life to grow be harmful?"

"A part of me is becoming demon dead, Dante."

He rolled off me to lie on the bed, his eyes staring up into the ceiling. "My mother told me. So?"

"So?" I repeated, incredulously. "I'm becoming *Damanôen.* Demon living. It's changing me, Dante. I'm growing fangs in human form and drinking blood. If it's changing me, how can it not change what is growing inside of me?"

"So you wish to kill our baby before it has even a chance to live? To end its life when you do not even know if it will be affected, as you fear."

I tried to roll over to face him, but the restraints would not allow it. Scooting back up toward the headboard, I sat up instead. "Dante, you of all people . . . you know what it's like to be cursed. If my child is different, not just part human, part Monère—that's bad enough—but part demon as well, it will be looked upon as a freak, a monster, a curse.

Something to be hunted down and killed as anything different, anything perceived as a threat would be. That's just how our world is."

"You are determined to view it as a curse. But what if it's not? What if it ends a curse, instead?"

"What do you mean?"

"You said that fate crossed out paths once more for a second chance. What if that second chance is this child that we have made together? Creating new life to balance the lives taken in the past. Mona Lisa." His blue eyes deepened. "Please, do not kill our child. Let it live."

The poignancy in those eyes, and the possibility of his words hammered like a giant spike into my heart. Broke a sob from me. Oh God. I didn't know what to do. What was true, what was not. I didn't know what was best for the baby.

Would a baby—*our* baby—truly undo Dante's curse? Would fate be so warped as to play our lives this way in this second twining? *Of course it would*, something in me whispered.

I trembled. Said in a tremulous voice, "Dante, whatever my sins in the past, I will gladly pay for them. But I don't want my baby to have to pay for the mistakes that we made. To bear the burden of our past deeds."

Sitting up, he reached a hand out to me and laid a rough, callused palm gently over my stomach. "Of all the things in the past I have done, this one thing, making fresh, innocent life with you . . . how could that ever be a mistake?"

I didn't know what to say or do or feel anymore.

As the silence spun out, he drew his hand away and rose to his feet, his expression closing down once more. "Come, we must be on our way. Do you need to use the toilet before we go?"

To my hot embarrassment, I did.

No matter how much I begged and pleaded and then

threatened, he would not undo the cuffs. I ended up using the toilet and then standing, a painful flush sweeping over my entire body, as he wiped me down afterward.

"You *cannot* expect to keep me like this for the next nine months!" I said, utterly appalled and humiliated.

"I will do whatever I have to do to give our baby a chance. You can stop this at anytime, Mona Lisa. Think about what I've said."

As if I could do anything else, I thought as he led me out into the bright sun. Even wearing a baseball hat, sunglasses, and light jacket, the warm solar rays must have pained him. If they did, he gave no indication of it.

Part of me wanted to lie, to give him the promise he'd asked of me—that I would not abort the life growing in me. But I could not bring myself to do that, to lie to him. I'd hurt him so much already—brought a curse down upon him and his family—how could I hurt him anymore?

How can you think about harming his child then? a voice inside me whispered.

I don't know that it is his child, I argued back.

Part of you believes it is his.

Hard to argue with yourself.

Now who's acting like the crazy one?

Go away! I told the bothersome voice as Dante seated me in the front passenger seat. Slumping back against the soft leather, I shut my eyes, blocking out the sight of him. Wishing it were as easy to ban him from my thoughts.

Think about what I have said, he had asked.

I did, as the miles rolled by.

I did.

SEVENTEEN

WE PASSED A sign announcing we were leaving Mississippi and approaching the Arkansas state line. One moment we were driving sixty-five miles an hour, the maximum speed limit, the next moment we were suddenly backed up in traffic, ten cars in front of us. There was some sort of road block ahead, with police lights flashing.

"You're heading north," I said.

Dante didn't bother answering.

In a few minutes, we would be entering another Queen's territory. I wondered if that would be better for us or worse.

"They're checking car registrations, making sure they are valid," Dante informed me, apparently already having ascertained the reason for the checkpoint up ahead. He seemed unconcerned, which I took to mean that his registration was current and up-to-date. A pity. The thought flashed in my mind and my body tensed: *Should I call out to the policeman for help?*

"Don't try it," Dante warned without looking at me. "I won't hesitate to hurt him."

"Damn you, Dante."

He smiled bleakly. "I have been damned for a long time now."

"Don't you dare try to make me feel sorry for you," I said in a low, heated voice as we pulled up to the waiting patrolman.

"I would not dare, milady." Rolling down the window, he gave an easy smile.

The patrolman didn't smile back. "I'll have to ask you to pull over onto the roadside."

"What's the matter, Officer?" Dante asked politely. "My registration is current, and I haven't been drinking."

"I just need to look over your driver's license and proof of insurance," the officer answered just as politely, but his tone was insistent. "It will only take a few minutes, sir."

Nodding, Dante pulled off the road as instructed and parked the car. Instead of walking over to us, the patrolman returned to his car. With our acute senses, both of us heard him clearly as he called in a match on the stolen car that had just been reported. He recited the license plate and requested backup.

Dante cursed.

"You're driving a stolen car?" I asked. Was he a common criminal as well as a kidnapper?

Those pale blue orbs turned and glared at me. "No, this is my car. Your people must have called it in."

Dante's door was flung suddenly open.

"Right on the first guess." Chami shimmered into view, holding a silver dagger to Dante's throat. He took possession of Dante's knife and gun, and reached for the car ignition keys.

"Uh-uh-uh. Keep your hands on the steering wheel," my chameleon chided in warning as Dante tensed. "I will not hesitate to cut off your head here in front of all these nice people," he said in a low, deadly voice.

Dante must have believed Chami's threat, I certainly did, because he kept his hands on the wheel as Chami removed the keys and pocketed them. When Chami eased back on the pressure of the blade, I saw a thin red line of blood trickle down Dante's neck from where the knife had cut into his skin.

I choked back my instinctive cry—*Don't hurt him, Chami*—swallowing back the words because I knew that if I tethered the violence on Chami's end, it would explode out from Dante.

Oh Goddess, please don't let them hurt each other.

Chami drew out a thin whistle and blew it, three short blasts. The frequency was too high pitched for humans to hear. But animals—and Monère—would be able to hear it clearly.

"Hey, what's going on?" the patrolman demanded, striding quickly back to us. There was only surprise not alarm in his voice at seeing a third person suddenly with us. From his tone, I could tell that he hadn't seen the knife yet.

"Milady, if you can kindly take care of the nice policeman," Chami requested, keeping his eyes and knife on Dante.

"That'll be a little hard for me to do, Chami. I'm handcuffed."

"To the car? Or just behind your back?"

"Behind my back."

"Hey you, in the black shirt. Step away from the car," the officer ordered, wariness in his voice now. He released the safety strap from his gun holster.

"Can you open the door and scoot out?" Chami asked. "I cannot handle both of them."

I had a moment to think, *Well, duh. I should have thought of that.* Then I was blindly groping for the door handle. My hands fell on the lever, pulled it, and I started to topple backward as the door swung open behind me.

"Careful," Dante barked, grabbing my shoulder. That

was the only thing that saved me from tumbling out of the car. He looked furious. There was no concern at all over the knife that was cutting deep into the side of his neck, trailing a small rivulet of blood down his shirt. He was focused entirely on me.

"Release her," Chami snarled.

When he was assured that I had my balance once more, he did, and launched himself at Chami with sudden, swift violence, knocking Chami's dagger aside with a swing of his arm, the warrior bracelet hidden beneath the jacket striking away the blade with jarring force.

They fell from my sight to the ground as I awkwardly wriggled out of the car, my heart pounding.

"Officer, help me," I cried with unfeigned terror. "He kidnapped me. Tied up my wrists."

"What the hell," the policeman muttered, his attention diverted to me. He lifted the gun he had trained on the two wrestling men, and strode around the car to me.

The officer's eyes locked with mine, and I had him. Power burned up from within me and spilled out in an invisible gush.

"You see only two men fighting. No weapons, no knife, no blood. A domestic matter that you do not wish to be concerned with," I said in a voice that throbbed with the power I had called up, compelling him to my will. "You will go back to your car and report that you were mistaken about the vehicle. The license plate was Alpha-Bravo-George, not Charlie. Then you will wave the other cars by, and drive away, forgetting about us."

The officer returned to his car, obediently radioed in the correction, and waved on the few cars that had slowed down to gawk at us. When he had cleared the road of traffic, when no other cars were in sight, he pulled away.

"Stop," I cried, rushing to the two warriors fighting in deadly silence.

Without any human witnesses to hinder him now, Chami winked out of sight—chameleon. An unseen punch sent Dante's head swinging back. He retaliated with a back-handed blow that caught Chami in the stomach, shimmering the chameleon back into view. Chami's dagger came stabbing down.

"No!" I screamed.

Dante caught Chami's wrist, the bloody dagger point an inch from his chest. His eyes locked on Chami, and I felt the roil of power spark the air. Saw those glacier blue eyes turn silver and take on that eerie glow.

"Cease," Dante commanded, and Chami stopped fighting. "Give me your knife."

Chami relinquished it to Dante, and Dante drew it back. To behead him!

"*Don't!*" I threw myself between them, unable to do anything else but use myself as a shield, with my hands bound as they were behind me. Dante's mesmerizing silver eyes glowed down at me, bloodlust filling them. "Don't hurt him. Please," I begged.

"He put you at risk. You almost *fell*."

"He doesn't know I'm pregnant."

"*He almost harmed the baby!*"

The almost mindless rage burning behind those words washed over me and set my body trembling, with the knife poised just over my neck where Dante had stopped its swift descent.

"Please, Dante," I whispered. "He didn't know."

But you did, the voice inside of me said. *You would have harmed your child knowingly and deliberately.*

For a moment, I wondered if he would kill us both.

Dante lowered the dagger, and I collapsed back against Chami with shuddering relief.

"Thank you," I breathed.

I didn't fight him when he drew me away from Chami.

Dante focused his will, those glowing eyes, back on the chameleon. "You will not move or speak for thirty minutes." When he released him from his gaze, Chami fell to the ground and lay there unmoving.

I turned back to look at Chami lying there helpless as Dante led me back to the car.

"He's in the sun," I said.

"Only for thirty minutes. Not the four hours I could have commanded instead."

His clipped words had me swallowing back my protest. Indeed, with but a few different words, the outcome could have been deadly instead of just a short discomfort.

I'd forgotten about battle lust, I realized, when he opened the car door and gently sat me back inside. All gentleness fled as he turned those pale, gleaming eyes on me. The color was blue once more. I gasped beneath their cold, burning light. Gasped again as he lunged forward and captured my mouth in a harsh, punishing kiss.

A whimper of fear escaped from my lips as the weight of his body pressed me back, and his warrior's presence, fierce and battle sharp, sparked against my own energy, making me aware of the ferocity he had kept chained. All that aggression, tightly leashed, he channeled now into me, in that kiss. In the coarse movements of his hands as he shoved up my shirt. On my bra, which he tore away with one rough pull, exposing my breasts.

I wrenched my face away from him. "Dante, stop!" I cried, struggling to push him off me as he lowered my seat down. "We're by the side of the road. Anyone can drive by and see us."

"*Don't fight me!*" His lips ran feverishly over my face in wild, nipping caresses, violence barely contained. Dangerous touches that both thrilled and scared the hell out of me. He was like a dangerous, roaring wildfire, threatening to consume all that it touched.

"You held my hand, stopped a kill. You left me no other way to channel my aggression. *Yield to me.*" His breath struck my face in heated gusts as he undid his pants. Then my pants and underwear were down by my ankles, my body nude and painfully exposed, my body, heart, and mind in terrible upheaval. Jesus Christ, we were by the fucking *roadside.*

His voice was gritty urgency, his eyes burning need. "Please," he whispered roughly, and swooped down, capturing my mouth, stealing my breath. Stealing the will to fight him.

I yielded in the face of his need, and stopped fighting him.

My body's soft acceptance of him eased some of that overwhelming urgency. And in that momentary lull, his need sparked my own.

Pulling my lips from him, I said, "No blood," in a hard, uncompromising tone.

"No blood," he promised and nipped my lower lip, three parts caress, one part punishment. Dominating male.

"Hurry," I murmured, so terribly conscious of our exposure. Of my nudity.

"First you tell me to stop. Now you tell me to hurry up and take you." Amusement mixed with the heated urgency of his movements, like fire and ice—how he made me feel.

He pressed between my legs, and I felt the bold rub of him naked and hard against my thigh. The utter outrageousness of our situation—by the open road!—the utter *dangerousness* of our situation—a powerful warrior still flying high from battle, and me, bound and helpless beneath him, with him poised over me, ready to take me . . . God help me, but it set a part of me on fire. Spiked my own desire.

His hand slid up my legs, cupped me. And with but that one touch, not even a caress, my core heated, grew moist and damp, wetting his palm.

"Oh God." He groaned, and with no other preparation, he thrust into me with gentle, insistent force. He pushed in, groaned as he sank into my honeyed wetness. Tunneled in deeper with a swiveling gyration of his hips that had me gasping and bending my knees to arch up against him.

He withdrew, pumped back into me with restrained ferocity, his eyes wild, burning with lust. Another withdrawal, another gentle push back in as he watched me with those uncanny pale eyes, making me feel like a helpless butterfly he had captured and pinned. It was a devastating feeling, mixed in with the wet, thrilling pleasure he evoked with each stroke. Too much, those eyes, piercing down into me as if they could see into the very deepest part of my soul. And perhaps he could. As if knowing his gaze was more than I could bear, he dipped his head, and I felt his lips warm against my breast. Felt his mouth take in a tight, pouty nipple, bite down on it.

I cried out, bowed up into him, and he pressed me back down into the seat with a deep stroke into my body as he sucked on my nipple, tugging on it with less than gentle force. He sank into me again with another insistent thrust, another fierce tug—those two simultaneous movements—and pulled light from me, spilling it out onto my skin, running it down over my body, the moon's captured glow within us. When the radiance spread to where his flesh joined inside mine, when my light touched him there, it set him ablaze. He lit up above me like a Christmas tree, beautiful to behold—his taut muscles, the driving urgency of his body, his male aggression tightly chained and channeled into me. A warrior, stark and powerful, bold and beautiful. Yet vulnerable in his need for my softness, for my light.

"Yes," I sighed as he rose and fell above me, my body taking him in with soft, willing submission. He shifted, braced himself up on one arm, freeing the other hand to run down my body, palm my bottom. His finger whispered over my anal rim in the lightest caress.

"Come for me," he said, his face harsh, tightly clenched above me. Another sweet deliberate press of his finger there, teasing my back hole while his thickness filled and drove tightly into my other entrance . . . that one added touch and I overflowed. My release spilled out, and I came for him as he had asked me to, helpless to do otherwise. I imploded beneath his stroking caresses, his inner one and deliberate outer one, and I shattered in a brilliant, shaking, shuddering climax.

He drank down my light, then gave into his own release. One more deep stroke, pushing through my spasming tightness, and I felt him grow still, jerk harshly inside as his wet ejaculation spewed into me.

Until that moment, I hadn't realized just how restrained his passion had been. Only in his climax did he truly let himself go. Throwing back his head, Dante roared his release to the heavens with a primitive cry. So primal, so beautifully savage he was with his neck corded, with the agony and bliss of release carved harshly on his face. One fixed moment where every muscle, every tendon in his body seized tight . . . then came the sweet thrill of release. The jetting bliss of satisfaction as he relaxed down over me. I felt his weight blanket me for a brief, lovely moment— too short—then he was pulling his body from mine, lifting himself off. His eyes were heavy-lidded, slumberous, as he crouched down beside me, opened the glove compartment, and took out a packet of wipes.

"Did I hurt you?" he asked. Even his voice was more soothing in its resonance now, like melted honey.

"No."

"Your hands?"

"Uncomfortable from the handcuffs. Can you release me?"

His eyes slid away as he pulled out a wipe. "You know I cannot."

Without another word, he cleaned me and dressed me. Maybe there was a limit to how embarrassed you could get. I'd apparently reached mine. I sat there and did nothing as he finished caring for me. Then wiped himself down and zipped himself back up.

He turned suddenly to look up into the sky. An eagle circled high above us. So high I almost didn't feel it—that faint, shimmering presence of another Monère.

It was Aquila shifted into his bird form. Drawn to our location by Chami's whistle blasts.

"*Maudrëa,*" Dante said, muttering an imprecation in a language so old it had almost been forgotten by all. He shut my door and went around to the back, opening the trunk.

My eyes widened in alarm as he drew out a rifle. "No, don't. You can't! It's Aquila," I said, twisting around in my seat. "You might kill him."

"That is my intention," he said coldly. He slid two bullets in, chambering the rounds.

I looked at him with horror, then turned my head skyward. "Aquila," I shouted. "Go away. Leave us!"

A shot rang out with a flat *crack,* and the eagle jerked, tilted. He fluttered in the sky for a moment, still airborne. Then he began to fall.

"No!" I moaned as I watched Aquila plummet from the sky, silent, graceful, so terribly still. Blood washed down his right wing, streaking his feathers like wine-red paint as he spiraled, until trees cut him from our sight, but not our sound. I heard the rustling of leaves, the snapping of twigs as he crashed through the foliage, a discordant cascade. Then that final, terrible *thud* as he hit the ground.

"Aquila." His name was a mournful, teary sound slipping unconsciously from me. My mind, my body felt numb. I didn't even register my own actions, my bound hands blindly seeking the door handle, lifting the lever. I wasn't aware of what I was doing until I was hauled halfway back across the seat toward the driver's side, with Dante's hard furious face above me. He reached across, slammed shut the door I had just opened.

"Stop it," Dante commanded. Shifting me back into my seat, he pulled out my seat belt strap. "Stop crying," he said. Only then did I realize that I was making harsh, guttural sounds deep in my throat. Like an animal that was being beaten.

I leaned forward, preventing him from latching the seat belt, and slid back against my door, twisting against his hold almost hysterically. "No, I have to go to him!"

"He's not dead," he said, giving me a little shake when I continued to fight him. "Mona Lisa, look at me! He's not dead."

His words calmed me down enough that I stopped struggling for a second. As soon as I did, Dante snapped my seat belt in place, then gripped my arms. "I just shot his wing, not his heart. He will heal."

"He fell so far. Was so still," I whispered brokenly. "And there was so much blood."

"He's not human. Only taking out the head or heart will kill us, remember? Listen. Take a breath and listen, and you can hear his heartbeat."

He slid his hand beneath his shirt, deactivating the privacy shield, and I heard it for an instant . . . a faint, rapid heartbeat out in the woods. The sound disappeared as he reactivated the charm. I sobbed then. Sobbed as if my heart would break as the car pulled onto the road, taking me away from my fallen men. Both of them injured because of me.

We drove for a time, not long, or at least it did not seem so, before he pulled off the road into a gas station, and parked in front of a minimarket. I sat there, staring straight ahead, not seeing anything. Numb. He glanced at me, then went inside, keeping an eye on me through the glass doors. No need. I was not running anywhere. I didn't have the heart or energy to do so. Lethargy had gripped me, a cottony distance separating me from the rest of the world and its trifling concerns. He returned with a soft drink, some chips, a candy bar. Driving to the back of the parking lot, he parked there, away from prying eyes. He said something, opened his mouth and spoke, but I wasn't aware of his actual words. Not until he lifted the can of soda and put a plastic straw to my lips, intruding into the soft bubble that surrounded me.

"Drink this," he said.

Because it was easier to do that than fight him, I took two sips before turning my head away and losing myself once more in the emptiness of not thinking, not feeling.

The door shut as he got out of the car and came around to my side. Opening my door, he crouched in front of me, ripped open the candy bar, and held it to my mouth. I looked past it without interest.

"One bite," he urged, nudging the chocolate against my lips.

I frowned. Felt a brief flare of irritation at the intrusion. What did he want, I wondered?

"One bite," Dante repeated, "and I'll leave you alone."

Because that was what I desired most, I took a bite and swallowed. The peace I sought, however, did not come. Not because of his actions. But because of another's.

Like the silent demon he was, Halcyon suddenly appeared. He was dressed in his usual shirt of white silk, with diamonds glinting at the cuffs. Only his attire was civilized. Not his actions.

His long, sharp nails sank with almost sickening ease into Dante's flesh, his fingertips half-buried in Dante's shoulder. Blood—and the demon's presence—stirred my unholy hunger to life, and it roared past my numbness, shattering it with a desire to feed that overrode my emotional state, that did not care if my men were hurt or killed. The only thing it cared about was the crimson, shiny blood welling up from beneath the thin barrier of skin.

My fangs burst forth, eager to sink into the meal that was bleeding before me. But it was not to be. With one casual fling, Halcyon sent Dante flying back into the copse of trees lining the lot. One quick glance at me, then Halcyon was gone, moving almost too fast to see, gone after the prey he had casually flung away.

"No!" I screamed, and wanted to howl with thwarted hunger, with terrible need. I could not think, could not feel with that overwhelming, driving thirst for blood overtaking me.

The sound of a door opening drew my attention to other prey as the gas station attendant came running out.

"Hey, what's going on out here?"

He was a bald, middle-aged man with a ponderous belly. But it was not his fat belly I was interested in, only his blood. I was on him in an instant, with no knowledge of moving, of snapping the seat belt, opening the door. His heartbeat surged faster, began to race like a thumping rabbit when he saw my fangs. How delectable, that fast rhythmic pounding, that stink of fear.

"What the—" He gurgled as I struck, fastening onto his neck. He was a big man, bigger than I, weighing almost twice as much, straining wildly, pushing against me with his hands to no avail. *Such a delicate creature. So easily broken*, was my impression before the richness of his blood filled my mouth and ran down my throat like the sweetest and most intoxicating wine. *Yes!* I mentally cried as I sucked and pulled with long, succulent swallows, drinking down that potent elixir of life. *This is what I need.*

My body sang with the richness pouring into it, and a moan slipped out, mixing with the juicy, slurping sounds I made as I feasted on him. A moan that came not from me as I first thought, but from the thing I was drinking from. Instead of pushing me away now, his arms wrapped around me. It was that protruding belly nudging against me, the odd, alien feel of it, that broke me from my thralling hunger. That made me realize, suddenly, what I was doing.

I pulled away.

If you feed your hunger instead of fighting it, you will be able to control it better. It does not take much blood.

Halcyon's words haunted me now as my eyes fixed upon the red blood trickling down the attendant's neck. He seemed completely unaware of the fact that he was bleeding, or perhaps uncaring of it as he reached out to me. I let his beefy arms wrap around me, draw me to him, and bent my head back to the man. Not to drink, but to lick the puncture wounds closed.

Stop bleeding, I thought, picturing it in my mind, and felt the blood grow sluggish, clotting beneath my tongue.

Something in me—something still so terribly hungry that had barely begun to have its need met—some demon part of me wept at the sight of that closing wound.

No! it cried. *More!*

But I denied it.

"Look at me," I said, my voice trembling, not with horror, but with the effort of restraint. When the man turned to me, I captured him with my eyes. "You cut your neck against the edge of a shelf. You will have no memory of anything that occurred out here. Nor will any further disturbance outside draw your attention for the next hour. Go back inside and cover your neck with some Band-Aids."

His arms dropped away, and he walked obediently back inside the store. My control stretched only so far. Only when he was completely gone from my sight—like a box

of chocolates covered up once more, hidden from view—
was I able to turn my attention away from him and toward
the woods.

Halcyon. That one thought of him and a vision of those
demon nails ripping open Dante's arm flashed to me like a
waking dream. In it I saw Halcyon turn and look at me. In
that brief moment of distraction, Dante struck him with his
dagger, burying it to the hilt in Halcyon's side.

I saw, felt the pain of it. And felt the anger, the *rage* over
the spilling of his demon blood. It spewed up like bubbling
lava from within Halcyon, making his eyes glow red.

Leave us, he commanded, and cut the mental bond between us.

I staggered at the sudden severing.

"No," I whispered. Casting my senses wide, I let them
guide me, following the pull of the Monère warrior and my
demon sire. It guided me to where they fought, and as I came
upon them, I saw with my eyes what I had seen in that vision:
demon blood dripping sluggishly from Halcyon's side, his
eyes red and enraged, the very air trembling with his fury.

His skin rippled as if a pebble had been skipped across
its surface, breaking the calm, stirring the demon beast that
lurked beneath. Dante circled him, knife in hand, his lower
abdomen torn into ribbons of flesh where Halcyon had
sliced him with his nails. His eyes glowed silver with his
own power and an aura of danger clung to him like a second skin. But Halcyon, it seemed, was immune to this mesmerizing power.

"No!" I said louder, drawing their attention.

Their forces hit me separately. Dante's luminescent silver eyes pinned me in place as he whispered, "Stop." And
the silent mental command Halcyon flung at me. *Stay.*

I froze in place, unable to move, mentally cursing them
both as they rushed each other, coming together in a flash of
tanned skin—one lighter brown, the other darker gold. Both

of them armed. But it was ten demon nails against one silver blade.

Foolish Dante was the aggressor, with Halcyon welcoming his attack with a cruel, taunting smile. They struck at each other savagely, moving with lethal beauty, a dance of fast movement, strikes and countering blows that was almost beautiful to watch were it not so frighteningly deadly.

Dante rushed Halcyon again and again with almost reckless daring, the silver blade flashing in his hand, his metal bracelets glinting darkly at his wrists. Were it not for the wrist guards, he would have been completely torn apart by Halcyon's nails, which were not even claws yet, just his normal inch-long nails as the Demon Prince wrestled back his beast's change, retaining his man form.

They came together again in a stunning flurry of strikes and blurring movement, and broke apart with new injuries scored along Dante's thighs, his arms. Halcyon had only the one knife wound, terrible enough—it had almost caused Halcyon's demon beast to emerge.

All I could do was watch, frozen by both their wills. And inwardly scream. I found I didn't have to wait for Hell. It had found and captured me, here and now.

"Do you know who I am?" Halcyon asked, his voice crooning, silky menace. Even in his human form he was a fearsome sight, his red eyes burning with Hell's fury, his long nails coated with blood, a cold smile twisting his lips.

"You are the Prince of Hell," Dante said, and lunged at him with the knife. Halcyon danced gracefully away, swiping downward as he did. His razor-sharp nails came up against Dante's blocking metal bracelet, scraped over it with a discordant screech.

"You know who I am," Halcyon said, "yet you do not fear me."

"Why should I fear someone who will never have any

dominion over me?" Dante growled, his silver eyes glowing brightly. He attacked again, pressing forward, uncaring of the new wounds he incurred, focused only on driving that knife again into the Demon Prince.

They sprang apart.

"How did you find us?" Dante demanded.

A fast, almost careless swipe of those nails, and the top of Dante's shirt was sliced open, spilling his amulet into view.

"Did you think your stone's small magic could keep me from finding my mate? My own blood?" Halcyon's smile turned mockingly cruel. I'd never seen him like this before.

As if he knew my thoughts, those burning eyes turned to me for a second. "I am not always nice, Mona Lisa."

Dante chose that moment to strike again. But this time it seemed Halcyon's inattention had been deliberate. The Demon Prince moved again, so fast I didn't see him stir, and Dante was suddenly pinned on the ground, the silver dagger now in Halcyon's hand.

"What's to stop me from killing you now?" Halcyon taunted as his fangs lengthened to sharp, cutting points.

"Nothing," Dante answered, his face impassive.

"You still have no fear."

"I do not fear death," Dante said. "It's not *staying* dead that torments me."

"I shall do my best to see that you stay dead." With that silky promise, Halcyon raised the dagger he had seized.

Dante's smile was brief, bitter. "Not even you can grant me that ease, Demon Prince."

Power surged, thrummed the air as the demon part of me came to the fore, shattering the separate spells that had been placed on me.

"No, Halcyon!" I screamed. "Don't. I carry his child."

I swayed, freed of the mental bonds, but had no power to move. All my energy had been used up.

"Don't," I whispered as I sank to the ground. Into dark swirling oblivion.

I WOKE UP to find two concerned faces peering down at me. To see pale blue eyes no longer glowing, and dark chocolate ones no longer demon red. Nothing like announcing you're pregnant and then fainting to get some attention.

I started to sit up, but was pressed back down by two pairs of hands. My handcuffs, I noticed, had been removed.

"Easy, *ena*," Halcyon murmured.

"Lie back down, *dulcaeta*."

Tender words—wife, beloved. Old words spoken in a tongue that I remembered from another lifetime. Tears sprang to my eyes. Those blasted, stupid tears. But fury was the cause of them this time.

"Get your bloody hands off of me," I snarled. "Both of you!"

Surprised, alarmed, they did and I sat up slowly. When all seemed fine, no tilting of the ground, no dots of whiteness, I snatched Dante by the two torn edges of his shirtfront. Yanked him to me.

"Don't you *ever* freeze me like that again." I bared my teeth at him and pushed him away.

Snatching Halcyon next, I caught him by the edge of his shirt and shook him. "And don't *you* ever command me to *stay*. Like I am your dog!"

I shoved him away, sick with them both, and slowly got to my feet, batting away the helping hands that reached out to steady me. "Don't touch me!"

The sight of me screaming and crying seemed to befuddle both demon and Monère warrior alike.

"Don't cry," Dante murmured, his hands opening and closing helplessly by his side.

"It's the hormones surging in you," Halcyon soothed. His words had the complete opposite effect of what he intended.

I exploded. Literally saw red for a moment. "It's not the fucking hormones! It's you stupid men." Then I was sobbing.

I angrily wiped the tears away and saw that they were tinged red. I was crying tears of blood.

"Calm yourself, sweetheart," Dante murmured. "It can't be good for the baby."

I literally shook with my fury. "And you two trying to kill each other in front of me after freezing me with your commands so that I can't even speak or move . . . *that's* good for the baby?"

The two men looked at me, then at each other as if seeking guidance on how to handle the pregnant, hysterical, part-demon Monère Queen.

The air trembled with another wash of fury. Then, like a cleansing wave, or perhaps because I could no longer sustain the energy for such wrath, the anger died away, leaving bitter dregs of its ash in my mouth.

"Are you going to kill each other?" I asked in a dull, flat voice, like soda that had lost its pop and fizzle.

They shook their heads.

"No," Halcyon said. "Dante explained . . ." He paused. "No."

"And you?" I asked Dante.

He looked at me with sadness, with weariness. "The Demon Prince and I have come to an understanding. We will no longer try to hurt each other. But you . . . What will you do?"

What will you do with my child?

I suddenly felt old and brittle and so tired of it all. The worry, the fighting, the hurting of so many people.

"You win," I said. I was going to leave it to a power, a

wisdom greater than mine. "I will do nothing to harm the child."

He bowed his head. "Thank you," he whispered.

"And what of your promise to let me go," I asked, "now that you have secured my promise?"

His head lifted so that I saw the flash of his pale blue irises. "Will you grant me these next few days until the Service Fair? After that, you have my word that I will be gone from your life."

"Will you?" I asked.

"Yes."

I nodded. "These next few days," I agreed. Turning, I walked back to the car.

We backtracked to where we had left Chami, and found a familiar green Suburban parked by the roadside. Chami sat in the shade of the big vehicle, moving once more, freed of the compulsion. Faint redness colored his face, neck, and hands, but that seemed to be the extent of his injuries. Aquila on the other hand, sitting next to him, was more severely damaged, but not as badly as I had feared. Dontaine and two of his men, Marcus and Jayden, who I recognized from the practice session, were field dressing Aquila's wound. Their surprise when they saw me accompanied by my kidnapper and my Demon Prince was enough to drop the men's jaws.

I brushed past them to kneel at Aquila's side. "You shifted back into your human form." Someone had loaned Aquila a shirt. His legs gleamed pale and naked beneath the cloth. "Were your injuries that grave?"

"No, milady," Aquila was quick to assure me. "Just bruises, some flesh gone from where the bullet struck me in the arm. Nothing broken, though. I shifted back into this form so I could report to Dontaine."

"Are you hurt?" Chami asked. His quick glance down at my belly, and his wary gaze past me to Dante, told me that he had heard us. That he had been a silent, frozen witness when Dante had taken me in his post-battle frenzy. He knew that I was pregnant, and that Dante was likely the father.

"No, I'm fine. The only one, in fact, who is not hurt." I stood, said to the others, "It's over. Halcyon and Dante will explain everything to you later. Or maybe just confirm what you all already know. I'm too tired for that now. I just want to go home." The last sentence came out plaintively.

When Dante moved to take my arm—I think I swayed again—my men drew their daggers against him.

Explanations, I realized, could not wait.

"Put your weapons away," I commanded harshly.

Dontaine and his men reluctantly sheathed their daggers.

Maybe it was the steel in my voice. Or perhaps it was just that they were used to obeying the orders of their Queen, unlike my other men. Whatever the reason, I was grateful to be obeyed.

"Dante is likely the father of the child I carry," I stated. "He is a guest, not a prisoner, for the next several days, until our next Council meeting, at which time he will be departing. I want no one else hurt in this matter. Do you understand?"

There was a chorus of "Yes, milady."

"Good. Let's go home."

EIGHTEEN

THINGS RETURNED TO normal, or as normal as they could be under the circumstances. Dante's family, who had fled when he had, returned when he called them back. No word was mentioned of this second snatching. Perhaps because all understood now why Dante had done what he had done. What perplexed my people, no doubt, was why I had even considered terminating the life I carried within me.

Still . . . understanding only carried you so far. They treated Dante differently now. Before, they had seen him as what he had appeared to be—a twenty-year-old, gifted warrior. The knowledge of his previous life—his infamous killing of me, and the curse laid upon him—had brought caution and mistrust to their eyes. Add to this the knowledge that he could compel other Monère—not just humans, but Monère warriors and Queens—and they looked at him not only with wary distrust but active fear, melting away in his presence, not meeting his eyes. Afraid to look into them. Even Dontaine treated him with careful caution, ceding these last few days entirely to Dante. The father of my child.

What was it about seeding life in a woman's womb that gave a man ownership of her body—in other men's eyes, at least—during the time she carried that living, growing being? A perception that none others challenged. My bed had remained empty since we had returned.

Halcyon had kissed me and returned to his realm. "Until the High Council meeting," he had murmured.

It was almost like a mantra muttered among my people and my men. *Until the High Council meeting*. Until the Service Fair when Dante, and likely the rest of his family, would leave us. Amber had called to say that he would not be coming that Wednesday as per his usual practice. He hadn't even tried to give an excuse. He'd simply said, "I will see you in a sennight." Seven days hence, when we would travel down to High Court, the seat of Monère rule here on this continent.

Dontaine slept in the next room—his room now—but he, too, made himself scarce, pressed no demands, made no requests for my bed. And the man the rest of them had ceded my body to . . . he also pressed no demands for my bed. Just my company.

During our days, when darkness fell—that was when our mornings began—he would sweep into Belle Vista and claim me. He had left me alone in my solitude that first night back. On the second day, he took me on a picnic, on a grassy knoll a five-minute stroll from the mansion, within the boundaries of my land. Chami and Tomas kept watch over us, but stayed a discreet distance away.

Dante fed me food from the basket Rosemary had prepared at his request. It was packed with odd things. Odd things for a Monère, but things I had acquired a taste for. Grapes and other fruits. Rolls of bread. Chunks of cheese, all kinds of cheese—smooth Gouda, sharp cheddar, smoked Brie. None of the others in the household ate this stuff. Only me . . . and Dante. He popped the cheese in his mouth and chewed with relish. When I looked askance at him, he said, "I grew up among humans, also."

"This time. What about your other previous lives? Do you remember them?"

He took his time chewing, then swallowing, while he composed his answer. "My memories are most clear of my last incarnation, and of my first life. That, I never forget. I get random flashes of other lives, occasionally. I think it's my mind's natural defense, that selective memory. Remembering everything would probably be too much for one single mind to handle."

The next day he drove us to New Orleans. We played tourist, ate dinner, and danced informally afterward in the carriageway outside of Preservation Hall, swaying to the music of the boisterous jazz band while Tomas kept an eagle-eyed watch over us.

The fourth day, Dante drove me to the county fair, set up in the next town over, while Aquila trailed behind us in another car. At the fair, he bought me pink and blue cotton candy, and treated me to carnival games. We popped balloons with darts, bounced ping-pong balls along the rims of fishbowls, and won stuffed animals, lots of them, which he continued to trade up for a bigger prize until we ended up with a huge, stuffed, purple Scooby-Doo almost as tall as I was.

We twirled on the merry-go-round, the only ride I was permitted on. He stood beside me as I bobbed gently up and down on my carousel horse. It was on the down sweep, with laughter bubbling from my lips, when he kissed me. Our mouths clung, with the sweet taste of spun sugar and the even sweeter enjoyment of the day flavoring our kiss. Then my painted steed started its slow glide back up, and we broke apart with the warm taste and touch of each other lingering between us like fine, heady perfume.

The fifth night, he took me on a picnic again on the

same grassy knoll, but this time it was different. This time
we were alone.

"No guard tonight?" I asked.

"No guard." Dante's silver-blue eyes gleamed at me, re-
flecting the moonlight. "I promised that we would stay on
the property, and asked them for privacy."

"Why?" My voice came out husky, soft.

"Because I want to make love to you tonight. Will you
allow it?"

He'd courted me these last few days. Courted me with
laughter, with fun. We'd played among the humans for a
few blissful, irresponsible days. He'd made me laugh, giving me a respite from my duties and burdens and fears.

"I want this memory of you and I," he said softly. "Will
you give me that to take away with me?"

The two remaining days until the next Council meeting
loomed like a shadow before us. We hadn't just played
among the humans . . . we'd played at *being* human. As if
he was a normal twenty-year-old boy, and I, a girl he was
dating, with the prospect of a happy, finite lifetime together
before us, with no other goal in mind than marriage, the
2.4 requisite kids, a house, and a nice-paying job to cover
the mortgage. It was a sweet, brief illusion. A paper dream
that would rip apart with the first tug of reality. But not
yet . . . not yet. With deliberate choice, I continued to drift
us along in that lovely illusion.

"Yes," I said. "I will allow it."

He fed me from his hand. Fast food—Chicken Mc-
Nuggets, french fries, an apple pie—and I greedily ate it
down. Food that no one else would have thought to buy for
me. His eyes caressed me; he looked at me so tenderly.
Why had I ever feared those eyes, I wondered?

Pushing aside the empty bags, he pulled me into his
arms and kissed me with lips warm and gentle. He laid me
down on the soft blanket, and I sighed at the feel of his

body against mine. I pulled the tie from his hair, freed its long length so that it spilled over and around me like a shining curtain of silken honey. He kissed me as if he cherished me, as if he loved me, raining soft kisses down my face and neck to the gentle slope of my abdomen. He paused there and pressed trembling lips against my skin.

"May I?" His hand hovered above my shirt, asking permission. I nodded, and his hand slid beneath the soft cotton to lay gentle claim to what lay below it.

I watched him, no words, emotions held at bay. Just simply watched as he lifted my shirt over my head, tossed it away, as he carefully undid my jeans, pushing down the denim. I quivered beneath his heated gaze, beneath the reverent touch of his hand splayed protectively, possessively, over my belly where our child grew inside of me. My eyes fell on a ring I'd never seen him wear before. I felt the cool metal band warm as it touched my skin. Watched as the smooth, ugly gray stone flared with power, changing into a sparkling aquamarine color. With that pulse of power, two life forces shimmered into view—mine, a pale shimmering golden aura just above my skin, and below it, *part* of it and yet separate and distinct, was a tiny, delicate blue bubble, not much bigger than a tennis ball.

"Is that the baby? Its life force?" I asked in an awed whisper.

"Yes." His eyes were moist and damp.

It hadn't seemed real before, just a nebulous concept . . . a child. It didn't even have a heartbeat yet. There were those that argued that true life did not begin until that very first beat. But seeing that little ball of energy centered within me, I could not deny the conviction that I carried life.

There's a little guy or gal growing inside of me, I thought, stunned.

Dante took his hand away, and with the loss of contact

our auras disappeared. "Forgive me," he said. "I just wanted to see it once. To know it this way. You have no need to fear me."

He thought that the stunned look on my face was from fear.

I shook my head. "I'm not afraid. It's just . . . the baby suddenly became real to me just now. How did you do that, make its aura visible?"

"The ring I wear. Here. I want you to have it." He started to remove it from his finger. I stopped him.

"No. Keep it, please." It looked old and valuable, the ring band crafted from the same burgundy metal as his wrist bands—the same distinctive bands his ancestral father Barrabus had worn. They were heirlooms he had somehow managed to keep from another lifetime, I realized with a shiver.

He mistook my tremor as fear of him rather than as what it really was . . . fear of our past. His face closed down and he started to draw away.

I sat up, caught his hand. "Don't go."

He stilled, like a bird poised to take flight. "The mood is gone."

I smiled. "You're right." I slid my other hand up his T-shirt, slowly revealing his sleek, lovely muscles. "Let's set a new mood, then. Undress for me."

With a perception that was new to me, I knew that he needed this moment . . . we both did. Another small step toward each other. Another knitting closure in our healing wound. As much as he needed this memory to take away with him, so did I.

"Love me," I whispered.

He did. With gentle touches and blazing eyes, not that eerie phosphorescent glow but with the shattering intentness of a man about to join his body with a woman he greatly desired. He ran his mouth over me, down me. Worshipped me with his touch, his hands, his breath, his long hair that glided over me like a thousand silky caresses.

The four preceding days of poignant laughter, of fun escape, had laid the groundwork, and now I was like a flower that had been stroked open by the sun, unfurling my petals, welcoming his touch.

With simple strokes he readied me. The graze of his fingertips down the side of my neck. The light brush of his fine-grained beard, rough, over the upper slopes of my breasts. The snuffling of his warm breath against my belly. The feel of the cool tip of his nose running down my thigh, raising goose bumps along the sensitive skin. Laughing softly, he nuzzled his way to the back of my knees and set his hands upon my feet, pressing deep into my soles with his strong thumbs. A jolt ran up through me and I caught my breath at the stunning reminder of that previous time when he had touched me there. The memory of it blazed between us, burning laughter away. Leaving only humming anticipation in its place.

He touched me in all places but two . . . no, three—my lower body where I wept softly for him, my peaked and aching breasts, and my lips.

"Kiss me." Yearning for his taste, I tugged at his strong arms, urging him up.

He answered my plea and kissed me. But not where I expected. He kissed me at the lowest point, where I hungered most for him. His breath fell on me first, giving me a second's warning before he delved between my legs. Opening me wider with his hands, his shoulders, he kissed my soft, glistening folds. I lay there, shocked, stunned, surprised, until that first, rough-delicate lick up one side of my nether lips. Then I moaned and spread my legs wider for him. Arched up as he lapped down the other side. Gave a muffled shriek as he delved deeper, stroked his tongue into my channel's wetness. Oh!

It was the worst tease, building me up slowly with devilish licks, teasing tongue, hot smoky breath. My body jerked
and quivered beneath his totally hedonistic appreciation of
me, of my wetness and desire for him. He rumbled his appreciation against me and the vibration was transmitted from
his mouth to my sensitive, weeping core. I moaned, lifting
my hips, twisting harder against him. He turned his face,
stroking the short stubbles of his jaw over my mound, scraping over my half-hidden pearl, stabbing it with sensation. He
rubbed against me like a purring cat, a brief, spiky caress
followed by the smooth, soothing rub of his soft, silky lips.

"Dante," I moaned, as he alternately stimulated me then
soothed me. And all the time he did this, his hands touched,
pressed, and caressed my feet, giving me sensation on top
of sensation in places I was not used to feeling so sharply.
It was as if his touch, there in those two spots, polarized
my entire body, spreading to my breasts, my womb, my
quivering thighs, my throbbing lips. His thumbs stroked
the arches of my feet, and my body tightened, flexed, my
hips lifting up into him. He purred and rewarded me with a
deep, penetrating stab of his tongue that both filled me and
left me aching for more. For something harder, thicker.
Much, much longer.

"Dante." His name was plea and demand, prayer and af-
firmation.

"Do you want more?"

"Yes!"

He slid his thumb inside me with a gentle thrust, and I
gasped. Moaned as he withdrew it, pushed it back in again
like a little miniature penis. Both of us watched as that single digit slid inside me, the fat head disappearing, the slender stalk swallowed up. Then watched it come back out in
reverse, wet and slick with my dewy desire.

Both the feeling of what he was doing with his thumb—
again nice, but like a tiny, teasing appetizer, not the main

course—and the fact that he was *watching* it so raptly as he exercised that deliberate, slow, in-and-out fucking movement . . . tightened me, inside and out, swelling my desire, and brought light to my skin, beginning its incandescent glow.

His lips and cheeks were smeared wet from my intimate fluid. I could see my essence coating him, could smell myself on him, and the light within me flared even brighter.

His eyes lifted, spearing me with his hot gaze, with the knowledge and awareness in them—that my legs were splayed wide, my body open to him, lifted up like a flower opening to the sun, welcoming his warm, stroking attention.

He rotated his hand, shifting the angle so that his thumb pushed against, instead of with my body's natural pathway, stretching the thinner posterior wall, flooding me with sudden, new, unexpected sensation. I bit back a cry, unable to help the involuntary squeezing down of my walls against that penetrating thumb that I suddenly felt with incredible sensitivity as it plowed a slightly different path inside of me.

"Touch yourself. Stroke your breasts for me," he murmured in a soft, gentle voice that was so completely at odds with the fierce shine of his eyes. Everything about him was like that. Gentle but intense. His angled-back thumb dipping in and out of me, his knowing gaze. His awareness of how hard it was for me to do as he asked. *Touch yourself for me. Give yourself to me that way.*

My hands shook as they lifted up, my head falling back, my eyes closing as I did as he asked me to do. As I touched myself while he watched me do it.

Closing my eyes made it worse instead of better, because I could feel everything more that way. His watching eyes. My cool hands as I stroked the soft, curving slopes of my breasts, brushed over my turgid nipples. As I cupped myself and squeezed as if it were his hands stroking over me. That was how I touched myself. Imagining it as his hands, not mine. His hands that circled my pebbled, pouting crests. That thumbed over them. Brushed over the sensitive nubs. Pinched the hardening peaks.

Pleasure rolled deliciously over me, and I opened my eyes. Looked at him. "Like this?" I murmured.

His voice, when he answered, was hoarse and thick, his eyes gone a smoky gray, as if clouds had swarmed across the sky. "Yes, like that."

I smiled at his answer, at his reaction. And what had first been awkward now became easy. It was as if the hands that were touching me were touching him also. Teasing, caressing. Soothing, tantalizing.

I circled my nipples with forefinger and thumb. Squeezed.

I bit my lips, tightening inside around his thumb. Held it for a moment in my tight, greedy grasp before it slipped from me, then pushed back in. I groaned and opened my eyes to find his eyes locked on the rosy red tips of my nipples, engorged and lengthened from my pinching caress.

I ran my fingertips around the flushed areolas, smiling like a game show hostess drawing graceful attention to a waiting prize. Yours if you gave the right answer.

"Or like this?" I asked, my voice sultry, low, like Eve offering up forbidden fruit to Adam. With slow seduction, I put my finger and thumb back around the hard little peaks and squeezed my nipples again with another slow, rolling moan, another delicious tightening of my body around his pumping thumb.

I pulled, tugging on those swollen tips for two long seconds, pulling them out. Then my fingers cupped and framed what I had wrought—my nipples flushed cherry red, fully elongated, jutting out like little fingers.

With a hungry growl, like a beast teased past what he would resist, he tore open his pants and swarmed up my body, latching onto a jutting nipple with his warm, wet mouth, sucking on it hungrily while his left hand covered my other breast in a frank claiming. *Mine!* that hand proclaimed as he wrapped his fingers around the turgid tip and squeezed with firm, possessive pressure.

I cried out and arched against his sucking mouth, his torturing hand, my legs bending up around his waist. His other hand slid beneath my bottom, grasped my cheek and lifted me, grinding my mound up against his hard sternum. The angle of it was just right, catching my swollen pearl in the place of greatest friction. His teeth scraped over my nipple, capturing it with the dull-sharp edges of his teeth, *pulling* on it. Simultaneously squeezing and tugging on the other tip with his clever fingers. One more stimulus added . . . the unexpected graze of his fingertips there along my anal pucker . . . and I climaxed. It rolled sharply, suddenly over me like a huge, cresting wave, sweeping over me, drowning me in shaking ripples, in tearing, convulsive sensation. My light and my pleasure spilled out from me like the sun bursting apart.

After the giant peak had passed, he slipped into me while I was yet shuddering in the helpless, quivering aftermath. As my light dimmed, his began to glow. It was like one of the most natural things in the world, that my ebbing spark of light would beget his.

He was so gentle, staying so still inside of me. As if he knew my sensitized nerves could not take any more sensation at that moment other than the slow, stretching slide of his hardness in my softness. Just his filling length where I craved him most. Where I held him deep inside me, my inner ripples stroking him like a squeezing hand.

There in that frozen moment, he was one of the most beautiful things I'd ever seen. Poised above me with effortless, waiting strength as I felt him throb deep inside me. The strong cut of his muscles lovingly defined. The sweeping breadth of his shoulders. The curve of his biceps and

more streamlined triceps. The gentle swell of his chest. His
sloping deltoids, starkly delineated. Ready strength gathered, held in abeyance, calm for the moment like storm
clouds slowly gathering on the horizon, biding their time to
unleash their torrent at just the right moment. That same
waiting gentleness of how he had slid into me. Thinking
about it, remembering the feel of it, that gentle friction,
stirred me from my postcoital languor.

I gazed up at him through half-closed eyes and felt my
body tighten once more at just the sight of him. The divine
illumination of his skin against the fading glow of mine.
He looked like an angel with his honey-brown hair spilling
in a loose, wild tangle around his face, framing those fierce
eyes in softness. He reminded me not of a playful cherub,
but of a warrior angel. A ferocious beauty that took my
breath away.

Holding my eyes, he began a gentle, graceful dance
with his body. Slow, poignant movements rocking in and
out of me. Poignant because his face, his eyes, the coiled
energy emanating from him in invisible waves that you
could feel . . . all spoke of the fact that he was not normally
a gentle man. But he was gentle now, for me, with me, inside of me. Slow, languid strokes made even more erotic
because of the unexpected pleasure of it. Like expecting a
storm to strike with fierce, pounding fury, and finding
sweet, gentle rain kissing your skin instead. That restraint,
that containment of all that he could have unleashed, made
me moan.

I lifted my heavy arms and legs, wrapped them around
my gentle lover, and drew him down to me. He kissed me,
the lightest touch, as he stroked within me in that soft and
easy way, his rhythm never changing, as if he were savoring the feel of it, the sweet intimacy of our joining. I savored him in turn, without demand, just appreciation, my
hands gliding over his shoulders, down his back, stroking

the muscles there that flexed and moved as he moved slowly, gently. My hands swept lower, reading him, feeling the tight clenching of his buttocks as he pushed into me, the easing of those muscles as he pulled back out.

The movement of his body above me was like lapping waves, ever constant. Even when I arched up into him, my skin brightening anew, asking for more, he kept to that maddeningly slow pace, that languid rhythm.

He spoke to me then, telling me how he felt, what he wanted to do to me, what he *was* doing to me. Coarse love words. And the rough frankness of the words he used was in such marked contrast with his movements, to the gentleness with which he made love to me. The dichotomy of it stirred my mind, my body, wound me even higher without a single alteration in rhythm.

He touched me no other way, just the turgid length of him in that maddeningly slow and intimate dance, graceful, beautiful, ever gentle. The light brush of his lips over my lips, my cheeks, across my eyes, feathering down my temples. The lightest brush of my nipples against his chest as he dipped and swayed above me, into me and out of me. The rough stroke of his words against my ears—gritty, male, shockingly explicit. Words that excited me, made me tremble, made me moan.

He stroked me slowly, sweetly, brought me once more to the edge that way, nothing more. Kept me trembling there on the brink for so long that it became like agony and ecstasy combined. Wanting and having. But not enough, not enough.

"Dante." I said his name over and over again feverishly. My body lifted into his, but he held me in his rhythm with a restraining hand upon my hip, not allowing a faster beat. When I tried for more, he stopped and stared down at me with those fierce, glittering eyes, withholding his body until I yielded once more to that gentle, maddening stroking.

He was deaf to my cries for "*harder, faster, more*," delivered first as a command, then as a plea. Nothing moved him from that torturing slow and easy pace. Not his tight, straining body. Not my inner clenching, my weeping need for him. Honey poured out of me. So wet was I that you heard the slurping sounds we made as he slipped in and out of me.

I finally surrendered and lay quiescent beneath him, just accepting his easy thrusts, what he chose to give me, with silent tears rolling down my cheeks with the pleasure and frustration he had built up in me. He lapped up the spilled wetness with tender strokes of his tongue.

"*Dulcaeta*"—beloved—"don't cry."

The endearment only made more tears flow.

"Please," I begged. Nothing else. Just that plea.

Looking down into my eyes, he gave a shuddering sigh.

"Thank you for this time. For this sweet gift," he said. He didn't alter the force or speed of his rhythm. But his hand slid beneath my thighs and I felt his fingers stroke my wet outer lips, probe over where he stretched me, penetrated me. He traced that sensitive, swollen tissue back to where it rucked up tight and became perineal tissue, and his touch there was even more sensitive, disturbing. My breath hitched, and my body clenched around his shaft as he grazed a fingertip around my back opening.

With eyes both tender and fierce, his voice gentle and rough, he said, "Come for me," and pressed down, sliding that moistened fingertip into me, penetrating me as his cock withdrew and stroked back into my sheath, easy, gentle.

"Come for me," he demanded. And I did. With crying blessed relief, I finally came. A rippling tremor that seized him, squeezed him so tightly inside me. A release that broke gently over me like the wash of calm waters against the still shore. A sweet convulsing easing that went on and on until I felt it trigger his.

Like the wash and play of our light—my shine dimming as his brightened—so did his release begin as mine ended. Extending it until it felt like one endless, gentle liberation. A letting go.

A rippling, shuddering, cleansing of the senses, washing us anew.

NINETEEN

W HEN DAYLIGHT CAME, it was with the thought of him, the lingering taste and feel of him as I lay there in my bed. He had imprinted himself on my body, in my mind. He'd been saying good-bye. And that had felt *wrong* . . . because I wanted him to stay.

Yes. A simple truth. I didn't want him to go.

I'll tell him, I thought. *I'll tell him tonight that I want him to stay.*

It was that thought that finally soothed me to sleep. And then I dreamed.

I *remembered.*

A MAN WAS inside of me and I was riding him with vigorous abandon as he sweated and glowed and moaned beneath me. He was on his back, chained to a bench, his hands and ankles restrained by silver shackles. It was Shel, the warrior cut down by Barrabus's sword in my last remembered dream, saved from death only at my intervention.

He had whip marks reddening his chest, his thighs. Some had cut through the skin, drawing blood. They were marks that I had deliberately inflicted on him, I came to realize with some shock. Not in punishment, but in love play.

We were inside a dark room lit by torchlight. A dungeon, I would have thought, with all the whips, crops, floggers, and chains along the wall, on the floor. But the bolted benches and the various wooden frames were padded, the chains lined with fleece. And Shel's moans were not those of pain but of ecstatic rapture.

Not a dungeon. A playroom, I realized.

My playroom.

I plunged down on top of him and felt his shaft, a huge, hard thing, slide into me. Beneath that I felt the pleasurable bite of leather straps. Without looking down, I knew that what I felt was a cock and ball harness secured tightly around Shel, making his phallus almost painfully hard and engorged, swollen to a very large size. The straps separating his balls lifted them into tight sacs. The sensation, I knew, was much more acute for him this way. When I next thrust myself down on him, I ground a bit against those stretched balls, and felt a powerful wave of energy spill from him along with his agonized cry of pleasure caused by the torturous pain.

"My Queen!" he cried. All the muscles of his body were strained tight as I rode him that way for a few more strokes. His hips were strapped down so he couldn't move, only I could, and I knew that the sense of helplessness devastated him even more.

"Don't come," I ordered, my voice cool and calm, utterly confident in the authority I wielded over the man I was fucking.

I shifted the angle forward, easing off his balls, and savored the feel of his penis sinking into me in that new position. Goddess, he was like rigid metal, so hard he was. The tightness of the bindings was such that his erection had to be almost uncomfortably hard by now, a discomfort that caused him to become even more erect. A vicious cycle of pain causing pleasure causing more pain.

It was a delicate, deliberate dance, mingling pleasure with pain, and I did it effortlessly, keeping Shel there at that razor's edge, my fingers stroking lightly, lovingly, over the raw wounds I had inflicted, pulling an almost frenzied groan from him. His body was twitching now with shudders.

"Mistress, please . . . I can't hold back—"

"You can. And you will. Or you will displease me greatly."

I don't know what disturbed me more. Hearing that cool, dispassionate voice. Or seeing the utter control I wielded so ruthlessly, so knowingly, like a priestess serving up pleasure bleeding on the altar of pain.

I watched Mona Lyra give in to her own pleasure then, throwing back her head and closing her eyes, enjoying the hard, swollen shaft she rode with increasing rhythm and almost fierce force, glowing with the moon's light. Utterly sure that Shel would obey her. It was odd thinking what she thought, feeling what she did. Seeing that gloriously, sexually dominant creature dancing with such abandon upon the man she ruthlessly used and pleasured. Seeing her as me . . . a much different me. I felt what she felt . . . the tightening pleasure, the bitter-sweet taste of coming ecstasy, heightened and sweetened by the control she wielded as her right. She was lost in abandon and utterly aware at the same time of the straining man beneath her, throbbing within her. Who grew even more excited, I saw, by her seemingly callous use of him.

When both their lights were blindingly bright, so bright they made the torchlight seem but a dim glow, she opened her eyes and looked down at him. Through her eyes, I saw Shel's light brown eyes darken until they were almost black, glazed with pleasure that was filled with the sweet bite of desperate pain, his face and body so strained they was literally twitching with tremors—a man brought sublimely to the point of breaking pleasure. He was like a man clinging to the edge of a cliff by just his fingertips, feeling the ground start to crumble beneath them and desperately fighting to hold on just a little bit longer, one more second, even as he felt himself begin to fall. Then and only then did I finally release him. Release us both.

"Come now," I commanded.

With tears in his eyes, his lips bloodied from where he had bit down on them in his frantic struggle to hold back the trembling tide of his release, he did with a harsh cry that filled the room. He came in a great shuddering, spilling tide inside of me, his hips bucking up into me as much as the restraints allowed as he convulsed almost violently, spurting, ejaculating into me.

Shel's release lifted me into my mine, and I felt it roar through me, a whitewash of ecstasy that ripped through my body, arching me above him so terribly tight for one powerful, blissful moment.

It was then, when we were both caught up in our body's rapture, helpless in its throes, that I sensed something wrong. Too late.

A blade swept down, and with one clean slice, Shel's head parted from his body. He died even while he was still inside of me, filling my womb with his seed. Light flashed—his energy, his life force being released.

His body, his solid flesh, crumbled into ashes. And just like that he was gone. I fell onto the bench, heard the clink of empty chains hitting the ground, saw the cock harness tumble down. And I screamed. With rage, with fury, with sorrow.

"Noooo!" It was an anguished cry torn from my soul. Then more quietly, more mournfully, "Oh Goddess . . . Shel."

Still shaking with the ripples of release, I looked up into the face of the enemy who had breached my fortress silently. Undetected until he took sudden form and substance before me now.

I'd never seen him before, and yet his face was familiar to me . . . to Mona Lyra. He stood before me like an avenging angel, the edge of his sword biting into my neck, drawing a slow trickle of blood. His face was like stone. Dispassionate, some would have said, but only if they could not see his eyes. His eyes were of the palest blue, like a glacier lake, and just as cold. Ghost eyes. Deadly and merciless. Around his neck he wore a glowing amulet, a brilliant orange stone speckled with black. On his wrists glimmered dark red warrior bands, ones I had seen before. I knew then who he was and why he appeared so familiar. I'd killed his father almost ten years before.

"No one can hear us," he said, making me wonder at the unusual magic he wielded. "Do you know who I am?"

I looked into those eyes. Felt the merciless impact of them. "You are Damian, Barrabus's son. Wounded in battle and then gone. Everyone thought you dead." For good reason. The battlefield had been coated inches thick with blood and ashes.

"I would not allow myself to die. Not while you yet lived." He spoke coolly, almost impassively, but his light blue eyes glowed with a dangerous, burning heat, flashing almost the color of silver, our greatest weakness. It was as if he touched that metal alloy to my skin when he looked at me with those blindingly bright eyes. I found myself unable to move, to strike out at him, my body chained by invisible bonds.

"Are you a demon?" I asked as fear trailed its chilly

fingers down my spine. I knew of nothing else that could have ensorcelled me like this. That had this degree of mental strength, holding me helpless beneath his gaze.

A small smile touched his lips, a feral gesture somehow. "Not yet."

"You didn't need to kill Shel."

"Do you mourn him? Feel pain at his loss?"

"Yes."

"*Good!*" The word exploded viciously out from him; and his body trembled with his fierce anger and satisfaction. His slight movement cut the sword deeper into my neck, the blade a cool silver burning in my flesh. "I want to give you as much pain as you gave me when you killed my father, and then my mother, too, for she ended her life the next day when she learned of his death. I want you to ache, to hurt . . . if it is even possible for an icy bitch like you to feel."

"I feel," I said with the heat of tears stinging my eyes.

"I hope you do. By the holy fire of Hell, I hope you do." Shaking, as if it took everything in him to do so, he withdrew his sword. Then with a casual strength that was even more frightening because I was helpless to move or fight against him, he lowered me to my back and secured my arms, wrists, and legs to the bench with the silver restraints. On top of that, he chained me with his will, a mental command my muscles were unable to disobey.

"Stay like this until I return for you."

I could not move. Not one single muscle of my body. I could only speak, and the dread that welled up within me spilled out into my voice. "Where are you going?"

He lowered his face down to me like a lover. Spoke to me in the soft, whispering tones of one. "To kill all who belong to you here in this castle. Your men, your women."

Everything in me shouted *no*. I gathered everything I

could to break free. Called upon the abundant power that had always been innate—and found myself utterly helpless.

With my eyes wild upon his implacable face, I drew on my last reserve, upon the pearly moles in my palm, the Goddess's visible favor upon me. With blessed relief, I felt them begin to tingle, to answer my call.

His sword came swinging down in a graceful arc. One cut with almost negligent force. I felt the reverberation of the blade bite into the wooden bench as my severed hands fell to the ground in a spurting fountain of blood, chopped off just above the manacles. The metal restraints fell to the ground with a heavy *clunk*, still attached to my dismembered limbs.

I didn't scream. Not aloud. Just in my mind. A scream that went on and on and on interminably. I opened my mouth and words spilled out. "I beg of you, don't kill them. Do what you will with me, but my people are innocent."

He looked down at me, his eyes pale burning flames. "No one in this war is innocent," he said in a gentle tone.

Panic choked my voice, fear twisting it ruthlessly. "Your father . . . your father was honorable. He would not have slain innocents."

"I am not my father."

"Don't. Please, don't. Just me," I begged with tears spilling down my face. With my blood spreading like an echoing sea of sorrow around me.

"Vengeance is mine, and it is terrible. Hush." And with that soft-spoken command, I could no longer speak. Could only scream in my mind as I watched him turn and walk out the door, go up the stairs. A moment of terrible silence, and the screams began. The cries of horror, the shrieks of pain that echoed and rang in the fortress. Cries that filled my mind and did not stop, even when all sound faded away and all heartbeats ended until I heard only mine and that of one other. His.

When he finally returned, I was light-headed and weak from blood loss, and from the pain that consumed my body, ravaged my heart, my soul. He released me from his mental control, freed my legs of the silver shackles. And a sick, almost mindless fury filled me. Swelled me with a hate so strong that it possessed me, expanding within me with a terrible, powerful pressure, even as I lay there physically helpless before him.

"I curse you," I said in a voice that was mine and not mine. In a voice that was deeper, more resonant, filled with a power that came not from me alone, but was channeled through my Goddess's Tears. They glowed from my amputated hands. "I curse you to a life that will never end. To deaths that are not true deaths. You will live again and again to die unceasingly, returning to an ever-diminishing seed until only you alone remain. May your soul be cursed in endless torment for what you have done today."

"It already is," Damian, the son of Barrabus, said. He raised his sword. "Know this before you go, witch Queen. I will lay waste to all that you hold dear. Anything and everything that you ever loved, I will destroy." And with that last promise, the sword, drenched red with my blood, my people's blood, came swinging down . . .

I AWOKE WITH a scream. With tears streaming down my face, sobs choking my chest. Arms held me, and I viciously fought against them.

"It's a dream. Just a dream, Mona Lisa."

My name and a face—Dontaine's—brought me to startling awareness of him and all the others who had come running at my cry: Thaddeus, the worried faces of Jamie and Tersa, Rosemary, Chami, Aquila, and Tomas. Everyone in the household.

"Oh God," I whispered. My people now, I thought, while

the shrilling screams of my dead and dying people from the past echoed in my mind.

"You had a nightmare," Dontaine soothed.

No, not a nightmare, I thought. *Something much worse than that.*

Memory.

TWENTY

I REMEMBERED HOW I died.

But it was the other memory, the memory of how all my people had died, that utterly devastated me. And the memory of the tool of their destruction. Damian . . . and myself.

Dante came to me as he had come all the nights before at the gloaming of the day. I studied him as he entered the sitting room where I had sat and waited for him for over two long hours, and gazed at him with memories both old and new. I saw him as he was now—young, easy, relaxed. Happy, even. And over that reality, I saw the monster in my dreams, the cold, burning eyes, the merciless face. I saw the bloody swing of the sword, heard the shrieks, the wails of my people as they died. It was as if ghostly images of the past clung and superimposed themselves over the slimmer body and younger face of the man before me.

I had not known that the curse Dante bore had come from me.

I'd cursed him. And I wondered if I had cursed myself

as well. You could not invoke such a thing without some of it coming back upon yourself.

I searched that face, looking for evil. But could not find it in him unless I saw it in myself also. He had killed, as I had killed. Sought vengeance, as I had sought vengeance in the end. We had simply used different means. Was his choice any better or worse than mine? I did not know. Both things that we had done were horrendous. I could see that, understand that in my mind. I'd reached that fair and logical conclusion after two hours of careful thought, deciding how to proceed. But my body was less logically governed. Coldness pervaded my body when he stepped through the door, and an almost wild, wrenching fear seized me. It was a reaction not governed by reason or will.

A riptide of primitive instinct sent my control splintering away, and I overset my chair, sent it crashing to the floor as I hastily stood and backed away from him like a wild animal trapped.

He stopped. Froze still. And that easy, happy light that had filled his eyes upon seeing me died away. All the warmth seeped out, leaving his eyes like pale, glimmering ice.

Seconds ticked by. A long, suspended moment of silence and ghosts, of life and death and everlasting rebirth.

"You remembered," he said. Two words that sounded the death knell of everything that might have been.

I nodded, feeling everything I had resolved die away beneath the primitive scream of horror and rage, of sorrow and pain choking my throat, trying to claw its way out of me.

I could not forgive. I could not forget.

I could not bear to be in his presence.

My body was equally torn between fleeing him, and attacking him. Tearing him apart.

Something closed in him like the audible shutting of a

door. His eyes dropped away from mine, and his head lowered.

"We go to High Queen's Court tomorrow," he said in a low, quiet voice. "Can you bear my presence for one more day, or would you have me leave now?"

He was asking whether I was banishing him as a rogue, or if I would allow him to reenter our society legitimately. Asking as if it did not really matter to him what I chose to do.

Now. I want you gone now! my body screamed. But the words that came out of my mouth in a hoarse, strained whisper were, "Tomorrow. You can stay until tomorrow."

He bowed and left.

For a long time afterward my body continued to tremble.

T HE NEXT NIGHT we went to High Court. The private jet took us there swiftly. I knew that logically, but those several hours locked together with Dante in the plane seemed endlessly long. When we landed, I practically leaped outside. Only when in the open space was I able to feel calmer.

We were settled now in the suite of rooms at the manor house that I had come to think of as mine. The Morells had been given guest rooms on another floor as per my request. An unusual request that Mathias, steward of the Great House, had complied with without a flicker of expression, although his eyes had widened a bit when he had first caught sight of Nolan and Hannah. By his reaction, I knew that he recognized them.

Other Queens and their entourages had arrived, many whom I'd never seen before. It was a full house, I noticed, as we entered the dining hall, which seemed to be the main gathering spot for now, at least until High Court convened in the next hour. I'd brought all of my men but for Chami,

who I had asked to stay behind to watch over Thaddeus,
Tersa, and Jamie—my Mixed Blood flock—and Rosemary. Eyes glanced curiously at me, but it was the powerful giant beside me who drew the most attention, the most
stares. Amber, my Warrior Lord.

It was not just the gold medallion necklace Amber wore
that proclaimed his elevated status, but the feel of his
power alone. A power unmatched by any other warrior in
that room. Not by Aquila or Tomas, my senior warriors.
Not even by Dontaine. It was only now, in comparison to
the other Queens' guards who filled the room that I could
see what others saw: that I commanded the strongest warriors here. My men's collective strength gleamed around
me like bright gemstones, sparkling more vividly than any
force the other Queens had. And shining most brightly was
Amber, like a raw diamond that had been chiseled free of
all flaws and weaknesses, so that every facet of him gleamed
now with unhidden radiance.

He was different than before, more confident. Grown into
his power and authority. He wore it now with assurance and
ease, a strong man with nothing to prove. With no fear that
his greater strength would mark him for death by his Queen.

He was so much stronger now. Not in degree of power,
that was unchanged, but with the quiet command he
wielded. Two of his guards stood by his side, and two virgin lads. They were all technically from my territory, but
they were really his, boys who had chosen to train under
him. The two eighteen-year-old boys had come to seek service with other Queens. To give up their prized virginity to
their new mistresses.

I'd worried for nothing, I understood now as we were
seated at a table long enough to accommodate us all. I'd
worried about Amber's vulnerability, the tainted legacy left
him by his infamous rogue father, and the fear and mistrust
by the other Queens that would always be there against

him because of that. But vulnerability came from inside a person. You were susceptible to hurt only if you cared what others thought of you. Amber didn't. The only Queen's opinion that mattered to him was mine, and he was secure in that. He was armored by the mantle of his own authority and by my trust in him. It was a rich, unknowing gift he had given to me, seeing him like this—proud and invincible to the poisonous arrows of others because of my love.

All those long, lonely nights spent apart from him were a worthwhile sacrifice, to see him like this now.

The Morells entered the dining hall, and all eyes turned to them. To the tall, bearded warrior and his healer wife that many had thought dead and departed. And to the two additions to their family—their sons, Dante and Quentin.

Here, where I had not expected it, was vulnerability.

The dining hall was a mass of patterned colors, each guard wearing the individual dress uniform of his Queen's court. My table's livery was gold and ivory, set against black trim. Sitting around me, my men were like an array of golden petals set around my black-gowned center.

Nolan, Hannah, and their sons wore simple clothing. There were no uniform colors declaring to whom they belonged. There had been no time, and no need perhaps, to have custom livery designed for them. They could have worn clothes that bore my Court's colors, but they hadn't. Probably a deliberate and cautious choice after I had requested separate quarters for them. They didn't know if I had I brought them here and washed my hands of them already. I had left them awash in a sea of uncertainty, and as a result, they were vulnerable now in this period of transition. As they paused at the threshold, all eyes in the room watched to see at which Queen's table they would sit. To see who, if anyone, protected them.

Nolan glanced in my direction, but with no acknowledging nod from me, no indication of what I wished, he began leading his family toward a table set in the opposite corner of the hall, farthest away from me.

A part of me wanted them to go there. To have Dante far, far away from me. Another part of me screamed that until they pledged themselves elsewhere, they were still under my care and protection.

The latter voice won.

"Join us." My words were spoken softly. But they were easily heard by Nolan. With a grateful look in his eyes, he changed direction and headed toward us.

"You are mistaken, Nolan. It is *my* table where you belong, is it not?"

The voice was a low, smooth, feminine one belonging to a Queen I was not familiar with. A tall brunette with blond-streaked hair. Not the natural kind that came from sun and surf. With the Monère's sun sensitivity, that would be very unlikely. No, these blond highlights had to have come from a bottle, from the human magic of a beauty salon. She sat in a corner table surrounded by six of her men dressed in forest green and yellow saffron. She wore the traditional long black gown of a Queen, but again, a human touch here—it was couture. One that had a label like Versace, or something of that ilk. She was a handsome woman with lovely blue eyes set in a strong, proud face. The only thing marring her features were her lips. They were too thin, making her mouth a tight, straight line, indicating a rigid, cruel nature or a parsimonious one. I'd be willing to bet it was both, that she was a greedy covetous thing, and not too nice on top of that.

From the look of ownership in her eyes as she gazed at Nolan and his family, and the sudden tension in Nolan's and Hannah's shoulders, I had a feeling that I was looking at their old Queen. The one who had not allowed them to marry. The one for whom they had faked their deaths in order to flee.

"No, milady," Nolan said quietly, continuing to guide his sons and wife to me. "We are sworn to Mona Lisa's service now."

"*No*, Nolan?" she said with a dangerous gentleness. "That is not a word that Mona Sephina's men ever say to her."

Sheesh. A Queen who referred to herself in the third person. I guess you could add "huge ego" to rigid, cruel, and greedy.

Her voice changed. Became hard and whiplike. "You are mine! I have not released you from my service."

It would have, of course, been impossible for things to go so smoothly for me. To think that just once I could come to High Court and not cause an uproar. I sighed and deliberately stepped over the line that would make this Queen my enemy.

"*No,*" I said, deliberately stressing the word that Mona Sephina's men never said to her. Poor schmucks. "They fled you and became rogues. Which means you lost what once belonged to you. Too bad, so sad. But," I shrugged, "that's our law." Mentally, I patted myself on the back for saying *our law*, and not *your law*. See? I was getting better. "I found them," I continued, "and now they are mine. Willingly," I added, unable to help adding that last twist of the knife.

My words stabbed her dead on. She rose to her feet with fury. Let me tell you, that gal had a lot of inches on her. She must have stood at least six two. Taller even than Rosemary, my Amazon cook, although maybe only half her girth. Still, she was a formidable thing, solidly built, almost half a foot taller than me, and outweighing me by at least fifty pounds. And the way she held herself bespoke of a confidence that had me thinking this Queen might really know how to handle herself in a fight. Gee, I really knew how to pick 'em.

"Thank you for reminding me of our laws," Mona

Sephina said, suddenly smiling like a cat that had just gulped down an unsuspecting canary. Nolan and Hannah froze, caught halfway between the two Queens squabbling over them.

Mona Sephina's eyes slid from the parents to focus on the children. And the acquisitive light that shone in those blue eyes as she looked over Dante and Quentin like something that already belonged to her made my stomach clench with foreboding.

"You are right," she said. "Once they went rogue, I lost all rights to my former master at arms . . ." Somehow, I wasn't surprised at hearing Nolan's previous rank. ". . . and to my healer. But *not* to the children they conceived while still under my rule."

"That law applies to simple bondwomen sworn to your service," Hannah said, speaking up in her children's defense. "It does not apply to healers. We have more rights. Our children belong to us."

"Unless you cast aside those rights and turn rogue," Mona Sephina said. Vicious satisfaction layered her words. "Then all your special rights are naught. Your sons belong to me. You two boys, come here."

"No," I said. I was deriving more and more satisfaction in saying that word to her. I was pretty vague on most areas of Monère law. I just knew what the others told me and what I picked up, as in now. But it couldn't be much different from human law, I reasoned. Open, as such, to any interpretation you could throw in and get away with.

"Not so fast," I drawled in a fashion that would have made Clint Eastwood proud, lounging back in my seat as relaxed as Mona Sephina was rigid. "They are no longer rogues. They belong to me now, remember?" I watched with satisfaction as a muscle twitched beneath Mona Sephina's eye. "As such, Hannah's rights as a healer still hold. Her children are hers."

"I dispute that," Mona Sephina said. And something about the way she said it, throwing it down like a gauntlet, made it seem more significant than the mere words themselves. And, of course, it was—my intuition was good about things like that. Not in other matters, like loving and trusting someone who had freakin' *killed* me in another life and slaughtered all my people. But in things like this, it was dead-on accurate.

An expectant hush fell over our dining hall audience, a collective breath held as if they were waiting for something more.

"I challenge your claim," Mona Sephina said, and the tense, waiting stillness dissolved with an almost audible sigh.

"What does that mean?" My question was aimed at Amber, sitting beside me. He and all my men had gone deeply still.

"In matters where the law is not entirely clear, a dispute can be settled by issuing a personal challenge."

"You mean, like where might is right, winner takes all? She wants to *fight* me?"

Amber nodded.

"There is no need." It was Dante who spoke, as I had somehow known he would. Of all the men here, even more than my own men, he would not want me fighting another Queen—not when I might be carrying his child.

He addressed Mona Sephina courteously. "Withdraw the challenge, milady, and my brother and I am yours. You need not fight to win us."

Mona Sephina studied Dante and Quentin for a moment, savoring the pain in their parents' eyes. Smiling triumphantly, she nodded. "Very well. I withdraw the challenge. Come to me now."

Dante did as she bid. Quentin followed him.

As they walked to her, I told myself that they were doing

nothing more than what they had come here to do—to find another Queen to serve. But the agony in Nolan's and Hannah's eyes, and the delight in Mona Sephina's over their suffering, was just *wrong*.

Another Queen . . . any other Queen. Just not her.

"Wait," I said, and Dante and Quentin halted, instinctively obeying me because in their hearts they still belonged to me. "I cannot agree to these terms." *Would not* agree to them. I looked to Nolan, the only one of my men of whom I dared ask this because of his right as their father. "Can someone else accept the challenge on my behalf?"

"Yes," Nolan answered. His eyes held understanding of what I was asking of him, and agreement to it. "If a Queen chooses a champion, he can fight in her stead. It would be my honor to serve as your champion, my Queen."

"I choose you then, Nolan. Thank you."

"Touching," Mona Sephina said with a sneer. "But I have already withdrawn the challenge. The boys are mine," she said and smiled slowly. "Of their own free will."

"I dispute that," I said. And calmly threw down the gauntlet. "I issue you a challenge in turn for them."

She smiled coldly at me. "You do not know our laws well, do you? I am not obliged to accept your challenge. Only a fool would do so, and I am not a fool, despite what you may believe. Nolan was my best warrior. I have none who could defeat him." She snapped her fingers at Dante and Quentin. "Come, as I command of you."

They started forward again. And again I stopped them with one word. "Wait."

There had to be something else, some other way. Power was only what you allowed someone to wield over you. I would not allow her to hold it over me or any of my people.

"We are at an impasse, Mona Sephina. I claim them, and so do you. I issue you challenge, and you cravenly decline it." She stiffened at my words. "I would say that leaves both of us with an equal balance of nothing. Dante and Quentin have come here to seek service with another Queen at the fair. If we both yield our claim to them, I will uphold that original intent. At the service fair, I will bow out gracefully, and leave you with a clear shot at obtaining them then. *Only then.*"

"You try to grant me a right I have no need of," Mona Sephina said coolly, "when they are mine already."

"We are at a stalemate then."

"No, we are not." Mona Sephina turned to Dante. "I withdrew the challenge as you asked me to. Honor your word to me now, boy."

Face stiff, he began moving toward her once more.

I stood, scraping back my chair. "Take one more step, Dante, and I will engage Mona Sephina in a fight over you right now, challenge or no challenge."

Dante drew to a halt, his jaw set in a hard, grim line as he turned back to stare at me with a look in his eyes that clearly said: *If I could get my hands on you right now, you would not forget it anytime soon. I thought you wanted me gone. Are you crazy?*

Maybe I was. If so, it was entirely his fault for getting me pregnant. All those hormones.

My gaze swung back to Mona Sephina and I watched as her eyes narrowed into slits. She looked like a big cat that was considering pouncing and seizing her two young prizes, only a short reach away. Her men were tense and ready beside her. I felt my own men gathering themselves for the fight about to erupt.

"What if *I* serve as Mona Lisa's champion?" Dante said into the sudden tense stalemate.

I saw Mona Sephina pause and consider it. He was young, only twenty years old, and the feel of his power was much less than that of her guards, all seasoned warriors. "I will accept those terms," Mona Sephina said, nodding abruptly. "If she does."

"Who will you choose as your champion?" I asked, not knowing why I did so. It would be the strongest of her men, of course, the one standing on her right. He was almost the same height as his Queen, but built like a massive bull. Power oozed from him like invisible heat.

"My champion will be Oswald."

Sure enough, the warrior I had eyeballed stepped forward. I glanced from Dante to Oswald, and back again. Distinguished bloodline or not, reincarnated warrior who had lived countless lifetimes before notwithstanding, Dante still looked like a young pup next to the big warrior he would face.

"Mona Lisa," Dante said softly, reading the resistance in my face. "It is my choice."

His choice. His right to fight for his freedom and that of his brother's. Although freedom was a poor word choice. More like the free will to choose which Queen they would bind themselves to in servitude. Yeah, that truth sounded so much better.

Was it worth it, this fight over something that may or may not matter much in the end?

I looked at Mona Sephina's thin lips, her cruel eyes, and thought: *Hell, yeah. It was worth it.*

TWENTY-ONE

WE ENDED UP bickering some more before finally coming to terms we both agreed upon. Dante had proposed archery, shooting at targets. His opponent, Oswald, had snorted, and proceeded to tell us what he thought of such a bloodless sport.

He got to choose the terms of the fight, Oswald insisted, since I had issued the challenge.

We all had to take a moment to rehash the events—Mona Sephina's issuing challenge, Dante's counteroffer, her withdrawal of the challenge, then my issuing it. Yup. I guess that's how things had pretty much ended—with my challenging her, Dante proposing himself as my champion, and my accepting him as such.

How his eyes had blazed when I had said those words—*I accept Dante as my champion.* How odd the twists and turns tricksy fate continued to bring into our lives.

Everyone poured out into the courtyard to witness the spectacle about to unfold.

Oswald had gotten his wish for a bloodier fight. His terms. Unarmed combat, four-legged form allowed.

I'd seen the look in Dante's eyes as Oswald had announced the rules. Just a faint flicker in his eyes, no other betraying movement. But somehow I knew that the last part of it had bothered him. I didn't know what Dante's animal form was or if he even had one. Could he even shift? If he could, it still had to be a new ability only recently attained with puberty, which usually took place around seventeen years of age in Monère males.

I spent another five minutes haggling, to no avail. Oswald's chosen terms stood. Shifting was allowed. The only concession I managed to wring from Mona Sephina was that the winner was the man who first pinned his opponent to the ground for ten seconds. I don't know if that helped Dante or made it harder for him. He gave me no hint, no clue as to what would help him. In truth, he didn't seem to really care what the terms were.

Both Mona Sephina and I agreed that the challenge was to be nonfatal. Death was not allowed. Would be punished, in fact, by awarding victory to the other side. No guarantee, but at least it would motivate Dante and Oswald not to kill each other. No male liked to lose.

Again, I didn't know if that hindered Dante or helped him. Maybe it would have been easier for Dante to kill Oswald rather than pin him; he was a big guy. But in this matter I was operating solely on my own preference. And I found that I'd rather Dante lose and live. In my heart of hearts, I did not want him to die.

Oswald stripped down to just his pants. Unclothed, he was an even more imposing figure with a thick chest, massive shoulders, and heavy, dense muscles that knotted his hairy body with solid strength.

Dante, on the other hand, was more elegantly built, with sleeker muscles. Like a ballet dancer rather than a burly wrestler. Even the way he removed his clothes was in marked contrast to the way Oswald had done so. Instead of rough, forceful gestures, it was a graceful, deliberate disrobing, with calmness, precision. He passed his sword and dagger into his brother's keeping. The wrist bracelets and necklace were removed next and also handed to Quentin. Standing beside each other, you could see the features that made them brothers. The similarities—the high-bridged noses, the long, lean cut of their faces. And their differences—the warm tawny brown of Dante's hair, his lightened blond streaks coming from the sun's natural touch, not a bottle; and Quentin's darker hair. One face smooth, almost girlishly pretty with big eyes and long lashes; the other face less refined, yet roughly beautiful somehow in its harsh imperfection.

It was in the eyes, though, where the true difference lay. Quentin's eyes were still soft, still young. Dante's eyes were those of an old soul, one that had lived long and hard. One to whom death, pain, and suffering were familiar knowledge.

When all items of clothing were removed by Dante, all but for his pants, he stepped forward into the cleared center, ringed by the curious throng that was composed of Queens, guards, maids, footmen, and various other housestaff. All who had come out to watch the fight.

The two opponents approached each other, and it was like watching a young David step forward to meet a hulking Goliath. I knew Dante's history, had seen him fight. With a sword he was almost unparalleled. But I did not know what he was capable of in unarmed combat, and the disparity between their sizes was frankly daunting. Dante's muscles seemed as naught next to the bulk of Oswald's more mature, brutish mass. They were of the same height, both just over six feet, but Oswald was almost twice Dante's weight. Twice his width.

With a grin, Oswald charged, going after Dante like a two-ton tank. They collided with resonating impact. Surprisingly, it was Oswald who went tumbling in the air for a dozen feet before crashing to the ground. The big warrior lay there for a moment, stunned by the unexpected outcome. Then he picked himself up, and with a roar, launched himself at Dante again. With coiled, springing grace, Dante met him in the air. Oswald swung. With a lithe twist, Dante ducked his blow, and landed one of his own. The force was enough to alter Oswald's course. One moment he was springing forward, the next second Dante snapped Oswald's head back with a solid hit that not only halted his forward momentum, but sent him flying backward in reverse.

Dante seemed to pack quite a punch.

Oswald landed with an impact that made the ground tremble. He shook his head, clearing it, and seemed to decide that a change in strategy was required. With a rippling release of power and a sparkle of light, he started to shift. Oswald's big, broad face pushed forward into a snout. His brown eyes lightened to yellow. His spine curved and he fell onto all fours. A short, hairy coat of tawny fur spilled over his skin, a tufted tail emerged, and a beautiful auburn mane thickened around his head and shoulders. With a great roar that showcased the long canines wickedly well, he completed his shift into lion form—a magnificent and deadly predator, even bigger now than he'd been in his upright one.

All eyes turned to Dante. Energy pulsed once, twice. But he didn't shift as everyone expected. Only two things changed. His eyes silvered, and his hands started to morph, to shorten, thicken, the bones becoming more curved. Two-inch long claws pushed out of his fingertips, sliding out like blades. A partial change. I'd only seen two others do that, shift only that one part of themselves. One had been Dontaine, my master at arms, and it had not been an easy thing for him to do—more of a slow and painful process. For Dante, it seemed as natural and simple as breathing. And his change was even more refined than Dontaine's had been. No fur. Just his human skin, though it was thicker and coarser now. There was no hint of what his animal self was, other than those long, curved claws. The only other person who had accomplished such a partial transformation so effortlessly had been Lucinda, Halcyon's sister, a demon dead princess.

From the murmurs that came from the audience, the light gasps, I took it to mean that the partial shift and the ease with which it was done was not a common ability. Still, impressive though it was, those claws did not seem an adequate match for Oswald's lion. I glanced at Nolan and Quentin's faces, and saw from their troubled expressions that they did not think so either.

The crowd backed farther way, giving them more room as the lion sprang. Dante stood his ground. At the last instant, he slashed and rolled out from beneath those powerful paws, scoring four diagonal cuts along the lion's underbelly. It continued in that same pattern, like a beautiful, vicious, choreographed dance—Oswald attacking and Dante dodging, scoring light hits when he could. But quick though Dante was, in his lion form Oswald was equally as fast. And he had four clawed appendages to Dante's two. On top of that, he had flesh-tearing canine teeth, making it five weapons in his arsenal to Dante's mere two. Inevitably, one of those swiping paws caught Dante. The impact sent him slamming to the ground, his left side ripped open, the white of his ribs showing through the torn flesh.

The excitement of the bloodthirsty crowd swelled, and their eager cries swallowed up my gasp in a sea of sound. But Dante's eyes turned from his springing opponent and unerringly found me. As if he'd heard my soft cry of distress. Could discern it from all the other noise.

Only when he was assured of my physical well-being, that I was fine and my reaction simply that of seeing him injured, did he turn his attention back to Oswald, back to the fight.

It left me shaken, that look, that keen awareness of me even in the midst of battle. I swallowed a scream as the lion fell on Dante.

Dante rolled away at the very last instant so that Oswald hit the ground not on top of his prey as he had intended, but past him. A hard, downward chop of Dante's hand, and the thick bone in the lion's foreleg broke with an audible *crack*. A sweep of Dante's legs, and the big animal toppled to the ground. Dante rolled on top of him, and drove his right claws through the lion's two back legs, his left claws stabbing through the upper forelegs, pinning the beast to the ground in a brutal, effective manner, with his body behind and out of reach of the great jaws.

The crowd fell unexpectedly silent at the sudden reversal. Into the silence, Quentin started counting, "One. Two. Three. Four . . ."

On the count of five, the lion tried to heave back up. With almost casual violence, Dante yanked his left claws out from the pinned forelegs and backhanded the beast across his head with a powerful blow. The lion fell back to the ground, knocked out for the remainder of the count. When ten was called out, Dante unhooked his right claws, wiped the bloodstains on Oswald's thick pelt, and stood up. Two soft pulses of power and the long, hooking nails shrunk back beneath the flesh, and his hands became just hands once more.

The crowd parted, making way for him as Dante walked back to his brother. He stood quietly, allowed Quentin to bind his wounds, then donned his necklace, arm bands, and clothes, in that order. With his dagger secured and his sword belted at his side, he strode to me and the crowd slipped back away from him . . . and from me, once they saw where he was heading. Only Amber, Dontaine, Tomas, and Aquila remained by my side.

Stopping before me, Dante went down on one knee, bowing his head.

"Your victory, milady."

Then, with no more fuss than that, he stood and walked away, his family following after him. Leaving behind a stunned audience of warriors and Queens and one particularly furious one—Mona Sephina, who gazed down at the still unconscious Oswald with tight, thin lips.

"That's a cool one," someone in the crowd muttered, voicing the sentiment aloud for us all.

Dante had taken down a warrior much older and more powerful than himself with an economy of motion, snatching victory from his competitor's grasp with simple, elegant savagery. He had defeated a warrior shifted into his animal form while he had remained in his upright one. Most disturbing of all, though, was that not once while Dante had fought Oswald had emotion touched him. No rage, no passion, no anger. Not even triumph in the end.

A cool one, indeed.

And far more dangerous than even they knew.

TWENTY-TWO

I FELT HALCYON'S presence after most of the crowd had drifted away. The sudden awareness of him was like that of a tuning fork being struck, leaving my entire body vibrating with every part of me conscious of him. I felt him, felt his thoughts, and knew that he was lending me some of his control. I tasted eagerness, concern, curiosity . . . and nervousness from him.

Why are you nervous? I wondered. Just a normal thought, one that popped into my mind. I was surprised when he answered.

Meeting you again. Wondering if you had changed your mind on becoming my mate. His words sounded as clearly in my mind as if he had spoken them out loud.

I saw him then, a slender man with skin a dark, vivid gold against the white silk of his shirt, his hair a sumptuous fall of black against the white and gold backdrop. Simple. Elegant. Breathtaking.

Your eyes flatter me. I am most common in looks and

appearance, he whispered in my mind. But I heard a smile in his voice. My own lips curved up in response.

You are all things but common to me, Halcyon.

Our hands touched, and his fingers wrapped around mine, golden brown skin against fair white. A lovely study of contrasts. What we were.

He lifted my hand to his lips in a gesture that only he could make so naturally graceful. "Hell-cat," he said, and kissed the back of my hand.

"Halcyon." I brushed my fingertips across his golden cheek and felt warmth flare up in his mind and along his skin at my touch. Amber and Dontaine greeted him politely, and he responded in kind to them, nodded cordially to Aquila and Tomas.

"It seems I missed quite a show," Halcyon murmured. But I felt the truth through that connection we shared. He had deliberately waited until it was over so that he would not distract me, though it had been hard for him to do so. To stay away, knowing that I was here.

I was both touched and flattered. And watched, entranced, as a light, scarlet blush touched that gold-dusted skin.

This connection between us both soothes and stings, Halcyon murmured wryly in my mind. *Nothing can be hidden when we are thus joined.*

Out loud he said, "I have something I wish to give you waiting in my quarters. Will you come with me there?" Silently he added, *You can quench your hunger in the privacy of my place.*

I nodded. Told Aquila and Tomas to wait for us at the Council Hall, while Amber and Dontaine accompanied me to Halcyon's abode.

"We'll meet you in a little while," I told them.

Bowing, Aquila and Tomas left.

Halcyon took my hand, set it in the crook of his arm,

and led me down a path that wound behind the Great House. We passed a few other small, private residences before we finally arrived at his. It was set farthest back, away from the other lodgings, closest to the bordering thicket of woods. His dwelling here was simple and comfortably furnished, smelling like him, I thought, as I stepped through the doorway.

We do not have scents was his amused thought.

Then what do I smell?

What you are picking up is my physic scent. And because he was not used to censoring his thoughts, I caught the rest of it. That it was something that was only normally sensed by other demons.

He caught my distress. "Forgive me, Hell-cat. That was thoughtless of me," he murmured, earning puzzled glances from Amber and Dontaine.

After we entered, Halcyon lifted his hand and stroked his palm over a stone mosaic design made of individual rocks embedded in the wall. As he passed his hand over it, a small, nondescript gray pebble set near the bottom began to glow, turning emerald green. I felt the thrumming energy slide over me and stretch wide to encompass the entire room.

"You already know what it is," Halcyon said with surprise.

"A privacy shield. A sound barrier. So that no one outside can hear us." I knew because Dante and his mother each had a similar stone.

Interesting, Halcyon thought. *Kámennae stone are quite rare.*

What type of rocks are they?

Have you not guessed yet? They are remnants from our mother planet, the moon. Taken from her core.

"You can speak to each other mind-to-mind," Amber said, breaking into our silent conversation.

"Yes," I confirmed, and felt apprehension flit through me. I had not told Amber of my new demon nature. The reason why I had asked him to come here now with Dontaine was so that I could explain it. So that he could see and know.

"I have a small part of Halcyon's demon essence in me that allows this communication. It is not something he infected me with," I added quickly, as concern and anger flared up hot and strong in Amber's eyes, changing his blue eyes into the yellow-gold color of his name. "It's something I took into myself through my own actions." And that of another Queen.

"An accident," I murmured, though it had not been so much an accident as ignorance. When I had sucked Mona Louisa's light and essence into me, it had been with the full intent of killing her. Infecting me with Halcyon's demon essence, which she had drank down into her, had just been an unforeseen side effect.

"Halcyon would not have knowingly done this." I put my hand over Amber's arm, and felt his thick muscles tighten beneath my grip. "It makes them vulnerable to those like me. They call us *Damanôen*, demon living, because we can sense them. In fact, it was their past practice to kill all those like me."

I felt Amber's energy flare anew beneath my restraining grip. "Halcyon's trying to save me, Amber, not kill me. One of the reasons why he wishes to publicly claim me as his mate."

"To give you his protection," Amber said in a hard, grating voice.

I nodded. "And as a diversion. We *want* people to think that Halcyon infected me because of my intimacy with him as his mate."

"Why?"

"To hide the real reason why I have become demon living."

"And what is the real reason?" he asked.

"I cannot tell you, ever. That is the real secret we are protecting. I'm sorry, Amber."

Those feral yellow eyes stared down at me. "If the cost of it is your life, then it is knowledge I can live forever without."

I squeezed his arm in gratitude.

"That's the reason why you wished to rid yourself of the babe," Amber said in sudden understanding.

"Yes. Even though the child could be yours, I feared how this change in me would affect it."

"It is not mine, Mona Lisa."

Amber's words startled me with their surety. "You sound as if you know this for certain."

"I do," Amber said. "Who have you shared your body with since this new life has sparked in you?"

Actually, I had to stop and think about it a moment. To rerun the past few days in my mind. "Just Dante."

"*Only* Dante. Since that first time you lay with him," Amber said.

"Why do you sound so sure about that?"

"We are the children of the moon. Beings tied close with nature and its rhythms. A Monère woman knows whose seed has taken root in her body. And she will instinctively desire only that man while his child grows in her."

"Oh." There was still so much I did not know about who and what I was. But with that explanation, my behavior of the past few days became clearer now. Why I had just slept in Amber's arms and then Dontaine's. How I had lain with them without making love with them, without desiring to do so, and why they had not pressed themselves on me. I realized the full significance now of that look in Dante's eyes when I had taken him into my body that last time of my own free will, of my own instinctive desire. He had known then, for sure. *Everyone* had known who the father of my child was all this time. Even me, deep inside.

Amber turned to Halcyon. Asked him, "What can we do to protect her?"

"Just be near her" was Halcyon's answer. "And be willing to donate your blood should she need it. The demon part of her lies dormant until it is triggered by the presence of another demon. Then bloodlust, an almost overwhelming hunger at first, rises up within her. She will be able to control it more as time passes. In the beginning, however, it will be more prudent to simply slake her thirst instead of trying to fight it. A small drink of blood will regain her much of her control."

"She is in your presence now and has not evidenced the bloodlust you speak of," Amber observed.

"Because I have linked us mentally, giving her some of my control. I wished to reach the privacy of my quarters before I unleashed it."

"You can do so now," Amber said. "I will gladly give her my blood."

"That is my role," Dontaine said, stepping up to my side. "She asked us to come with her here so that she can explain this to you and drink from me." He bent down to me, tilting his neck to the side. And with an abruptness that was like a curtain tearing away, Halcyon's control was removed.

Need crashed over me in a sudden deluge, and hunger, thirst, flared up inside me. My teeth morphed into sharp, piercing fangs and plunged into the white neck offered up before me. I drank him down mindlessly, reveling in the rich, piquant lifeblood flowing into me, gulping it down greedily at first, then more savoringly. Such bountiful flavor. Such abundant life. The taste was incomparable, and the need it filled beyond description. Dontaine moaned against me, clutching me to him, and I pressed my body against him willingly like a cat rolling sensually in catnip.

Unthinking need receded, and awareness returned. *Enough*, I thought, and felt the blood slow and thicken beneath my tongue. Reluctantly, I pulled out of that rich vein I had so easily tapped, so easily piercing that soft, tender flesh.

Perhaps it was because I was more familiar with it now that the thought of drinking blood no longer repulsed me. I hadn't fought it this time, and control and thought had returned more quickly, easily.

I stepped back from Dontaine and looked up at Amber, let him see my fangs, the blood coating them. Another deliberate thought, and I shrank them down, felt them become normal teeth once more.

There was shock in Amber's eyes, and I reacted without thought to it.

"No, don't turn away from me," Amber said, pulling my stiff body back against his much larger one. "It was just the surprise of seeing it. Even after you had told me, it's not the same as *seeing* it for the very first time."

"Let me go, Amber," I said, my voice low, hard, closed down.

"Never." His arms tightened around me. "Don't run away from me."

"I repulse you."

"No! It was just . . . different, new. Forgive me."

Another pair of arms came around us, glowing with soft light. Dontaine's blond hair brushed feather-soft across my face as he drew up against me.

"That was wonderful," he murmured in a thick, dreamy voice, nuzzling behind my ear, positioning his neck a whisper away from my mouth. "Drink from me some more."

The unfeigned eager press of his body against mine was

a soothing balm healing the cracks of my uncertainty. Pulling an unwilling smile from me.

"You sound like a cat that has just lapped down cream, instead of being the one who was drunk down," I observed.

"What you made me feel was far better than any cream could ever taste." Dontaine rubbed his face and body against me with a soft, sensuous purr. "Sweet blessed moon. That was almost as good as being inside you."

"You felt pleasure?" I asked.

"Beyond your imagining."

"Did it hurt?"

He drew back just enough so I could see his face. "Only when you first bit me. Then it disappeared and all I felt was this amazing pleasure rolling over me, filling me."

"It will get even better when she gains more finesse," Halcyon promised.

A delicious shudder ran through Dontaine's body. "I can't wait." And the way he said it brought another smile to my lips.

I patted Amber's hand, letting him know that I was all right. "It's okay," I said softly. "It's new to everybody. We're all learning how this works."

He let his arms fall away. Instead of stepping away from him, I turned and wrapped my arms around Amber, burying my face against that broad chest that made me feel so safe. He was my anchor in this world, and I clung to him as such.

He pressed a kiss to the top of my head, then set me from him, crouching down so that we were face-to-face. "I would have you take blood from me next time. It would please me . . . as Dontaine is making so damn obvious," he said with a slight smile.

"Next time," I promised, feeling my world settle once more back onto its axis.

When all was tranquil once more, Halcyon presented me with a beautifully carved, small wooden box, inlaid with ivory and gold. "I brought you here not only to feed, but to give you this," he said, putting it into my hands.

It was a gift from my mate.

"Oh, Halcyon." I lifted stricken eyes to his. "I didn't think to get you anything."

"You have given me the gift of yourself. All else is immaterial. Do not distress yourself. It is truly not so much a gift as my claim on you for others to see. Open it."

I did and gasped. Inside was an exquisite cameo necklace with Halcyon's likeness. It was framed around the rim by scroll-like writing. At the bottom was engraved the image of a fierce dragon. But the most striking part of it was the bright, glittery metal of the necklace itself, something that would catch every Monère's eye.

"The chain is silver," I said.

"Yes, I had it made thus in your honor. For the only Monère Queen to whom silver is not a weakness but a strength."

The touch of silver against a Monère's skin usually drained them of their power, made them only human strong. I was not only not weakened by it, but seemed to have an affinity for it, able to call any weapon made out of silver easily to my hand.

"Even the demons know this about you," Halcyon said.

"What does this say?" I asked, tracing a finger over the characters carved around his likeness.

"The character on the left means *royal*, the one on your right that you are touching means *consort*. The dragon denotes my lineage and is the crest of our family line." His dark chocolate eyes met mine. "Will you wear this?"

The picture of him, the words "royal consort," and the dragon crest all denoted his claim and protection over me. But the silver it was set upon was a tribute to me, to my individual strength. It was a melding of us both, thoughtfully done.

"Of course." My fingers fumbled a little as I reached behind, unfastening the silver cross I wore. It had been the only thing found on me as an infant. Something left by my birth mother, I had thought, and had been my most cherished possession, something I wore always. Even after I found out it had been Sonia, the midwife, who had given it to me, who had loved me as my mother had not, I had still worn it as a familiar comfort. I took it off now, a symbol of my past, and fastened Halcyon's cameo in its place.

I smoothed my hand over the cameo, which I left prominently displayed, not hidden under my dress as my other necklace had been. Outside where everyone could see it and know who I was—the High Prince of Hell's chosen consort.

"You honor me, *ena*." Halcyon breathed the last word out like a soft caress. I knew now that it meant *wife*. And flushed a little at the meaning of it, the acceptance of it. His light kiss was as gentle and tender as the endearment he had whispered.

"Come," he said, placing my hand once more on his arm. "Let us go attend to Council affairs."

TWENTY-THREE

THE FIRST ITEM of business we attended to, as it turned out, was the public presentation of me before the other Council members. I entered the large domed chamber on Halcyon's arm, and all eyes immediately zoomed in on the cameo necklace I wore as he led me up the tiered steps to my seat. A small collective stirring occurred when he sat, not in his usual place across the room, but in the armchair next to mine. A not-so-subtle political power statement, clearly allying himself with me.

There were over thirty Council members present, filling the chamber almost to capacity. A dozen new Queens numbered among them, and I wondered at the turnout. Wondered if it was because of me. Whether the rumors of the new Mixed Blood Queen and her recent Court antics had drawn them here. Or if it was because of another event unbeknownst to me. The way they were all looking at me, I was laying bet on the former.

The new Queens' eyes were not all outright hostile like

Mona Teresa's was. I'd mentally dubbed Mona Teresa the Fire Queen for her flame-colored hair and spiteful nature. *Nasty* would best describe her and most of the Queens I'd met to date, for that matter, all except Mona Carlisse, the only Queen I counted as a friend. Sadly, she was not present.

I was willing to reserve judgment on the other Queens arrayed here. And by the cool reserve in their eyes, they seemed inclined to do the same with me. There were more healers, denoted by their maroon garments, filling out the assemblage, along with a couple more white-robed ladies. All women but for three men: Halcyon, Amber, and Lord Thorane. Amber was new, granted a seat on the Council by his new status as Warrior Lord, one of only two that existed. Lord Thorane, the Council speaker, was the other. Had Gryphon still been alive, he would have sat here among us also.

It was an open session, meaning that guards and other spectators stood back along the walls, watching the proceedings. The Council members were arrayed in rings around a central clearing, the area where the petitioners stood and presented their cases.

Lord Thorane opened the session, and sure enough, I was the first matter of business called. It was actually Halcyon's name that was pronounced, but since I was the matter he was presenting before everyone, he drew me to my feet and walked me down the steps into the center.

Of everyone present, it was the Queen Mother who dominated over us all. Not just in status but in palpable strength. Hers was a presence I had always felt. But for some reason, I felt her even sharper now. Her power and age tasted acute to my senses, not at all mellow like you would imagine it might be from someone as advanced in years as she was. Unlike everyone else present, the Queen Mother was obviously old. Wrinkles marred her face, testament to the passage of time and her enduring presence through it.

Halcyon bowed and I curtsied before her. Not as graceful as he, but then again, I hadn't had over six hundred years to perfect the gesture like he had.

"Queen Mother. Honored Queens. Ladies and gentlemen of the Court," Halcyon said, addressing the others. "It gives me great pleasure to present my chosen mate before you, my royal consort, Queen Mona Lisa."

Nothing more than that. They were simple words stirring a complex reaction that rippled around the room. The distress caused by the announcement was obvious, but no one dared voice anything out loud in front of the High Prince of Hell. Couldn't blame them. Never knew when you might suddenly find yourself in his realm.

The Queen Mother acknowledged his announcement. "Prince Halcyon, this Monère High Court is pleased for you and your mate, Queen Mona Lisa, High Lady of Hell." I started a little at that unexpected title. "We wish you joy and happiness," she said, bestowing the words like a blessing. I bowed my head, accepting it as such, touched by it. Happiness and joy. They were two things that seemed so ephemeral in my life, like precious liquid I could only cup in my hand for a few brief moments before it trickled through my fingers, lost.

"Thank you, Queen Mother, members of the Council." I inclined my head to the others. *No curtseying, you are above them now in rank,* Halcyon had told me. Taking my hand, Halcyon led us off the floor, back to our seats.

When the next order of business came up—my petition to have the west Mississippi portion of my land set up as a separate and independent territory, with Warrior Lord Amber recognized as the official ruler there—it passed with not one single opposition.

Halcyon's amusement whispered in my mind. *Why are you so surprised?*

I didn't expect it to be that easy. Not even Mona Teresa opposed it. I think I like being your mate. Everyone is being much nicer to me.

Halcyon's mental laughter rolled richly through my mind. *And so they should. But it is in their own interests to agree with your proposal. It is only your land being offered up, not theirs. They do not have to give up any of their own territory. Why should they not agree? Likewise, they would see separating a powerful Warrior Lord from your side as to their benefit.*

A part of me was saddened by the accuracy of Halcyon's words. My intent had been to elevate Amber, to align him beside me. But in doing so, I *had* separated him from me. Put physical distance between us.

Do not be so sad, Hell-cat, Halcyon murmured as he tasted the melancholy lacing my thoughts. *Amber knows and appreciates what you have done for him. You have not lost him any more than you have lost me simply because I cannot walk beside you every day or be with you every night. You are our home. We shall always return to you.*

His words and the honest emotions behind them—feelings that he could not hide from me when we were linked this way—comforted me. I was blessed despite myself.

High Court adjourned several hours later and the real festivities began. Tents were erected on the sprawling lawn, and trade counselors were inundated with service people seeking new positions in other courts. Men, women, a few families, warriors, and tradesmen. The greatest number at this fair, however, was the assemblage of young boys. Eighteen-year-old virgins were gathered like a flock of colorful peacocks at the largest central tent, arrayed in their best finery with hair neatly combed, nails buffed, and shoes polished. They looked like high school boys going out on their prom night. Only the dates they took home tonight would be the Queens who had selected them. And it would not be just a kiss that was taken but their virginity.

"My goodness, why are there so many boys here?" I felt their eager attention hone in on me, a Queen, as I walked by on Halcyon's arm, the Demon Prince on one side of me, Amber, my giant Warrior Lord, on the other.

"It is the first gathering after winter solstice," Amber explained. "Most of the boys who are of age seek their Virgin Claiming during this first session of the new year. It's considered good luck to enter your manhood during this time. Summer solstice is another popular time. I see my two boys near the center there."

"My two are at the end," I said softly, finding them easily in the crowd. Quentin and Dante. Their clothes were less gaudily bright than the others. They were dressed in simple attire that enhanced their more developed physiques.

They stood out in other ways. They were older, for one, a striking and obvious difference. The other boys stood on the cusp of manhood, eager and young. Quentin and Dante had taken the step over that line already, denoted by their calm assurance, their more noticeable reserve. Men in maturity of mind and spirit. No longer boys.

They were also far more beautiful in my eyes. The simplicity of their clothes drew attention to the lean, masculine beauty of their faces, to the greater breadth of their shoulders, their more muscular arms and chests. And any Queen who had witnessed the fight between Oswald and Dante knew firsthand what a superb warrior Dante was, so different from the other young lads here. His wounds had been healed by Hannah, probably as soon as she'd been able to lay hands on him, and he seemed none the worse for wear from his earlier challenge.

Quentin served as a bridge, standing between his brother

and the other virgin boys. Dante stood at the end, positioned halfway between that tent and the next one, which housed older warriors seeking positions, a more desperate lot. They were quieter, more somber men, less than a handful. It was in this group that Dante technically belonged, because he was not a virgin. Not anymore. Yet neither did he really belong with the older men.

Dante's apartness seemed to have intrigued the Queens. He had not one but five of them looking him over, perusing him with interest. But even surrounded by Queens, his gaze unerringly found mine.

Instead of looking ecstatic as he should have been at so much interest, he looked . . . desolate. He answered their questions politely and allowed them to look him over like a stud they were considering buying. He didn't preen as the other young lads did, he simply endured it, tolerating it with a dispassion that bordered on frank disinterest.

"I will leave you to attend to your matters here," Halcyon murmured. "There are matters I wish to discuss with the other Council members before the next meeting." It was a considerate gesture on his part. He had made public his claim on me, and now was allowing us separate time to each attend to our own affairs. Maybe he even thought I wished to choose one of the boys for myself and didn't wish me to feel constrained by his presence. Drawing my hand up, he kissed the back of it. Then he was gone, gracefully winding his way through the crowd, leaving me in Amber's care.

"Dante and Quentin seem to be quite popular," I observed, eyeing the two Queens who were circling Quentin; he had his admirers as well. "I can understand Quentin, but why the interest in Dante when he is no longer a virgin?"

"But who did he lose his virginity to?" Amber asked. "You. Very few unclaimed males have that distinction. And with his lightly tanned skin, they cannot help but wonder if he has acquired some of your gifts, such as your rare gift of walking under the sun without burning. Can he do that now?"

"I don't know," I answered in a muted voice. "My best guess is probably not. Dontaine gained nothing from lying with me. My gifts don't seem to transfer so easily anymore." Not since I had taken the demon essence into me. Perhaps it was better that way. It would have been a disaster if I had been able to pass the demon taint as easily as I had passed on my other abilities before.

A Queen, one of the new ones I didn't know, stroked a bold hand down Dante's backside. Seeing him being fondled ignited a maelstrom of unpleasant emotion within me. She was either daring or stupid. Or simply arrogant, as all Queens naturally seemed to be, sure that her touch would be welcomed. With Dante, none of the other Queens had dared that liberal stroking and caressing that the other boys not only encouraged but preened beneath. There was a dangerous stillness to Dante's reserve that the other Queens had sensed and respected. All but this one.

Dante's gaze broke away from me to focus on that other Queen, the one who had dared touch him. His expression, one that I could not see, made her hand fall away. Though she didn't back up or do anything so obvious, her arrogant, inspecting saunter around him increased the distance between them.

His attention drifted away from her like an annoying gnat already forgotten and returned to me. The other Queens saw where his eyes wandered, and gazed speculatively at me.

Hope had flared in Dante's eyes at the sight of me. Hope that he had quickly hidden. But I had sensed it still.

Don't make me go, those eyes cried. *Keep me.* No words spoken aloud or heard in the mind. Just that look. Those burning embers of hope.

Something twisted painfully inside of me.

I can't . . . I can't keep you. You're too dangerous. You killed everyone I ever loved before.

Reading the answer in my eyes, he gazed at me like a thirsty man looks at a fountain of water he knows he will never drink from again. Desolation filled the pale blue depths, extinguishing that last wild hope. And with it gone, it was as if a flame had been snuffed out, leaving them cold, dead, and empty. His eyes dropped away from mine.

"You should come away," Amber urged, a silent witness to our byplay.

I almost did, even started to turn away, but stopped when I caught sight of another Queen. This one I knew and hated bitterly. Mona Teresa. Her flame-colored hair glinted beneath the moonlight as she sauntered her way down the line of virgin boys, her six guards following behind her. The guard closest to her I recognized as the man who had raped Tersa on his Queen's order. Guilt and hatred burned in me at the sight of him.

With a careless caress here, an intimate handling there, Mona Teresa sampled the virgin lads. The boys quivered beneath her touch, just like the horseflesh she casually treated them like. Disappointment was keen in their eyes as she passed them all by, to stop and linger before Quentin, drinking in his perfect male beauty. With a smirk aimed my way, she continued on down the line to Dante, whose beauty was more harsh like a natural gemstone. Less refined, more primitive. Knowledge was in her eyes, and purpose.

"She knows," Amber murmured, oddly echoing my thoughts. "She knows his history. And yours."

What he was really saying was: *She knows he killed you before, and wants him because of that.* Gossip about his past and mine must have spread like wildfire after the challenge and his unexpected win. If news of my pregnancy had been whispered of as well, Dante would become a hotly desired acquisition for any Queen. Especially one who hated me.

"I've already offered for him, Mona Teresa," said the Queen circling Dante.

"And has he accepted it, Mona Annabella?" Mona Teresa asked with a mocking smile.

"He has not given his answer yet to any of us," Mona Annabella returned, her dark eyes flashing with spite. "You're welcome to tender your offer and see how you fare."

I was a little shocked to hear he had had offers. More than one. What was he waiting for?

"Come away," Amber urged again, but I could not. I had to watch. Had to know to whom he would go.

Mona Teresa tilted her head. "Join my service, Dante, and I will promise you ten years in my bed."

She made it sound like a generous offer, making me wonder how long virgin boys usually lasted in a Queen's bed before she tired of them and moved on to new untried flesh.

"I will consider it," Dante said in a voice that held no eagerness, no joy. No word of thanks.

The other Queens tittered and Mona Teresa's eyes flashed. But her voice stayed slitheringly calm, like a snake just before it pumped venom into its prey. "Fifteen years in my bed if you accept my offer now."

He looked at her with no change in expression, and repeated his words from before. "I will consider it."

Denial of her offer by his very lack of acceptance.

If he saw Mona Teresa's dark flush of anger, it concerned him not. All caring seemed to have left him.

"How dare you!" Mona Teresa hissed, fury lacing her words. Lunging at him, she raked her nails down the side of his face.

The apathy left Dante. His features hardened, and his

eyes flashed to dangerous silver. Amber and I were both
moving forward together as she lunged at Dante again.

A normal young Monère male would have fallen back
beneath a Queen's attack, nothing more than that. Dante
was not a typical Monère guy. He had been raised among
the humans. He had lived countless lifetimes. And in another time, he had been a warlord of such feared renown
that songs had been sung about him and legends told.

Dante didn't step back or cower under Mona Teresa's
attack. He stood there, and with a simple block of his arm,
he swept aside her clawed hands with insulting ease.

The other boys watching gasped as if he had done the
unthinkable. And perhaps he had, I don't know. Maybe
there was some stupid law saying that you couldn't defend
yourself against a Queen.

Mona Teresa's six guards drew their swords and advanced with lethal intent on Dante.

"Stay here," Amber said urgently, grabbing my arm and
dragging me to a halt. "For his sake. And for yours."

*Oh yeah, I'm pregnant, carrying his child . . . a pre-
cious life that he believes to be his chance at breaking the
curse.* It stopped me as nothing else could have. Satisfied
that I was staying put, Amber left me and rushed to
Dante's aid.

I wasn't used to that. Staying back and being safe when
my men were in danger. I cursed myself now for not bringing Tomas, Aquila, and Dontaine along. I had thought to
spare Dante's pride and my own raw nerves.

"Kill him!" Mona Teresa ordered her men. They rushed
him and everyone scattered back away from them, all but
Quentin. He stayed at his brother's side. A noble gesture, I
thought, but a useless one. Both of them were unarmed.

"Stop," I yelled, fighting the only way left to me—with
words. "You attacked him, Mona Teresa. He merely de-
fended himself."

"He dared raise his hand against me. Everyone here is witness to that," Mona Teresa said, almost spitting with outrage. "It is my right to demand his head for that. Kill him! I want him dead."

"No! He is still mine, under my protection." But my words did nothing as mere words often did. Only might mattered here.

Amber dived into the melee, his sword drawn, and three of Mona Teresa's men turned to meet him. The sound of clashing metal filled the air. And it was not just the sound of sword striking against sword, but sword scraping against Dante and Quentin's bracelet guards. It puzzled the warriors who attacked them for a moment because the metal bands were hidden beneath their shirts. A few block and strikes later, though, the cut cloth gaped open, revealing the wide bracelets hugging Dante's and Quentin's wrists.

The two brothers fought one guard apiece. They dodged and twisted lightly on their feet, and the swords either slashed empty air or came up against those deflecting wrist guards. It would have been a mesmerizing thing to see, almost like a graceful, twisting ballet, were it not so deadly in intent, and so unmatched. One sword against six, with Dante and Quentin fighting without weapons. But that I could do something about.

Walking closer to the crowd, I scanned the gathering onlookers, searching specifically for other Queens and their guards. With my strong affinity for silver, I could call any silver dagger to my hand. I could do the same with a sword, though not as easily since swords were rarely silver. No need to be when the main purpose was to cut off your opponent's head with them—simple steel did that easily enough. For nonsilver weapons, I usually had to familiarize myself first with the taste and smell of them. Amber's blade had smelled like ancient battle and had tasted like spilled blood. The remembered scent and flavor of it rushed back into my mind, and I focused on two older, more powerful guards, reasoning that their swords would be most like Amber's.

My palms stretched out, my moles tingled and pulsed. Nothing.

A second throbbing pulse with a deeper, pulling power, and yes! The two swords slid from their scabbards and flew into my hands, hilt-first.

What do you know? It worked.

"Dante! Quentin!" I called, and tossed the swords to them when they turned their faces to me. They leaped, caught the weapons in the air, and landed lightly, spinning back to face their opponents.

Now they were evenly matched, three swords against six. Okay, actually overmatched, with the advantage ours now. But I wasn't too concerned about being fair, not when Mona Teresa hadn't sweated it. And talking about that redheaded bitch. She'd drawn her dagger and looked as if she was considering hurling it into Dante's back, a coward's blow.

Eyes narrowed, I extended my hand again. Her dagger— it was silver, wasn't that nice?—flew to me like a bird, coming to rest neatly in my palm.

I tsked. "Nuh-uh-uh. No backstabbing allowed."

"You unholy mongrel bitch." Drawing her other dagger, nonsilver, she came at me quickly. I barely had time to think—*Should I run?*—before she was on me. Okay. I had time to think about it, and do it. But, goddamn it, I didn't *want* to run from her. What if I ran and she turned back and buried her blade in one of my men's backs like the treacherous bitch she was? And she might. Because she knew, as I did, by Dante's and Quentin's deft handling of their swords, that her men were outclassed. I, on the other hand, could fight her with impunity by our laws, Queen against Queen. I could even kill her if I needed to, though that was not my intent. I'd caused enough uproar as it was at High Court already. No need to add another Queen's death to the mess, especially coming so quickly on top of the other one I'd been involved in. Two of them, I think, would be stretching even the Council's tolerance, Halcyon's new High Lady of Hell or not. To be on the safe side, I tossed away the silver dagger I'd snatched from Mona Teresa and faced her unarmed. My blade might accidentally-on-purpose bury itself in her black, cowardly heart if I faced her with a tempting weapon in my hand.

She slashed at me quick, like a serpent striking. I twisted to the side and grabbed her hand as it came flying by.

"Mona Lisa, no!" Amber cried, catching sight of us. He quickly cut down the two remaining men he fought—the third one he had already dispatched—and ran toward us, dropping his sword, coming at us unarmed.

I was distracted by the sight, concerned with Amber coming between us, two Queens. Because even though he was a Warrior Lord, our supposed equal, he still was not really equal in the Council's eyes. If anything happened to Mona Teresa, Amber would be blamed and punished. Maybe even killed.

I froze, my attention drawn away from my opponent, which is never a smart thing to do. She kneed me in the stomach. It was a blow I could have easily blocked had I been paying attention, but I wasn't. It caught me with full, stunning force, and I felt something delicate, something fragile, tear inside of me. Then I felt pain. Stunning, incapacitating pain as I crumpled to the ground.

"*Noooo!*" someone roared. A man's voice—Dante's—but sounding as I'd never heard him before. Amber reached us and pulled Mona Teresa off me, unarmed her. He held her a safe distance away from me, letting her kick and punch and claw at him as he turned his eyes to me. "Mona Lisa."

Then Dante was there. If his voice had sounded frightening, the look on his face was even more so.

"Get that bitch away from her," he told Amber in a voice so nakedly vicious that I shivered. "Quentin, find Mother. Bring her quickly."

His hands when they touched me, though, were gentle. So gentle they brought tears to my eyes. A horrible fear gripped me as I smelled blood and felt wetness pool beneath me, flowing out between my legs.

"Oh God, Dante. Our baby . . . I'm so sorry." Wet tears stung my eyes, streaming out almost as quickly as the blood gushing from my womb. I writhed painfully in his arms as a terrible cramp seized me, hardening my belly.

"Easy, *dulcaeta*," he soothed. His eyes, turned that ferocious, glittering silver, left mine and speared someone in the crowd. "Go find a healer," he growled, and the man quickly ran to do his bidding. When the spasm passed, he eased me gently onto his lap and laid his hands over mine, two sets of hands protectively covering my belly.

"Easy, sweetheart," he murmured. "Don't cry. It's okay."

But it wasn't okay. And I couldn't stop crying, couldn't stop cramping. I cried and bled as he rocked me, and felt his own tears splash down to mingle with mine.

"I'm sorry, so sorry," I whispered feverishly against him, over and over again, stopping only when another spasm gripped me.

Soft hands pushed our hands aside. I looked up, and through my pain, saw Hannah kneeling at our side, Quentin and Nolan standing behind her.

"Let me see, milady," Hannah said urgently. I stopped fighting her and she ripped open my dress at the waist and laid her healing hands quickly over my bared belly. I felt her seeking warmth sink down into my flesh, and like that, the pain, the cramping eased. The bleeding slowed.

"My baby?" I asked, voice trembling.

"I'm sorry," Hannah said in a bare whisper. "It's gone already. I could not save it."

Gone already. Her words echoed hollowly within me as she finished the healing. When it was complete, Dante gently eased out from beneath me, laid me back down. When he stood, I saw that he was drenched in my blood. In our baby's blood. He turned those fearsome eyes on Mona Teresa. She stood about thirty feet away where Amber had dragged her. The look in those silver eyes held the same awful expression I had seen once before in my dreams—that look of vengeance, of terrible retribution.

"You killed my unborn child." His words rang out loudly like a death knell. "I will take the lives of your men in return. Be grateful it is not your own life I will seek this retribution on. But I promise you this: If I am to remain cursed, I shall see to it that you share in it with me."

He turned toward her guards, and long hooking claws almost eight inches in length unfurled from his fingertips with a hiss of energy—twice as long as they had been when he had fought in the challenge against Oswald. He had been holding back, it seemed.

A few of Mona Teresa's guards had risen to their feet, helping their more severely injured comrades. The six warriors took one look at those claws, that maddened face, those silver gleaming eyes, and scrambled hastily for their swords. Some of them even grabbed it up in their hands before Dante reached them. He walked to them slowly, surely. In no seeming hurry to deliver the death he had pronounced upon them.

Two of them rushed at Dante, with sword and dagger in hand.

I said urgently to his father, "Give him your sword."

"He doesn't need it," Nolan said, watching his son.

Dante turned their blades away like a careless afterthought, deflecting the blows with his wrist guards. Then in a move so fast you weren't able to track it with your eyes, he sliced them open.

Splashing blood. Tearing cries.

Their intestines were still spilling out from their opened bellies when he sliced down again with those claws and took off their hands. Swords dropped down, daggers clattered to the ground with bleeding limbs still attached.

Turning his back on one eviscerated warrior, Dante concentrated his attention on the taller one, the guard who had raped Tersa. Another slice, aimed higher, and the man's head came flying off. A flash of light, a puff of dust, followed almost immediately by a second shower of light and ashes as Dante spun around and took off the first warrior's head, so that they were like two strobe lights going off in quick succession.

The coldness of his execution, his deadly accuracy with those claws, and the lethal consequences of them, struck pure terror in the remaining four men. They fled, or tried to.

"Stop," Dante commanded. His silver eyes were glowing now, and even standing where I was, distant from where they fought, I felt the power that flared out with that command. They froze, all four of them unable to move, unable to fight against that compulsion. And everyone watching him—Queens, powerful warriors—gasped in fear and realization at what he was able to do.

The four guards stood captured by his will as Dante walked to them. When he stood before them, he said, "You are free."

They moved. All four going in different directions, trying to escape him. Not one of them tried to attack him.

Dante moved even quicker. Nothing but a blur, then four more flashes of light. Ashes puffed over him, coating him gray, so that he looked like a ghostly specter. A horrifying creature drawn from your darkest nightmare.

For a long moment there was nothing but awful silence.

Then the silence was torn apart as Dante threw back his head and screamed. A terrible roar of grief and heartbreak howled up to the heavens. To the distant moon.

One loud, trembling moment . . . then he was gone. Vanished before our eyes.

EPILOGUE

KNOWLEDGE IS A funny thing. I'd always reacted badly to loss, shutting myself down, going into a shocklike withdrawal, like when Gryphon, the first man I ever loved, had left me for another Queen. Then again when he died, was killed by her. It was a lesson I had learned early in life. Don't love things, don't grow attached. Because it hurts too much when you lose them.

I'd thought that my extreme reaction was because I had been abandoned as a newborn, then cancer had taken Helen, my adopted mother, from me when I was six, and I had been sent to live in a series of foster homes. But I knew now that the foundation had been laid long before in another lifetime, by another man. A man whose baby I had carried for a brief time. I mourned that loss, that little spark of life. A surprise. Or perhaps not so surprising. When I finally wanted something, that was when it was usually taken from me.

Maybe it was knowing why I reacted so violently to loss that bolstered that most vulnerable part of me—my psyche.

I did not fall into a numbing decline as my men feared I would. I just simply grieved, mourning not only the loss of the baby, but the loss of the babe's father also.

Quentin was accepted by a young Queen, Mona Maretta. A brave acquisition. Or perhaps bravery had nothing to do with it. Maybe she had simply coveted his perfect male beauty.

Dante had disappeared. Gone, I thought, but not quite as gone as everyone might have wished. When I returned home the next day, Lord Thorane called me with the news that Dante had slaughtered all of Mona Teresa's warriors. Not just the six that had accompanied her to High Court, but the other twenty-four men that had remained behind in her territory. Dante had appeared there the next day like a wrathful god, taking his vengeance out on the rest of her men. Just the warriors this time, sparing the housestaff, showing more mercy than they realized. None of her guards, though, were left alive. He'd cut them down, one by one, eviscerating them, breaking their legs or chopping them off so they could not run away. Then he had proceeded to calmly tear them apart, limb by bloody limb, or had sliced them to pieces until they had begged to die. In the end, all that remained was blood and ashes, scattered empty clothes, and echoing cries.

Upon returning home, seeing the terrible carnage, and hearing her housestaff's frightful tales, Mona Teresa had flown immediately back to High Court, seeking their protection from "the madman," as she called Dante. Her frenzied cry for justice, however, fell on flat ears. We were Monère, after all. Children of the moon. Creatures of supernatural power. If you were not strong enough to survive, then you did not deserve to—that was the rule under which we all existed. All but the Queens, that is. Only the precious Ladies of Light were afforded greater protection by the Court. Protection, yes, but not retribution.

Mona Teresa, by her actions, however unknowing they

had been—and that was suspect—had caused the loss of Dante's unborn child and injured another Queen. A Queen who was the High Prince of Hell's chosen and acknowledged mate. She was lucky, she was told, that only Dante had sought reprisal.

Oddly enough, Dante's actions, reminiscent though they were of the slaughter of my own people long ago, didn't frighten me. Maybe it was the anguish in his eyes when I was losing the baby. The protective gentleness with which he had cradled me in his lap and called me beloved. Whatever he had done to me in the past, the curse I had laid upon him and his line was as equally awful. They canceled each other out; that was my hope, at least. And life, each life was different. I had to believe that. We'd messed this one up a little, but not irrevocably. Not yet. We still had a second chance to right the wrongs of the past. Or at least not repeat them.

Was the curse lifted from Dante? I don't know. Had that life we created together, however brief, been enough to break it? If so, that would mean that when Dante died this time, he would not return again. And I found that thought oddly painful.

Nolan and Hannah flew back home with me, having decided to stay in my service.

Why, you might ask, as I did?

"Because of the way he looked at you. And the way you looked at him. He will return to you," Hannah said. And their presence was a double guarantee of that. As his mother put it, "With us here, where else does he have to go?"

Maybe I'd gone a bit crazy, because the thought of him coming back didn't frighten me the way it should have.

My mind said one thing, but my heart said another. And what my heart said was, *Yes, come back to me. Come back soon.*

ABOUT THE AUTHOR

A family practice physician and Vassar graduate, Sunny was finally pushed into picking up her pen by the success of the rest of her family. Much to her amazement, she found that, by golly, she actually *could* write a book. And that it was much more fun than being a doctor. As an award-winning author, Sunny has been featured on *Geraldo at Large* and *CNBC*. When she is not busy reading and writing, Sunny is editing the works of her husband, literary novelist Da Chen, and being a happy stage mom for her two talented kids.

Mona Lisa Darkening, the fourth book in her acclaimed Monère series, will be released in January 2009. For excerpts, contests, and other news, please visit www.sunnyauthor.com.

TURN THE PAGE FOR A PREVIEW OF THE NEXT
NOVEL OF THE MONÈRE
BY SUNNY

MONA LISA DARKENING

COMING SOON FROM BERKLEY BOOKS!

IT WAS THE first day of spring. It was also the time to Bask, to draw down the silver rays of the moon and let its renewing light seep into us. *Us* being the Monère, the children of the moon—what I was, what my people were. Creatures descended from another planet. We were blessed with supernatural speed, strength, and beauty. As a human and Monère Mixed Blood, the first ever to be a Monère Queen, I had the first two. Missed out on the last one, though. Oh well. Better to be fast and strong, in my opinion, than beautiful. And able to Bask, to draw down our home planet's renewing light and energy and share it with my people. Oh yeah, that gift was perhaps the most crucial of all, and the one I was most thankful for. Because without that renewing light, we lived only a hundred years, a human's lifespan, instead of the three hundred years our lunar birthright gifted us with.

If you asked my people, I think they'd take the ability to Bask over their Queen being a raving beauty any day. Or rather night. As a people descended from the moon, we were children of darkness. When the sun set, that was when our day began. Then again, maybe you shouldn't ask my people, because even though my looks were plain—not hideous, but definitely not beauty queen material either—they treated me as if I *were* a raving beauty. The men, at least. The men who were my lovers.

Under the moonlit shadows of the darkened night, I glanced at the two of them by my side. Amber, my rugged Warrior Lord, who loomed a head taller than other men. Whose great strength lay not just in the heavy muscles roping his massive body, but in the love and devotion gleaming from his dark blue eyes. That—the pull of emotions in him—weakened me more than his obvious and splendid body strength. I physically swayed toward him before I caught myself. Not yet, I thought, but soon . . . soon.

Beside him stood Dontaine, my master at arms, my other lover. Blond, fair of face and body, a sumptuous feast to the eyes. Whereas Amber looked like a harsh god of war, Dontaine was like a Greek statue—a Greek god. A living Adonis with sun-kissed hair, splendid green eyes, and a body any woman would want to worship with her hands, her tongue, her mouth . . . any part of her body. He, too, looked at me with love, though I don't know why. Out of all my lovers, he was the one I rejected the most. The one I used the most. Used literally for blood.

It was an odd night, a special night—the vernal equinox. *Aequus Nox*, which meant *equal night*—when day and night were of equal length, and the sun crossed not only the Earth's equator, but the celestial equator as well. Even more special, it was one of the rare times when the full moon coincided with the first day of spring, the season of renewal. Perhaps that was what was causing this strange restlessness within me—a skittishness, a feeling of something not quite right. Spring fever likely.

My people were gathered around me, and I recognized

more of their faces now, recalled their names. Intricate, interweaving strings bound us all together, and I was slowly learning the many loops and circles. I'd worried over that, my lack of connection to my people, over four hundred of them. But like many things in life, names and familiarity with the people behind the names came slowly with time, and hopefully—thankfully—I would have plenty of that. Time.

I had survived to see another full moon emerge in its brilliant, round glory. Quite an achievement, tainted as I was with demon darkness. If the whims of fate had swung another way, I would have been dead by now, killed by Prince Halcyon, the ruler of the demon dead realm. Instead I was his lady, his mate—the High Lady of Hell.

And where was my Demon Prince? Presiding over his people in that other distant realm, Hell, while I presided over mine here in the living realm. I was missing the festivities of *Aequus Nox*, one of the big demon holidays. At least that was how it sounded to me when Halcyon had explained it. Were it not the full moon, the time when we Basked, I would be down there with Halcyon, mixing and mingling and being introduced to his people. A daunting thought because his people had fangs and drank blood—my blood if they had the chance. But then, so did I. Have fangs and drink blood, that is.

I was a human and Monère Mixed Blood Queen with demon dead essence residing in my living being. Quite a tongue twister and mind bender. The poetic term for my condition was *Damanôen*, demon living. A rare state of being because most of my kind had been slaughtered as soon as they were made, usually by the demons those very unwise Monères had blood raped because, alas, that was what sparked our living dead state. Why would a Monère do that, you might ask—drink a demon's blood? Because it gained them a demon's strength, which was even greater than a Full Blood Monère's. But, shhh, don't tell anyone that, it's a secret. A secret that demons would—and have—killed to protect.

The downside, and there always was one, was the physical manifestations that occurred along with that stolen power. It was pretty hard to hide what you had done—what you had *become*—when you started sprouting fangs. Now don't get me wrong. Fangs are no stranger to the Monère. Lots of us had them. But only in our animal-shifted forms. Not in our human forms. Of course, my fang-flashing happened only when the niggling presence of another demon triggered the demon essence in me. Then *wham!* It was like turning into the Incredible Hulk. Only instead of becoming green and muscle-bound and horrendously ugly, my teeth morphed into fangs, my nails sharpened into dagger points, and I had the uncontrollable urge to suck down blood, any which way, any damn how. Pretty hard to keep hidden a powerful urge that almost took you completely over until you satisfied that hunger with a sip or two of blood. By the time you gained back your control, the gig was pretty much up.

Halcyon had come up with an even better idea. Don't try to hide it. Simply make them think it had occurred for another reason, hence my official recognition as Halcyon's mate. When I finally manifested my demon traits in front of Monère witnesses (those that tattled), which was bound to occur someday soon, they would think that I was becoming what I was becoming because I'd been contaminated by my demon lover through sex. Sex, after all, was how Monère usually shared and acquired gifts and power. And since such a relationship had never occurred before, a demon taking a Monère mate, all would blame it on that. And perhaps on the fact that I'd been down to Hell a time or two.

The real cause of this all, though, was the former Queen of the Louisiana territory, Mona Louisa. She'd swallowed down Halcyon's blood, and I in turn had sucked her light and demon-tainted essence into me. That was another secret, what I could do, Mortal Draining. It made me feel guilty that the blame would be placed on the wrong person, on Halcyon instead of me and that former bitch Queen that no longer existed, except sometimes in me. Mona Louisa was dead but not entirely gone. I felt her occasionally in my dreams.

As a vulture in her other form, she'd been able to fly, and sometimes I dreamed of soaring through the sky, of smelling death and rotting, decaying flesh down below, carrion meat. Even more odd, outside of dreams, in my waking state, in my *demon* awakening state, my eyes changed from my normal brown to cool crystal blue—Mona Louisa's eyes. A creepy thing, that.

I shrugged away my morbid thoughts and concentrated on the here and now: the full moon riding like a giant beacon of light above us, and my people waiting expectantly for me to draw down its life-extending rays. There was no real science to it. I just opened myself—best way to describe it. Every child of the moon felt that distinct pull when the moon came into its full and ripe roundness. It was like an invisible, tugging rope reaching down to try and open up a door inside of you. I simply stopped resisting and let whatever was being pulled inside of me flip open and become a conduit . . . a conduit of lunar light. It shone down on me now like a spotlight, filled me up, filled me to bursting, then overflowed out from me.

Little butterflies of light flittered down from the heavens, swooped into me, and spilled out like a cresting tide, washing over my people, darting into them, bowing their backs, lighting them up like flickering candles set aflame. We shone brilliantly for a long spun-out moment in time until that lunar light was swallowed and absorbed into us. Until we no longer glowed and skin became simply skin once more, not incandescent light, incandescent energy.

The last two times I'd done this, the *only* two times I'd done this, that was it. Over. *Fini*. Not so this time. This time was different. This time something hazed my vision. Something hazed the moon, actually, because that was what I was looking at.

Like a veil being thrown across its bright surface, a shimmering darkness swept across the moon like spilling ink, blocking out the light like an eclipse, only faster, much faster. It occurred in the blink of an eye, so fast that I almost doubted what I was seeing. *Would* have doubted it had I not felt it as well—a weight like a descending hand reaching down to cover me. Not that gentle tugging sensation but something much more heavy and forceful.

My people cried out in alarm and I could do nothing to stop it or respond to them as a black power slammed into me, closed like a gripping hand about me, and swallowed me down into a dark and fathomless void.

Enter the tantalizing world
of
paranormal romance
MaryJanice Davidson
Laurell K. Hamilton
Christine Feehan
Emma Holly
Angela Knight
Rebecca York
Eileen Wilks
Berkley authors
take you to a whole new realm
penguin.com

M4G0907